# A VILLAGE IN JEOPARDY

The villagers of Turnham Malpas are in for a shock. With Sir Ralph now dead, his fortune and title go to a newcomer, Johnny Templeton. He could not be more different to his well-loved predecessor. And he is soon in conflict with long-standing members of Turnham Malpas — particularly Craddock Fitch, who is determined to obstruct Johnny's plan to buy back the Templeton estate. There are villagers who have their own crises, but the local gossip surrounds Marcus and Alice March. Finally, after they had longed for a child for years, Alice has become pregnant. However, she has grown close to Johnny, prompting doubts about the child's parentage. Now Alice must make the most difficult of decisions — whether to follow her heart or her morals.

*Books by Rebecca Shaw*
*Published by The House of Ulverscroft:*

THE NEW RECTOR
TALK OF THE VILLAGE
VILLAGE MATTERS
THE VILLAGE SHOW
VILLAGE SECRETS
SCANDAL IN THE VILLAGE
VILLAGE GOSSIP
TROUBLE IN THE VILLAGE
A COUNTRY AFFAIR
COUNTRY WIVES
A VILLAGE DILEMMA
COUNTRY LOVERS
COUNTRY PASSIONS
INTRIGUE IN THE VILLAGE
WHISPERS IN THE VILLAGE
A VILLAGE FEUD
ONE HOT COUNTRY SUMMER
THE VILLAGE GREEN AFFAIR
LOVE IN THE COUNTRY
THE VILLAGE NEWCOMERS
A VILLAGE DECEPTION

REBECCA SHAW

# A VILLAGE
# IN JEOPARDY

*Complete and Unabridged*

# CHARNWOOD
*Leicester*

First published in Great Britain in 2012 by
Orion Books
an imprint of
The Orion Publishing Group Ltd., London

First Charnwood Edition
published 2013
by arrangement with
The Orion Publishing Group Ltd.
An Hachette UK Company, London

A catalogue record for this book is available
from the British Library.

ISBN 978–1–4448–1558–0

Published by
F. A. Thorpe (Publishing)
Anstey, Leicestershire

Set by Words & Graphics Ltd.
Anstey, Leicestershire
Printed and bound in Great Britain by
T. J. International Ltd., Padstow, Cornwall

This book is printed on acid-free paper

# Inhabitants of
# Turnham Malpas

| | |
|---|---|
| Willie Biggs | Retired verger |
| Sylvia Biggs | His wife |
| James (Jimbo) Charter-Plackett | Owner of the village store |
| Harriet Charter-Plackett | His wife |
| Fergus, Finlay, Flick & Fran | Their children |
| Katherine Charter-Plackett | Jimbo's mother |
| Alan Crimble | Barman at the Royal Oak |
| Linda Crimble | His wife |
| Lewis Crimble | Their son |
| Maggie Dobbs | School caretaker |
| H. Craddock Fitch | Owner of Turnham House |
| Kate Fitch | Village school head-teacher |
| Dottie Foskett | Cleaner |
| Zack Hooper | Verger |
| Marie Hooper | His wife |
| Gilbert Johns | Church choirmaster |
| Louise Johns | His wife |
| Greta Jones | A village gossip |

| | |
|---|---|
| Vince Jones | Her husband |
| Barry Jones | Her son and estate carpenter |
| Pat Jones | Barry's wife |
| Dean & Michelle | Barry and Pat's children |
| Revd Peter Harris MA (Oxon) | Rector of the parish |
| Dr Caroline Harris | His wife |
| Alex & Beth | Their children |
| Marcus March | Writer |
| Alice March | Musician |
| Tom Nicholls | Assistant in the store |
| Evie Nicholls | His wife |
| Johnny Templeton | Heir to the late Ralph Templeton |
| Dicky & Georgie Tutt | Licensees at the Royal Oak |
| Bel Tutt | Assistant in the village store |
| Don Wright | Retired |
| Vera Wright | His wife and cleaner at the nursing home in Penny Fawcett |

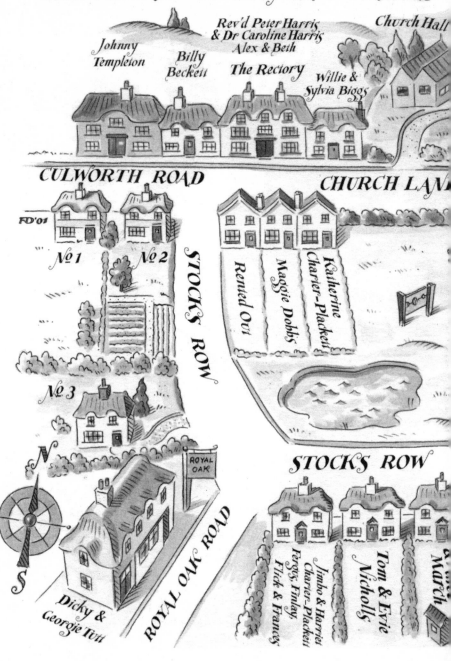

# The Village of Turnham Malpas

Johnny Templeton

Rev'd Peter Harris & Dr Caroline Harris
Alex & Beth

Billy Beckett

The Rectory

Willie & Sylvia Biggs

Church Hall

CULWORTH ROAD

CHURCH LANE

FD'01

No 1

No 2

No 3

STOCKS ROW

Rented Out

Maggie Dobbs

Katherine Charter-Plackett

ROYAL OAK

STOCKS ROW

N

S

ROYAL OAK ROAD

Dicky & Georgie Tutt

Jimbo & Harriet Charter-Plackett
Fergus, Finlay, Flick & Francey

Tom & Evie Nicholls

Anne March

# 1

Johnny Templeton stood in the shade of the Old Barn looking across the manicured lawns to the big house . . . Turnham House. His heart filled with envy. No, not just his heart; the whole six feet of him radiated envy. He was consumed by it. Why on earth had his family sold the place in 1945 when Bernard Templeton had been killed at the end of the war? Why hadn't they hung on till better times? Scrimped and saved, made do . . . simply tried harder?

But they hadn't, so here he was, the inheritor of his great-great-uncle Ralph Templeton's fortune but with no family estate to show for it. He'd asked round the village but the answer was always the same. Things were bad at that time, you see, they explained; the English were exhausted by the fight to beat Hitler, hungry, despairing. Yes, he'd heard all the excuses but none for him were viable, not for him, Johnny Templeton: inheritor of the Templeton money, the stocks, the shares, the valuable prestigious office block in London, the small house in the village but not *the house* that truly belonged, bone for bone, brick for brick, to the Templetons. One day he vowed it would be his, back in Templeton's hands as it truly should be.

A figure wended its way across the immaculate lawns heading for Turnham House. Oh! It's Alice! That momentary flash of guilt he always felt when he saw her quickly passed, as it always did. Slender and comely, she walked on, unaware she was being watched. He kept himself hidden in the shade of the oak tree. That new wing, patently at odds with the Tudor house, would have to be demolished. It stood like some thoroughly unpleasant out of place addition, out of time, out of tune with the ancient Tudor brick.

Obviously Craddock Fitch had influence in the council planning department, otherwise it would never have been allowed. He appeared to have influence in all sorts of quarters, his name cropped up so often. The Craddock Fitch Cricket Pavilion. Now that really had annoyed Johnny, that some upstart businessman from the North of all places, could calmly come along and claim the ancient cricket field for himself. The Templeton name belonged there.

Johnny had never heard of his late relative, Sir Ralph Templeton, until the solicitors had traced him to his massive office suite in Rio, from which he controlled the family's impressive hotel business, and had surprisingly imparted the news of Johnny's incredible inheritance in this spectacularly beautiful village.

Deep in his inner core, he immediately felt it rightfully his and he'd accepted the inheritance with alacrity. At that instant he had understood why he always felt like such a misfit in Brazil. His natural habitat, then, was England, that tiny island off Europe he'd only ever seen on a map. His whole family had risen up in dismay. Leave Brazil! What about the business? How can you leave all this for some crumbling house in some obscure place like England that's lost its empire and traded itself down to a third-world country? You must be mad! Brazil's where it's all happening! You can't leave us. But he had, saying, 'I should at least give it a go. See what it's like.' He was so wrapped in his thoughts, he didn't notice that Alice was on her way home now, and was walking straight towards him, her lovely sweet face alight with pleasure at seeing him so unexpectedly.

Alice confidently placed her hand in his and tiptoed to kiss him; the fragrant, gentle, undemanding brush of her lips against his stirred him as always. His hands slipped around her shoulders and they stood embracing in the cool shade of the oak; illicit though it may be, neither could resist.

'You didn't see me? So deep in thought!' Alice said. 'I'm doing a recital for the students — just been to confirm everything.'

Johnny tenderly stroked her face, following the line of her nose, her cheek, her jaw and wondered in amazement how someone so beautiful could choose him as the light of her life.

'No. Yes. I was. Deep in thought. Love you.'

Alice smiled up at him and straightened his hair where it had been blown awry by the wind, admired his adorable smile and wished, how she wished . . .

'If you were free . . . ' Johnny got no further because it was futile to do so; he'd trod that path so often, dreamt about it, wallowed in the joy of what would never be.

'Got to go. I have a pupil coming shortly. Be seeing you.'

Johnny bent his head and kissed her, gripping her to him as though their parting would be too hard to bear.

Alice pulled herself away, hating their parting as much as he, and dashed for home.

Home. Where she would find Marcus in his attic, writing. Marcus. She'd loved him since the day they'd met at university, except now, with their plans still on the back burner after twelve years of marriage and realistically likely to be forever shelved . . . the glow had gone. Marcus still loved her and never seemed to notice she acted differently. She recollected how they'd had to give up on having babies, give up on Marcus having success one day; perhaps next year this latest manuscript would be the one that finally made it. They both pretended to everyone what a brilliant writer he was, that one day a publisher would recognise the merits of his work enough to *buy* it. Alice felt the burden of being the only wage earner. Their food, their clothes, their daily living expenses all depended on her music and the interest on the capital her parents had left to her, and there were days when all inspiration left her and she hadn't the heart to open up the piano, play an instrument, neither sing nor teach, not anything at all.

Then Johnny had arrived in the village and her whole world had changed overnight. She met him for the first time one evening when she and Marcus had gone to the pub. It was a cold, dark, miserable night. If she hadn't been so bored by the thought of yet another evening reading through what Marcus had written during the day

4

and worse, giving her opinion on it, she would never have bothered to persuade Marcus to go.

The bar was busy for a Monday, and Alice's attention was immediately taken by the crowd clustered round a new face. They were all laughing and talking and admiring the man and she could see why. This new face had a certain grace which she found attractive. She liked the short spiky blond hair, the long, prominent nose that gave him a curious puckish look. His eyes were not blue as one would have expected with such fair hair, but very dark brown with a permanent twinkle as though he found life perpetually exciting. Who was he?

Harriet called across, 'Alice! Marcus! Come and meet our new neighbour.'

Marcus trailed behind her, reluctant to meet new people.

Harriet said, 'Now see here, Johnny, this is Alice and Marcus March. They've lived in the village for yonks and you must get to know them. Alice is our resident musician now, teaches singing mainly, but also piano and wind instruments, and this is her husband Marcus, who is a novelist. We wait with bated breath for the publication of his first novel!'

Harriet watched Johnny's reaction to Alice. It was as she thought it would be: Johnny was worshipping at Alice's altar immediately. How did she do it?

'A musician? It's the first time I've shaken hands with one and I must say you're a very pretty one, a true English rose, and just the right kind of hands for a musician — long delicate fingers but with strength there too.'

Then he turned to shake Marcus's hand and did so with enthusiasm, except Harriet noticed Johnny's eyes were on Alice all the time. Marcus didn't appear to notice this, so self-absorbed was he.

In a moment Alice was squeezed in beside Johnny, with Marcus left on the outside of the group. Johnny called across to Georgie to order their drinks and the joking and laughter recommenced. But for Alice it was the beginning of an affair she had never intended to start, let alone sustain, having her own strict rules about fidelity within marriage; she belonged to Marcus and no one else, for ever.

But it all happened so easily. Because her hours were haphazard, fitting in with her Ladies' Choir requirements, individual piano lessons sometimes after school or during the evening, concerts occasionally in the evenings, she was out and about at odd times of the day so Marcus, who never particularly noticed her whereabouts anyway, had lost track of her comings and goings. If she had an instrument with her or her music case he accepted without query that she was teaching. So Alice's freedom of movement aided and abetted their affair, and Johnny, free as air, neatly fitted in. Within weeks Johnny was established in Sir Ralph's old house, now finally refurbished after the fire, sparsely furnished to be sure, but enough to please two lovers vastly more interested in each other than the decor.

At first Alice felt guilty, but that fell away as the weeks advanced due to the pure joy Johnny's lovemaking gave her. There'd been nothing so fulfilling in her life before, so amazingly, so beautifully glorious, that she wondered how she had thought that Marcus was satisfying her. The first time with Johnny had been the biggest hurdle because of her obsession with fidelity but after that it got easier and easier.

Occasionally guilt reared its ugly head and Alice spent days thinking about where this was leading and wished he'd never come to the village, and then was overwhelmingly glad he had, because this was *living* like never before.

That evening she and Marcus dined on steak, fresh green salad and sauté potatoes followed by raspberries and cream. Marcus sat back replete, drank down the rest of his wine, dabbed his mouth and said, 'You seem to have a lot of pupils at the moment. Especially ones who want teaching in their own homes.' He raised an eyebrow at her, a habit that had set her heart racing at one time.

'I have a crop of young ones whose mothers find it easier if I go to them, because they have other children and can't leave the house easily. Sometimes it goes the other way and they all want to come here, which is a pest for you when you want to write.'

Marcus shrugged. 'I don't mind, not really. Tucked away in the attic with the door closed it doesn't bother me.'

'We need the money, Marcus dear.'

Marcus heard the criticism in her voice and sighed impatiently. 'Alice! Don't you think I know that already? I'm very conscious of being

7

beholden to you. If your parents hadn't bought this house for you I couldn't be doing what I'm doing. The expense of a mortgage would be beyond us.'

Alice didn't pick up on this obvious opening gambit of Marcus's because it inevitably led to a terrible row. Instead she changed the subject. 'I've got a new pupil in Little Derehams who looks rather promising. He's eleven, suddenly decided to learn the piano, and lo and behold I do believe he's going to be brilliant. I mean really brilliant, if he can stick at it.'

'Who is it?'

'Lucas Nightingale, a relative of the Nightingales at the farm. He's such a dear boy and so keen. I haven't told either him or his parents what I think about his talent. I'm leaving that to his first exam results. I'm so excited about him.'

'You've never mentioned him before.'

'Couldn't quite believe my luck. It makes it all so worthwhile when you get a pupil like him.'

'Well, he's being taught by the best.'

'Thank you, Marcus, that means a lot to me.'

'I'm not much good at anything.'

'You do yourself down.' Alice stood up to clear the table, knowing if she didn't that she'd be given the familiar tirade about how no one in their right mind would pass up the chance of publishing his novels. Didn't publishers *want* to make profits nowadays? 'Pass me that dish, please.' Marcus ignored her, so in overreaching to pick up the dish herself she dropped it and it smashed on the floor. It was her granny's favourite vegetable dish, filled with memories of

8

Granny and eating glorious meals with her army of cousins at the refectory table in Granny's huge kitchen. Alice burst into tears. Marcus tut tutted and stirred himself to get a dustpan and brush because he hated untidiness. Alice cried aloud for the mess she was in, thinking . . . if only . . . if only . . .

But crying achieved nothing, for she'd wake up in the morning still in the same position she was in now, unless she took serious steps to change her life . . . but she baulked at that because she'd promised to stay with Marcus till death did them part.

★   ★   ★

However, next morning, their affair, which until that day they had miraculously managed to keep secret from everyone, became known. Beth Harris, who was having a few days at home in the Rectory to recuperate from a bad attack of flu, was standing at her bedroom window looking out at her favourite view across the fields towards Turnham House. Suddenly she saw a movement closer to home and saw Alice using a key to slip in to Johnny's house, next door but one, via his back door.

Her mother came in. 'Beth! Here's your breakfast! Get back into bed, darling; you don't want to make matters worse for yourself standing by that cold window.'

'Mum! Is Johnny Templeton having piano lessons?'

'I shouldn't think so. I know for a fact he

9

hasn't a piano. Why?'

'Maybe it's singing lessons, then.'

'What do you mean?'

'I've just seen Alice March popping in through his back door using her own key, carrying her music case.'

'Alice March?!'

'The very same. This breakfast looks lovely. Thanks.'

'Well, I never.'

'You don't suppose . . . ?'

'Beth! Really, there'll be some perfectly reasonable explanation for it. After all, she's married to Marcus.'

'You can't be supposing Marcus is God's gift to Alice March. He's so boring, so full of himself, so hand on heart whilst gazing heavenward with a soulful expression on his face, saying 'I am a writer' when he obviously isn't, otherwise his books would have been snapped up. Compared to him, Johnny is the absolute gift. This tea is just right; why is it mothers make the best tea ever?'

'Because they make it with love.' Caroline took a mock bow and then left, shouting, 'I'm going — see you lunchtime. Bye!' from the bottom of the stairs.

Beth would have given anything to have been a fly on the wall next door but one, because Johnny was the best in her opinion. Handsome, wealthy, charming, amusing, with fascinating twinkling eyes that said anything and everything. As for Alice, she was beautiful, inside and out. Beth paused for a moment considering exactly what quality it was that made her so. The perfect balance of her features? Her figure — which any man in full possession of his faculties, no matter his age, would consider alluring — her singing voice? Exquisite! Yet she was modest, sweet natured, quiet, genteel. They were in fact the perfect couple, and if she left Marcus for Johnny Templeton, Beth Harris for one would applaud her.

If Beth *had* been a fly on the wall in the house next door but one, she would have witnessed the two of them in each other's arms, hugging as though they were about to part for ever.

'Darling! Darling! I'd marry you tomorrow, believe me, I would. You just have to say the word,' Johnny murmured.

'Is nothing impossible to you? No mountain too high to climb? No river too wide to swim, no problem too difficult to resolve?'

'All it needs is decision. Positive thinking on your part is all that's needed.'

'I do believe you are filled with so much conviction you'd fly without wings.'

'I would, if I needed to. Leave him. Come to me.'

Alice stepped away from him. 'I can't. He's so vulnerable.'

Johnny threw back his head and roared with laughter. 'For heaven's sake! Too vulnerable! What is he? A man or a mouse?'

'Both.' Alice laughed at herself. 'But what would he do without me?'

'Alice! He's not ninety years old and infirm, he's forty whatever. That's the new thirty, didn't you know?'

'But who'd read his manuscripts? With me not there?'

'Maybe if he started meeting people, travelling around, being busy, his writing might improve, because he's not very successful doing what he's doing, is he? How long's he been trying?'

'He gave up work two years after we married to give himself time to write. So that's ten years.'

'How many times has he got close to being published?'

'Once, they asked for the rest of the novel, but when they read it they turned it down. We were foolish enough to celebrate when they asked to see the whole manuscript. The disappointment somehow, instead of discouraging him, made him more determined to succeed. More certain he was doing the right thing.'

'Is it not painfully obvious to him that he's not doing the right thing? *Living off you?* That's not a man's way of doing things.' As he spoke Johnny knew he was in the wrong and should have kept his opinions to himself.

Alice sprang away from him as though he'd unexpectedly threatened her with his fist. 'Johnny! My God! How could you make a remark like that? I'm ashamed of you. Ashamed! What an accusation to make. He's trying to find himself, like we all do. Can't you see that?' Her face flushed with righteous anger, her hands trembling and on the brink of stormy tears, Alice grabbed her music case and fled. Johnny followed her to the back door, calling her name but to no avail. She was down the path and running along Pipe and Nook Lane as fast as she

12

could. Johnny slammed the back door.

Alice ran blindly across the village green; she couldn't go home — Marcus would see her tears and she'd no excuse to hand, so she escaped into the village store and hid behind the tinned soups. She should never have shamed Johnny in that way, because those very same thoughts had crossed her own mind several times when money was short, and Marcus had never offered to help by trying to get a job. He was a qualified Health and Safety Officer, a job he'd hated and was glad to leave when he began that creative writing class the year they married and got bitten by the novelist bug.

Alice snatched a tissue from her skirt pocket and dried her tears. She'd always wanted babies and now she'd been forced to give up even *imagining* a baby in her arms because if she started now . . . well, life would be impossible. But ten years of wishing is a long time to be patient, so that was that. She chose a carton of Harriet's Country Cousin Tomato and Basil Soup to make her sojourn behind the soups more credible.

She happened to be the only customer at that moment so Jimbo, doing duty at the till, was glad to talk.

'Hello! Alice! How's things?'

That did it. To her horror, and Jimbo's, she burst into tears.

'My dear, come, come now. Let me make you a coffee and we'll sit and talk a while. Let your old Jimbo sort things out for you. Come along, sit in the coffee corner; I make a good listener.'

13

Alice blew her nose and tried to compose herself while she watched Jimbo refresh his coffee machine. She couldn't even thank him for the coffee because she was so choked up.

'Now when you're halfway through that coffee you can tell me all about it. I can't let my beautiful Alice have tears running down her face without trying to help.' He whisked a snow-white handkerchief from his top shirt pocket and gently mopped her face.

They sat in silence and weren't disturbed by customers, a state of affairs of which Jimbo did not approve. He loved to hear his doorbell ringing; it was his measure of success.

Alice knew she couldn't say a word about Johnny so she feigned that her unhappiness was due to not having babies, which was true anyway.

'You see, Jimbo, I've always wanted at least two babies but time is running out. We're told there's no reason why we shouldn't, but we just can't.'

'Ah! That is difficult. I've no advice to give because Harriet and I would have had a baker's dozen if we hadn't taken steps, as you might say.'

'There you are, you see and I bet you never gave a thought to how lucky you were. It's so unfair.' Tears threatened again.

Jimbo put an arm around her shoulders and squeezed her tight. 'Dispensing advice isn't part of my shopkeeping duties but for what it's worth — ' he took a deep breath — 'you've got to keep at it, so to speak. You know, lots of *passion* and *very* frequently. Play the sex siren, entice him even when you're not in bed. In fact

14

sometimes it's better — ' He was about to explore the subject more deeply when Harriet walked in.

Alice flushed and shook his arm from her shoulders, Jimbo straightened his bow tie, which he guessed by now must be spinning round all of its own accord, and got to his feet. 'So take my word for it, that's the best recipe for tomato soup Harriet's ever made.'

Harriet eyed the two of them with interest. 'Ah! There you are, darling. Hello, Alice. Beautiful day, isn't it?'

'Yes. I'd better go.' Alice paid for her carton of soup, stuffed it into her music case and melted away out of the door, leaving Harriet standing looking at Jimbo with both her eyebrows raised.

'Well?'

Jimbo checked his bow tie again and then grinned. 'Well. In all the years I've run this store that's the first time I've given intimate advice on marital relations.'

'Don't make a habit of it, please.'

'I shan't.'

'Good.'

Together they burst out laughing.

'Which part of the procedure did she ask you about, husband dear?'

'It's not funny. She wants children and it's just not happening because they can't afford to.'

'I suspect she's having an affair.'

There was nothing Jimbo loved better than gossip and he eagerly inquired, 'An affair? Who with?'

'You swear not to say a word if I tell you?'

15

Jimbo nodded.

'Two nights ago when I was coming home late from WI, Johnny's kitchen light was on and they were standing in the kitchen having a rare old kissing session. I crept past trying hard to be invisible.'

'Why were you coming home via Pipe and Nook from WI?'

'Because I'd been to the Rectory to pick up some WI papers from Caroline, and Peter was deeply involved with a visitor at the front door so I went out the back way rather than disturb their conversation.'

'Have you told anyone else?'

'No.'

'Johnny Templeton!' Jimbo repeated the name. 'Johnny Templeton! No! I say! How could you keep that to yourself?'

'Because I'm not an old gossip like you and I like Alice and if she's having some fun with Johnny Templeton, I don't blame her, married to that idle good-for-nothing. I've never liked him; he's too full of himself.'

'I know what you mean.'

As he replied to Harriet he became aware of Marcus at that precise moment saying, 'I'm hoping you've got your goat's milk in by now. We've run out and I do prefer it to cow's milk — so much more taste to it, I always think.' He smiled at them both. Jimbo quickly pulled himself together and nodded. 'Indeed we have. It came late last evening. Got held up with all that flooding round the farm. Two pints as usual?'

As Marcus opened the door to leave he turned

back to speak to them. 'I don't like walking in somewhere and the conversation stops dead. Not customer friendly. No, not at all. However, seeing as I am well brought up I shall overlook it this time. Good morning to you both.' And with that he left.

'That'll teach us not to gossip in the shop,' Harriet said with a nervous laugh.

Jimbo laughed. 'Do you think he heard us? You can't have shut the door properly — that's why we didn't hear him come in.'

'I'm not going to lose any sleep over it.'

'He'll never come in here again.'

Harriet headed for the back office. 'Well, considering how little they spend in here it won't make us bankrupt.'

Marcus wandered home replaying the snippet of conversation he'd heard and wondering what it all meant.

Alice was already home, making a quick lunch for her and Marcus, and, while she sliced the granary loaf, spread the peanut butter and looked in the fridge for some fresh fruit to round it off, she thought about what Jimbo had advised. But from somewhere deep in her heart Alice knew it wasn't really Marcus she wanted to have babies with, not any more.

# 2

Johnny did not see Alice for three whole days and was beginning to worry. He was a prime marriage target back home in Brazil and he'd been out with whole regiments of women, many of whom were paraded in front of him by their eager mothers, but not one of them had affected him as Alice had. She was everything he wanted in a wife, with surprising depths not at first apparent; an overall gentleness that hid an amusing, joyous, highly intelligent, strong woman, ready for love and ready to give it. The stumbling block was her faithfulness to Marcus.

All credit to him, Marcus was tenacious, but just how blind was that tenacity? Would he still be trying to write a book that had a commercial future twenty years from now? All the while Alice's singing talents were being drowned in the need to make money to support them both. Didn't she see what Marcus was doing to her? When she had real talent that could take her to the heights of her profession?

An idea struck him while having a leisurely read of the morning paper after his breakfast the next day. He'd been in the village almost a year and never entertained any of them in his own house. Lots of rounds of drinks in the Royal Oak but never in his own home. He'd have a mad burst of activity putting the final touches to furnishing it and then the invites could go out.

The guest list would have to be carefully crafted to get the right blend of people. He always felt one needed an objective or at least a reason for a dinner party, but what was his? Getting to know the real movers and shakers in the village? Cosying up to Craddock Fitch to assess the chances of buying the big house back into the Templeton fold where it belonged? Usurping Craddock Fitch's influence in the village by buying as many of the houses as he possibly could, thus limiting Craddock's influence? Making Marcus look a fool so Alice saw him for what he was? He scrubbed that last idea out immediately as he, Johnny, was not that kind of man and it would only throw Alice, because she was so loyal, right back into Marcus's arms. That last idea strengthened Johnny's decision.

He immediately left his house and walked down Stocks Row to put his idea into action by going straight to Alice and Marcus's and ringing their doorbell. Hopefully Alice would answer the door. His hopes were dashed when he could hear someone clumsily thundering down the stairs right from the top of the house, and then the door opened revealing Marcus looking very much like a man flogging himself over his writing, judging by his three-day growth of beard. He was wearing the oldest sweater imaginable and trousers that matched, giving a kind of complete tweedy brown/green/grubby image right down to his sloppy brown/green slippers.

'Good morning, Marcus. Nice day.'

'It is. What do you want? I'm working.'

19

'Sorry, never know the best moment to call on a writer. Bad time, is it?'

Marcus nodded self-importantly. 'It is.'

'Well, I'll be quick then. I'm holding a dinner party in a couple of weeks, and I'd like to invite you and your wife . . . Alice, isn't it? Is there a best night to suggest?'

Marcus, looking as though he was struggling to come down to earth from whatever heavenly plains he'd been on when the doorbell rang, muttered, 'Never on Thursdays; that's always ladies' choir night. Nor Tuesday nor Wednesday — those are heavy teaching nights. Possibly Friday would be the most likely.'

'Perhaps . . . Alice . . . isn't it? could let me know definitely? Which is best?'

Marcus nodded. 'I'll ask her.'

'You'll know everyone who's being invited. They're all village people. I look forward to hearing from you.' He gave Marcus a beaming smile. 'Get back to your writing before you lose the thread. Sorry to interrupt.' He stood outside on the doorstep looking across the green. Who next? The Rectory.

Johnny rang the doorbell. Somewhere upstairs a vacuum cleaner was in full swing. He guessed it wouldn't be Caroline wielding it, didn't imagine that would be her scene. He heard footsteps and then the door opened.

'Good morning, Peter. And how are you this bright day?'

'Fine, thank you.'

'Time for a word?'

'Should have been in Penny Fawcett at nine — I always go to the market there, but another

20

ten minutes won't harm. Come in the study.'

The door closing shut out the noise of the vacuum. 'It's Dottie cleaning upstairs. How may I help? Please sit down.'

'It won't take long. I've decided to invite people to supper — a Friday, more than likely. Would that be convenient, a Friday night for you and Caroline?'

'It certainly would; we'd be delighted. Any particular Friday night?'

'Don't know yet, just checking in preparation for settling on an actual date. Just the usual people, Craddock Fitch and his highly surprising wife . . . '

Peter asked, 'Oh! you mean the big age gap?'

'Yes.' Johnny grinned.

'They are very well suited actually and very happy.'

'I didn't mean anything by it, just that you get a surprise when you see them together. There'll be Jimbo and Harriet, though I haven't asked them yet, and Alice and Marcus, and that's as far as I've got.'

'Sounds a great set of people. Thank you. How are you settling in, Johnny? Must be a far cry from Brazil and running hotels.'

Johnny tapped the side of his nose, saying, 'I have plans, great plans and I'm here to stay. Won't keep you. I'll send invites and make it official. I'm off to see Craddock Fitch now — any tips for dealing with him?'

'Self-made man, very generous towards the church, considers himself the village benefactor, but . . . '

Johnny begged for further enlightenment. 'Yes?'

'The village preferred your uncle Ralph's discreet approach to giving. Craddock likes everyone to know he's the first one with his cheque book out. Likes everyone to know who's doing the giving and they resent that.'

'Ah! Right. Old Uncle Ralph did it with better grace, you mean?'

Peter had to smile. 'Yes, I suppose you could say that, though I've nothing against Mr Fitch. He's very honest and plain speaking and I like that in a person.'

'Oh! So do I. Won't keep you. A Friday night it is, then.'

'Yes, we'll both look forward to it.'

'I'll see myself out. Bye!'

He stood outside the Rectory wondering what to do next. Should he take the car? No, he wouldn't; he'd walk up there, give him a chance to enjoy the approach to Turnham House. He ambled up the drive admiring the layout of the park, and best of all the glimpses of the house through the bank of trees, suddenly arriving there with the full panoply of the whole front of the house before him. Something very primeval coursed through his veins. He couldn't deny it; he coveted this beautiful Tudor house like no other thing in the whole of his life. He'd bought hotels in the past and been passionate about their acquisition but this . . . something in his blood urged him to go for it, whatever the cost.

Johnny quickened his pace and marched in through the open front door, his senses almost overwhelmed in admiration of the beautiful entrance hall with its lofty ceiling and the big windows flooding the space with clear morning light . . . and the walls! Ah! The ancient panelling that went all the way round, and the huge inglenook fireplace, the biggest he'd ever seen, filled with a great bowl of exotic flowers. The staircase was to die for. It was all completely breathtaking. The construction business students working here this week were incredibly lucky to be studying in this wonderful building.

Still in shock he approached the receptionist. 'My name's Johnny Templeton. Is there a possibility I could speak to Mr Fitch? Mr Craddock Fitch?'

'And your business, sir?'

'Oh! An invitation for him and his wife to dinner at my house.'

'You're from the village?'

'Yes, I am,' Johnny said, remembering to speak in that stiff English way that he had had to learn since he came.

'Very well. Would you care to take a seat and I will ascertain if Mr Fitch is free.'

*Ascertain.* Hmmph! Honestly, thought Johnny, how stuffy can you get?

She returned to say Mr Fitch didn't know him and why should he want to go to dine with someone he doesn't know?

'He'll see me. My name is Johnny Templeton; he knew my late great-great-uncle, Sir Ralph Templeton.'

'Ah! Right. I see. I'll go tell him.'

The receptionist returned a moment later

smiling from ear to ear. 'He'd be delighted; do come through.' She didn't tell Johnny that Mr Fitch had said he intended a big put down for the miserable little upstart, asking him to dinner! Huh!

But when Mr Fitch shook hands with Johnny he changed his mind about him. There was a strength in his grasp that Craddock couldn't ignore, and a charm and a similarity to Ralph which he liked. Despite being furious that Ralph always got his own way about things by being pleasant to one and all, he'd actually had great respect for him and envied his ability to charm everyone he met. This prepossessing young man with his good looks and his openness, charmed him in just the same way Ralph had done. And after all, he had inherited Ralph's aristocratic nose, so that counted for something.

They shook hands and Craddock suggested he sat down. Would a coffee be welcomed? It was about the time he always had his.

'I'd be delighted; walking up here has given me an appetite for one.'

Craddock dinged his bell and his PA emerged from the room next door, nodded her agreement to get the coffee for him and disappeared.

'I see you admiring her. She's a well-mannered efficient girl. I wish she'd worked for me years ago. The last one I had got herself sacked for insolence. Can't abide insolence.'

'All depends on how you treat them, how much insolence you get in return.' Johnny grinned as he said this.

'Mmm. All depends how they treat me. I don't

pay wages to no-brainers.'

'Neither would I. Well paid, but they have to work for it.'

'My sentiments exactly.'

Johnny was impressed by the silver coffee service and the elegance of the silver tray and the beautiful porcelain cups. This was class and breeding, even though Craddock's accent betrayed his humble beginnings. Still, what did it matter so long as he was honest and pleasant and willing to sell him the house? He wanted it on the same level as he wanted Alice March . . . with an all-consuming passion.

'I'm organising a dinner party for a few friends from the village. Would you and your wife count yourselves among them and come? I'm planning it for a Friday night in about two or three weeks' time. There'll be eight or ten of us. Would Friday be a good evening to choose?'

'Excellent. I'll tell Kate. You've met her, have you?'

Johnny nodded. 'One night at the youth club I spoke about Brazil, and I saw you both in church one morning when I read the lesson.'

'Of course, yes, you did, I remember you now. You read it to the manor born.' A reluctant smile of approval flitted across Mr Fitch's face.

Johnny heard a hint of sarcasm in his tone but ignored it. Wouldn't do to antagonise the old man, not right now. 'Lovely house you have here.'

An almost tangible glow appeared around Craddock's head as he replied, 'Indeed, yes. I love it. Inordinately proud of it I am, I have to say. Superb, isn't it?'

25

'What I've seen, yes.'

'This room makes me feel completely at home, as though I'm made for it.'

Johnny took a moment to admire the amazing antique desk that was Craddock's and the ancient shelving holding books he secretly felt Craddock must have bought just to fill the shelves as appropriately as possible: leather bound, gold lettering on the spines. Oh, yes! Not bought for their intrinsic value, that was obvious. But he had to admire the room and respect the man's love of the place. Johnny was intensely aware that Mr Fitch wouldn't give up this house of his without a struggle.

A silence fell between the two of them while they sipped their coffee. Johnny couldn't think what on earth to say except *I'd like to buy your house* and Craddock seemed to be thinking about matters far away from this wonderful room.

Johnny got to his feet. 'Mustn't keep you any longer. I'll be sending the invites out in a week or so. Glad you're able to come. Thanks for the coffee! Good morning.'

Now, who next? He needed a female to pair up with himself and make a proper balance. Did he know any lone females in the village who would fit in?

That lively old lady he met one morning out taking her constitutional around the cricket pitch? She would do very nicely. Now where did she live?

He'd ask in the pub. The doors were open and there was a sound of activity in the bar. Johnny checked the time: eleven fifteen. Just right.

'Good morning, landlord! Coffee please. Latte if possible.'

'Name's Dicky.'

'Dicky, of course.' Johnny stood at the bar to await his coffee and surveyed the scene. There were three obvious tourists sitting close up to the inglenook fireplace, and a young girl sitting by herself, reading a book while drinking coffee, and he decided she was stunning. He'd catch her eye. He raised a hand and smiled at her and she smiled back. She was beautiful in repose and even more so when she smiled. She acknowledged his greeting and then rather shyly tapped the table as an invitation to join her. So he did. As simple as that.

'I'm Johnny Templeton.'

'I know. Oh! Look, here's your coffee. Do sit down.'

'Love to. And you are . . . ?'

'Beth. It's short for Elizabeth.'

'You live in the village?'

'All my life.'

'Haven't seen you around.'

'I'm at university. I'm home at the moment, because I've had a really bad bout of flu that's knocked me for six.'

'Which?'

'Which flu?'

Johnny smiled. 'No, which university.'

'Cambridge.'

Not only beauty, but brains too. 'Oh! My word! I thought all girls who went to Cambridge wore round steel-framed glasses, flat shoes and looked in need of a makeover.'

Beth laughed. 'Honestly! You're way out on that score; there are still a few like that but most of them are right out front in the fashion stakes.'

'Studying?'

'Archaeology.'

'Ah! Right. Never got the chance myself. Just went straight into the family business. I'm envious of your opportunity. Must be a wonderful experience, Cambridge.'

'It is. I'm privileged.'

'And I'm privileged having coffee with such a lovely-looking lady.'

Beth pulled a face. 'Oh! Please, what a line!'

'Sorry. But you do have the looks, there's no doubt about that. My compliment was well intentioned.'

Beth's next remark took Johnny completely by surprise. 'You prefer beautiful women then?'

'I must admit it does add to the pleasure if they're good lookers.'

'Well, she's certainly that.'

Alarm bells rang in Johnny's head, so he feigned puzzlement to give himself more time to think. 'What do you mean?'

'Rather . . . *whom* do I mean.'

This was dangerous ground. Johnny raised an eyebrow.

'Alice March.'

'Yes, I do know her.'

'We know you do.'

'We . . . ?'

'People in the village.'

'Ah!'

'You didn't honestly think no one would guess, did you? I can't say I blame her. You must be a godsend to her, compared to that puffed up ridiculous husband of hers.'

'Mmm!' Johnny looked at her calmly.

'Lost your power of speech?' A wicked grin spread across Beth's face. 'Must go, I'm supposed to be making lunch for my dad and I've got to shop first.'

'Who is your dad?'

'The rector.'

'Right!'

'Go for it, I say; she deserves someone like you. It's been a while since we had a romance in the village. Murder, yes, burglary, yes, a very charming conman, a wedding, yes, but not an illicit romance. At least it gives us all something to talk about.' Beth picked up her book and her purse, smiled sweetly at him and left Johnny in turmoil.

So they all knew. So what? Let them. He didn't care how much gossip they stirred up; to hell with it. Alice was meant for him and he was determined he would have her for his own. He'd leave a message on her mobile, even though she had forced a promise from him that he never would communicate with her by phone. He hadn't worked out her reasoning for this rule. Surely Marcus didn't check her phone, did he? Who did he think he was? Well, damn it, he was sending her a text this minute because he couldn't wait another moment to hold her to him, to smell her, thread his fingers through her hair, see her splendid eyes shine with bright stars brought about by laughter.

*Must see you, Alice. Sorry for making you angry. Please forgive me. Johnny.*

He sent it immediately and left for home.

Ten minutes later he heard her key in the kitchen door.

# 3

The ladies' choir that met in the church hall every Thursday evening was made up of women from a wide area. Several were from Turnham Malpas but a larger number were from the surrounding villages. For a start seven came from Little Derehams and five from Penny Fawcett. In total they usually numbered between twenty-five and thirty members attending each practice. The choir was almost entirely in the charge of Alice March, except occasionally Gilbert Johns, the county archaeologist and church choir master, held Alice's baton. This Thursday it was Alice in sole charge and the choir were not convinced that her mind was as fiercely focused as it normally was.

She fiddled about sorting her music, changed her mind twice about their first voice exercise, called someone by the wrong name and was nonplussed when the person she was looking at didn't reply, and finally sent half her sheet music spinning to the floor as she sorted through to find the important piece they were practising for a competition in Culworth only two weeks away. 'I'm sorry about this. Let's start again,' Alice mumbled.

Harriet collected together her music from the floor and handed it back to her. Alice tapped her baton on her music stand, brought the accompanist in with a nod and they began, but it

31

was a ragged rehearsal. The choir members, accustomed to her usual streamlined performance, were confused by her distracted manner and when she brought the rehearsal to an abrupt end a quarter of an hour early they knew something was afoot.

Alice always stayed a while chatting to anyone who needed to have a word with her, but tonight she hastened off full of excuses for not going to the Royal Oak with the usual crowd for a drink before they trundled home.

In the bar, they pulled two tables together, worked out whose turn it was to pay for the round and sat down to wait to be served. Caroline, guessing the nature of Alice's distraction, tried to point the conversation away from Alice to the charity coffee morning being held in Little Derehams on Saturday morning.

'You haven't forgotten about the do at Sheila Bissett's on Saturday morning, ten till twelve? They're rather short of gifts for the Bring and Buy. I'm sure Sheila will be grateful for help . . . with . . . that . . . ' Her voice trailed away as she realised no one had heard, because little pockets of whispering were going on all round the table.

Harriet, also being privy to Alice's romance, tried equally hard to steer the conversation, but failed miserably.

'What the heck', said someone from Penny Fawcett rather more loudly than necessary, 'is the matter with Alice? She made a real balls-up of conducting tonight. For what good she's done she might as well have packed up before she started. Anyone know?'

'Well, normally I feel on top of the world after a good sing but not tonight. Her mind wasn't on the job at all. She was a right waste of space and not half.'

Harriet tried to intervene but was interrupted by Sylvia Biggs. She suggested that perhaps Alice was sickening for something nasty. 'There's a lot of flu about, and bad coughs.'

Then the drinks arrived and by the time they were sorted the conversation about Alice had gripped them all.

'I say! You don't think she might be pregnant after all this time?'

A roar of laughter went up from the Penny Fawcett contingent, mixed with remarks of 'chance 'ud be a fine thing!' and 'now how likely is that, married to that pathetic little man?'

Caroline, as Alice lived in Turnham Malpas, swung to her defence. 'It really isn't right to talk about her like that. It's probably as Sylvia said; there's a lot of coughs and colds about and I should know, being a doctor.'

This did quieten the chatter about Alice somewhat, but the Penny Fawcett singers all sitting next to each other wouldn't let it rest and giggled and spoke too loudly for the others' comfort, so the conversation broke into two halves.

They were all silenced by the arrival of Johnny Templeton. As the inner door swung closed behind him he looked immediately at the group from the Ladies' Choir, and the welcoming smile he'd had on his face fell away completely. He stalked across to the bar and, leaning forward so the other punters couldn't hear, he asked had Alice been in?

'Not tonight, Johnny, no. She usually does on choir night, but not tonight. Sorry,' said Georgie. Curious to know more about their supposed romance, she followed this up by asking was he expecting to meet her in the bar? He could leave a message if he liked.

Johnny looked ruefully at her, wondering whether to confide, but decided not.

'No, thanks, I won't.' He marched out, not looking to either side of him, allowed the outside door to slam, which it did viciously due to the vigour of Johnny's push, and stood outside listening to the stillness of the village and watching the little Jack Russell that belonged in the Rectory wending his way home alone. He gave two enormous barks, which appeared far too loud for a dog of his size, and in moments the front door opened and he hopped inside. Johnny heard Beth's voice greeting him with such enthusiasm that for a moment he almost wished Beth was greeting him and not the dog.

He stayed a while longer, studying the comfortableness that the sight of the village gave him, felt his bones stir in response and contemplated how every house in it had once belonged to the Templetons. And he wished . . . oh! how he wished . . .

The door of Alice's house opened and, as he watched, Alice slipped out, closing the door after her noiselessly. She glanced up before crossing Stocks Row and saw Johnny watching her. Her beautiful, beautiful face flooded with life and she began to run towards him, her arms widespread. As she flung herself into his arms the door of the Royal Oak opened and the Penny Fawcett choir members came out en masse.

Their gasps of surprise shocked Alice into hiding her face in Johnny's jacket, but it was too late; they'd seen her and gave her a loud cheer of enthusiastic support. Luckily for her she didn't hear their comments as they piled into the Penny Fawcett minibus in the pub car park.

Johnny hurried her into his house, shut the door behind them and clasped her to him. He sensed there was something very different in the way Alice had rushed towards him, as though she had made a decision from which there would be no turning back.

They kissed and kissed — guilt had been swept away, the need for secrecy lost in an abandonment, that Johnny had not experienced before, even with his many lovers.

'Alice!' he whispered, pulling her closer.

'Johnny! I can't live without you; I know that now, as an absolute certainty. Tomorrow I'm telling Marcus I must have a divorce.'

It was as though his very being had been splintered into a thousand pieces by her unexpected declaration. The shock waves made Johnny release her, saying shakily, 'You mean it, don't you?'

Alice stood back a little so she could look directly into his face. 'Don't *you* mean it?' The shock she could detect in his eyes frightened her and made her see very clearly what his real reaction truly was. He should have been thrilled; he'd got what he wanted. But she knew beyond any doubt that Johnny was appalled. How could she have got it so wrong?

Her voice shrank to a hoarse whisper. 'Marriage isn't what you want, is it? I can see that. I thought you *did*. What have I done wrong? Has nothing you've said to me been the truth? Oh! Johnny! What a fool I've been! What a fool.'

Before Johnny could think rationally Alice had left, closing the door so very quietly behind her, leaving him standing alone, his head spinning with conflicting thoughts. Wasn't marriage to her what he wanted above all? Why hadn't he shouted at the top of his voice, 'Yes! Yes!' But the words she had used were like a fatal echo of the words he'd heard so often before from women who he knew all too well fancied his fortune and his position in Brazilian society much more than him.

# 4

Alice, having crept out of her cottage knowing Marcus was ensconced in the attic writing, had to creep back in hoping he hadn't noticed her absence. She plunged into the easy chair beside the wood-burning stove in the kitchen, for she needed its warmth, too deeply hurt for tears. Her throat tightened unbearably, her skin burned with shame, and her heart beat so fast she felt she'd run a full marathon.

She couldn't even think. She'd take two painkillers, see if that helped. She deliberately chose to use chilled water from the fridge to help swallow them and to cool her raging heart. After another half hour crouched in the chair, her face hidden in her hands, and the painkillers beginning to soothe the pressure in her skull, Alice forced her hands away from her face and sought to answer her own questions.

What had she left of life? Nothing. An appalling tremble took possession of her limbs that no amount of self-control could stop. This was a night when, if anyone at all crossed her, she — and she was a pacifist through and through — could deliberately set about killing them by cold-bloodedly slashing their throats. Would Johnny be her victim or Marcus . . . or both?

With her mind swamped with murderous thoughts, the trembling slowed. All the crime dramas she'd ever watched on TV paraded through her consciousness, so when Marcus thundered down the stairs shouting, she was completely unaware, as though the real world had spun into space and left her the only person alive, curled in her favourite chair, paralysed.

'Alice! Alice! Where are you?' Marcus called.

She heard him rush into the sitting room, calling her name up the stairs out the back door, again and again and again. The excitement in his voice was obvious. She'd never heard him so elated since . . .

'There you are! I've had an email from a publisher asking me to let them have the full manuscript of *Killer at Large*. They want to see it! Isn't it wonderful?'

Seeing as he was all she had left now, Alice summoned every ounce of her strength in an attempt to match his excitement.

She sat slowly upright in the chair. 'That's marvellous. Best not get our hopes too high, just in case.'

'No, you don't understand. They say 'with a view to publication'. They're lyrical about it, full of praise! Here, read it. Read it.'

Alice felt the piece of paper being thrust into her hand, automatically looked down to read it, but the printing was a blur so she made a pretence of reading it.

'That's wonderful! At last!'

'I knew I'd make it one day. See here, look, they're saying about the possibility of me writing a trilogy! I've known all along I was on to a good thing with this novel. Something about it, you know, something special.' He grabbed her shoulders and squeezed them tightly. 'At last it hasn't all been in vain. Now they can all stop mocking me, looking down their noses at me. Now it can be me doing the patronising. Aren't you thrilled? Say something, woman!'

She unwound her legs out of the chair and made the effort to stand up. 'Shall we have a toast?' How the glasses and the bottle of sparkling wine appeared on the kitchen table she'd no idea, but they did, because there they were and it certainly wouldn't have been Marcus who'd got them out.

'Well, I must say you don't seem very thrilled. Can't you summon something up to show how delighted you are at my success? You're not envious, are you? You are! That's why you're so quiet. That's just not fair. You're my wife; you should be thrilled for me. Just think of the money! It could be millions! At last my just reward! All those hours struggling away in that damned attic, always short of money. Now comes my moment! Oh! Sparkling wine! That's more like it!'

Alice's hand shook as she poured it out. 'Here you are! To Marcus March's success in the publishing world! At last!' They clinked their glasses and Marcus saw how her hand trembled and he said with triumph in his voice, 'You're quiet because inside you're absolutely thrilled. I feel humbled by that. I knew one day I would make you proud.'

The wine made Alice's head spin as she listened to Marcus going on and on about success, apparently completely forgetting that this had all happened before and come to nothing. She found his writing obscure, deeply depressing and very scary, but maybe that was what publishers demanded now, not a manuscript bright and uplifting, which was what she would have written. On and on he went, talking about publishers sitting at his feet praising his novels, worshipping at the altar that was Marcus March.

'I say, Alice, do you think I should have a pseudonym? Something double-barrelled say, or Marcus *something* March? Or something completely different?'

Alice didn't answer. Unlike Marcus, she wasn't seeing a room piled high with copies of his very first novel in a major London publisher's office; she was seeing the look of horror she'd glimpsed in Johnny's face.

That night Marcus decided it was *the* night for making love. If they didn't have a bit of hanky panky tonight, when would they, filled to the brim with success as he was? So he began his ritual that she knew led to making love and filled her with dread; it was a poor substitute for Johnny's. She feigned her pleasure as she had done so often before, but this time it was grim because Marcus couldn't step up to the plate. When he rolled on to his back angry because he'd failed, he blamed it on Alice. She turned on her side and finally allowed the bitterness of her situation to fully surface and crucify her.

★ ★ ★

After an almost sleepless night Alice rose half an hour earlier than normal and showered, allowing the hot water to slough away her sorrow for a full ten minutes instead of the three she would have allowed herself had things been happier. She threw on a T-shirt and a pair of loose trouser bottoms, and heard in her head that hymn of national mourning, 'Oh God, Our Help in Ages Past'. She went down the stairs, one stair, one note, one stair, one note till she reached the kitchen.

Marcus rolled downstairs an hour later, kissed her on the top of her head and squeezed her shoulders.

'I'm looking forward to today.' He sat down to eat his breakfast determined not to allow last night's disappointment spoil what could be the first day of his new life as an international author. So, Alice thought, this is what I am spending the rest of my life with. This self-obsessed man who cares for no one but himself, so convinced of his own brilliance in every aspect of his life. He's going to be even more unbearable if his book is published. How could she possibly bear it another moment?

Marcus broke the silence. 'I've decided.'

'Mmmm?'

'I'm going up to London to hand my manuscript in personally and meet the people who will be dealing with it — make a big impression, you know, and be absolutely certain that it will be published exactly as I want it. I won't tolerate any interference. It's my book and it has to be done my way.'

Alice answered him after a long thoughtful drink of her tea.

'Has it occurred to you that they might have very different ideas from you of how they'll deal with it? You know, this character doesn't work well, or it would be better balanced if . . . after all, it is your first book.'

'Pass the milk. Quite frankly I shan't put up with it. It's my book, I know I've got it right and I shall stick out for having it published how I want it done, just exactly as it is. They've no right to interfere.'

'You seem to forget, Marcus, they will be *paying* you. And you, being new to publishing, might just have to fall in line with their thinking.'

Marcus cleared his mouth of toast and said officiously, 'Look, what do you know about publishing? I'll tell you. *Nothing.* I shall have it my way. *Full stop!*'

Alice stood her ground. 'This will be my last word on the matter. You could find they have decided to change it as they have determined, and you, if you object, could find yourself without a publisher.'

'Rubbish.'

'They're not a charity, Marcus. They're in it to make money and they will have strong ideas on exactly how they will treat it. Don't come home crying to me when they've turned you down. It's happened before and it could happen again.'

Marcus paused to look at her over the rim of his cup. 'You have so little faith in me. I praise you for everything you do, but when it's my turn for the limelight you're scathing and practical. I was right: you are envious of me. I'm doing what I said I would and no one is going to stop me. I shall need money for London so watch our bank account — we don't want to go into overdraft. I'll go get dressed. Is my best shirt washed and ironed?'

'Yes.' Alice almost added 'and good riddance to you', but she didn't. She needed to retain a measure of self-respect, though why she did she didn't know, when all her life was being slowly destroyed by people who she had supposed loved her, and there was nothing she could do about it.

While Marcus dressed she sat with her elbows on the kitchen table, hugging yet another mug of tea, wondering what Johnny was doing at this very minute. She pictured him in that beautiful house that had been Sir Ralph's with its new decorations, its brand-new kitchen, the inglenook fireplace in the sitting room fully restored. It had needed doing after the fire. That fire was all so terrible, with Muriel burned to death and Ralph dying so quickly afterwards from a broken heart. They'd been so very happy together. So had she, but where was all that now?

Marcus came clattering down the stairs, his arrival in the hall impeded by his suitcase.

'You're going for a few days then?'

'Of course. I can't do it all in a day. There'll be talks with marketing and publicity and editors. I've got to start as I mean to go on, up there in front, in charge.'

'Perhaps that all comes later when the contract is signed. You forget they haven't bought it yet; maybe a bit of appreciation might be a good idea.'

'Alice! Where are you coming from? You haven't the faintest idea how to go about getting

43

a book published. You leave it all to me. I'm not having any book of mine ruined. You'll see! Right, I've got my credit cards. Have you any cash, just till I get to a cash point?'

'There's a twenty-pound note in my purse.'

'That's not enough; you know the price of things in London.'

She rummaged through her purse again and said, 'I have another fiver, that's all. You've cleaned me out.'

'That'll have to do. Wish me luck.' He stuffed the notes into his wallet.

'Good luck. I hope it all goes well.'

'I've just thought, Alice. I don't know how long I shall be away. I can't leave the car in Culworth railway station for days. Give me a lift.'

'I'm not dressed. You'll have to wait — won't be long.'

Almost steaming with impatience Marcus said roughly, 'Just pop your coat on over your pyjamas. You're not getting out of the car; no one will notice.'

Desperate to get him out of the house, she did as he said — her coat on, in the front passenger seat. They were off, with Marcus driving like a madman. How they reached Culworth Station without having a serious accident Alice didn't know. She sat white-faced, gripping her seat as he overtook on bends and ignored speed limits: a journey that took half an hour on a quiet day took them twenty minutes in the early-morning traffic. Marcus dragged his case from the boot, waved a careless 'goodbye' and disappeared into the ticket office.

Alice sighed with relief. She was glad to see him go. This wild confidence which had overtaken him didn't bode well. He could very well come home with nothing and the whole process would start again. Money, of the kind Johnny had, interested her not at all, though she could see the advantages of it when she compared Marcus and Johnny. Marcus had no choices; Johnny had them all. If he wrote a book he could afford to publish it himself without thinking twice about it.

Oh! Johnny! Where did we go wrong? She shuffled her legs around the gear lever to get into the driving seat and, as though she had called him up just by thinking of him, she saw him in the rear-view mirror. Getting out of a taxi right there behind her. The driver hefted two huge suitcases out, Johnny paid him and strode towards the station platforms, his gait barely affected by the weight of the cases. Two big heavy suitcases! That must mean he was going wherever he was going for a long time. Perhaps for ever. Alice felt as though she'd been winded by a heavy blow aimed right in her solar plexus. She tried sucking air into her lungs but that didn't work, so she sat crippled by searing pain. God help us! Now what? The car windows were closed but she tried to shout 'Johnny!' at the top of her voice. She silently moaned, *Please, please, Johnny, don't go.*

Loud tooting alerted her; she was in the way. The car refused to start up, her tears blinded her, both legs refused to do as she wanted. In fact no part of her worked properly, not just her legs. Finally the engine fired and she stole slowly away, ravaged by grief.

Alice drove all the way home like a somnambulist, holding up the traffic and not caring that she did.

# 5

The news of Johnny's abrupt departure had spread through Turnham Malpas by teatime that day. The news of Marcus's departure took a while longer, but the significance of both their exits from the village was minutely examined in the Royal Oak.

'They *say* a publisher has offered to buy his book, but with him never going anywhere how can he write books anyone would want to buy?'

'How much will he get for a book, do you think?'

Willie shook his head. 'No idea. Could be millions; could be peanuts.'

'The rector saw him setting off when he was coming back from his run, didn't speak because Marcus drove out of the village so fast he couldn't have caught 'em if he'd had wings,' said Dottie. 'She was with him, he said, so she must have gone to bring the car back.'

'If he gets millions for it, I'll eat my hat,' Don ventured. 'Can't think how a man like him would write anything worth anything. He has one subject of conversation and that's . . . him. If you talk to 'im it's all about 'im and 'is writing, nothing else. A whole book about Marcus March! Huh!'

Sylvia said, 'He might surprise us all. Who knows what goes on in his head? I feel sorry for Alice — lovely talent she's got; she could go far but she's the one with the money to earn, slogging away teaching when she should be flying high singing in important places.'

Maggie hunched herself over the table so they could hear her more easily and whispered, 'I reckon he's a bully.'

'No! Do you think so, really?' they all said in unison.

'Sometimes in the summer I go out my bottom garden gate and feed the geese at night before they go to sleep, and one time, May or June time it was when the nights are light, I heard him having a right go at her. Shouting and carrying on. I'm not saying he hits her — how could anyone, her being such a lovely girl, well . . . woman. I couldn't hear her saying a word, even though she has that powerful voice, her being a singer like she is. I reckon he's on the nasty side.'

'He's full of himself, that's for certain, but he's so boring! Never going anywhere, never talking to anyone, crouched over his blessed computer. Bet she's glad he's gone,' Sylvia said.

Dottie, more interested in the glorious Johnny than Marcus March, suggested that Alice could be a lot more upset about Johnny going. 'They could have had a great time while the hopeful novelist's in London seeing his publisher. I wonder what's made Johnny go, all of a sudden. Maybe he's got bored with living in a village. I mean, just think of Brazil and all that money he has with them hotels!'

'I thought they made a lovely couple, both of 'em good looking and him with his money. Alice could really do the big time with her singing.' This was Maggie having her say, filled with envy at the prospect of beautiful dresses and all that applause, which reminded her of choir practice. 'Hell! What's the time? Sylvia! look at the time; we're going to be late!'

'It's not choir tonight. Today's Friday!' protested Dottie.

Sylvia leaped to her feet. 'Yes, it is, it's the extra, extra practice because of the competition. Where's my music? Here it is. See you all later. Come on, Dottie, hurry up.'

They rushed into the church hall to find, instead of Alice, Gilbert standing ready to begin.

The two of them shuffled into their places, apologising to Gilbert with brief nods of their heads.

'Good evening, ladies. I'm standing in for Alice tonight; she has a touch of flu. She's told me all she wants me to go through so we'll press on. There's the lovely Mia, with hands poised to play the first of Alice's voice exercises. Shall we begin? I hope you don't mind having to put up with me.'

Having to put up with him? They most certainly could. It was difficult to put into words what it was about Gilbert that was so attractive, but attractive he most certainly was. Everyone in the choir was bewitched by him. They knew he was married to Louise and that they had five lovely children, that he never ever flirted with any of them because he had no interest in any women other than his wife, but still they were intrigued by him; he wore the same clothes summer and winter, shirt unbuttoned almost to the waist, sleeves rolled up, cotton trousers, heavy sandals on bare feet, and it didn't matter if it was freezing — he had never been seen wearing a coat or sweater. This gave him a very positive aura of masculinity, besides which he had dark, deep-set eyes, a year-round tan, and a tumble of curly hair that, though clean, appeared never to have known the strictures of a hairbrush. As for his voice . . . there weren't words to adequately describe the deeply pleasing timbre of it, both speaking and singing, which made their knees turn to jelly. So, yes, they sang their hearts out . . . just for Gilbert.

'Now we've warmed up we'll have a go at singing 'Amazing Grace'. Overdone and oversung but nevertheless that's what's on the agenda for the competition and far be it from me to ignore it. Passion, ladies, and a tinge of deep sadness mixed with triumph. Who sings the solo voice?'

'Me.'

'Come out to the front, Laura.'

'Can't I — '

'Out here right by me, please.'

So Laura went out to the front, as one did if that was what Gilbert wanted.

'I think, Mia, you might not have accompanied this with a slightly syncopated rhythm, but that's how I want it. This song is always drawled along and that heightens the sugariness with which it is already overloaded. We want hope, not sugar. So we shall sharpen the pace and add a hint of syncopation. Thanks.'

50

Gilbert lifted the baton and they were away. After three false starts they got going with it and finished triumphantly with Laura's solo voice putting the final exquisite touch to it.

'Excellent! Excellent! Laura, that was magnificent. You're so good, all of you. Try for a little less of the vibrato, if you please though. I like the voice to be pure.' He bunched his fingers and touched his mouth like a Frenchman would, and they all felt their hearts beat a little faster. 'Mia! We'll have those two last lines again.'

Eventually Laura from Penny Fawcett sang the lines five more times and then got it absolutely right as far as Gilbert was concerned. 'Excellent, very moving but without sentimentality; just how I wanted it. On we go. I think you'll have a head start singing it this way at the competition. I'm seeing Alice at the end of rehearsal so I'll tell her what we've planned.'

The choir members were exhausted by the time the rehearsal finished, his more vigorous approach making it harder than with Alice. While many went back to the Royal Oak, Gilbert did as he said he would and went to report to Alice.

He knocked on her front door and walked in. 'Alice!'

'In the kitchen!'

'I said you had a touch of flu. OK?'

'Thanks.'

'It was good. You've trained them well. They are very keen.'

'Laura — all right was she?'

'Excellent.' He went on to outline the songs they had covered, then Gilbert said, 'I'm ready

51

for a cup of tea. I'll make it, shall I?'

Alice nodded.

'Then you can tell me why you asked me to say you had a touch of flu, which you very obviously haven't.'

'There's nothing to tell.'

'The village grapevine tells me Marcus has had a communication from a publisher. Surely that's good news?'

'Yes, he has, but this has happened before and when they saw the whole manuscript they turned it down. He's absolutely confident that they mean it this time, but I'm more cautious.'

'They've asked him to go see them; that must mean something, surely?'

Alice shook her head. 'They asked to see the rest of the manuscript and talked about a trilogy, but they didn't say to go to see them. He's determined that he should so he can control things from the word go.'

'I don't think it works like that . . . '

'Exactly. I've said that myself but he won't listen.'

'That's it then; you're upset because you're on your own.' He raised a disbelieving eyebrow and she found him difficult to resist. 'Well? Don't tell me if you really don't want to, but we all know about . . . Johnny.'

'He's gone too, loaded with two big suitcases.'

'Ah!'

'So . . . '

'But, my dear girl, you have Marcus. You married him, so you must have some feelings for him.'

'Gilbert! I don't want to say any more except I'm devastated about Johnny going. That's it. Devastated. I honestly am.'

'In those circumstances all you can do is maintain your life as best you can, soldier on and eventually the pain will ease. Sitting curled up in a chair in front of a fire letting the world pass you by is no solution. No solution at all. You have your life to live, and you'll have to get on with it. Don't let the rest of your years be ruined by one man who decided to walk away. Although you can't see it now, maybe it's all for the best.'

'I hear what you say. Thanks for listening.'

He smiled kindly at her. 'I won't stay for that tea. Good night. Call on me any time. I shan't mind and neither will Louise.'

Alice said nothing, but managed a small smile.

Louise smiled too when he told her about Alice's dilemma. 'I feel for her. It happened to me. That's why I came back to live here. I really didn't want to, not with Mother querying my every move.'

'Really? You never told me that.'

'Yes. Got badly let down by a chap I'd organised a bank loan for. Lost my job over it too. The heart rules the mind so often. I knew he wasn't sound but . . . I loved him and he said he loved me and was full of promises, till he got the loan and then reneged on it. But there we are. Fortunately, coming back home meant I met you.'

'Well, I'm glad.' Gilbert placed a smacking kiss on her forehead. 'You realise it's Johnny Templeton, not Marcus, that's the trouble?'

'Of course. Who can blame her when Marcus is a bore and totally selfish? I wonder what's made Johnny go away? They seem so right for each other.'

'No idea. Alice didn't say. I'd put money on the choir winning the competition. The best is Laura Turner from Penny Fawcett.'

Louise laughed. 'They won't like that! Can anything good come out of Penny Fawcett, I ask myself?' The two of them laughed. Then one of the children woke crying with a nightmare and that put an end to their laughter.

★   ★   ★

About midnight, just as Alice had finally got to sleep, she was disturbed by someone knocking loudly at the door. She heard Marcus's voice and braced herself.

'You put the bolts on,' he said angrily when she opened the door.

'I thought you were staying in London. What else would I do?'

Marcus flung his suitcase down on the floor and stormed into the kitchen. 'I need something.'

'Like?'

'Tea and toasted teacake, or a scone or something, please.'

'Right. Can I ask how it went?'

'No.'

'OK. Tea and toasted teacake coming up.' Alice kept silent and busied herself getting it ready for him. A teacake was always his comfort food and by the looks of his face comfort was needed.

They drank tea and Marcus gobbled down his teacake and asked for another.

'Right.' In that case, things were worse than she'd imagined.

When he finished the second teacake Marcus was able to speak. 'Half the people I needed to see were away at a sales conference. Those I did see said thank you very much for the complete manuscript, but they weren't in a position to discuss anything at all till the commissioning editor had decided about it. I said, 'Decided about it? Do you mean he is uncertain about it?' The reply to that was that it was a matter for the commissioning editor when he'd read it all and decided whether or not they wanted it.'

Marcus drank his tea right to the bottom, leaned back in his chair and said, 'So I had to come away not knowing.'

'That was bad luck, going when the people who mattered weren't there.'

'I don't need your sympathy, thank you very much.' He shuffled about angrily trying to get comfortable, but knowing he wouldn't. 'I could be waiting weeks for a decision.'

'Possibly, yes. They need to be sure it's the right book for them. After all, if they publish it they are putting a lot of money behind it, as well as time and effort.'

Alice hadn't intended to be provocative but Marcus jumped up and just before slamming the door behind him said, 'My book doesn't need to be considered; it's too good for them to miss!'

Alice was very aware she'd made a big mistake after this parting shot. Nevertheless, what she'd said was true; his problem was he couldn't face his disappointment after all his cock-a-hoop boasting last night.

Marcus still had hope of success though, whereas she had none at all. Oh! Johnny! Oh! Johnny, please come back. I'll apologise a thousand times for my foolishness, if only you'll come back. Just to see you, even from a distance, would be enough for me.

She and Marcus spent a restless night because Marcus didn't sleep a wink, so next morning Alice felt completely ghastly, which didn't help her cope with Marcus's bad temper. He cheered up eventually, after some tactful ego-boosting comments from Alice, and hastened up to his attic with the intention of beginning the sequel he was convinced they would be begging him for.

The doorbell rang about half past ten and it was Harriet standing there, bearing a gift of flowers.

'Alice! Gilbert said you were ill, so I've brought you flowers to cheer you up.'

'Come in! It was a false alarm; I feel much better this morning. Thank you for these, much appreciated. Have you time for a coffee?'

'Are you sure? If you're not well . . . '

'I am and I could do with some company. These flowers are lovely. I'll stand them in water and arrange them later.'

'Will it disturb Marcus? Oh! Of course, no, he's in London.'

'He's back actually, but he's busy writing so we won't disturb him.'

Harriet loved Alice's kitchen — the inglenook fireplace made it so homely. They sat either side of the fire enjoying their coffee and chatted.

Harriet asked her about Marcus's success at the publishers', reminded her about the coffee morning of Bridget Cleary's in aid of the flood victims, and then mentioned about choir practice the previous night. 'Gilbert added a new hurdle for us to master.'

'What was that?'

'Singing 'Amazing Grace' in a syncopated rhythm.'

Alice would never work out why she took umbrage at this statement, but she did. It felt like the last straw after yesterday.

'You must be mistaken.'

'No, it's true and I have to say it certainly gave it some oomph! Made it go with real gusto.' Harriet immediately sensed she'd made a huge mistake in mentioning the change. 'I'm sorry, I didn't mean — '

'He never told me that was what he'd done.'

Harriet faltered. 'Well, I suppose we could always go back to — '

'We will go back and have it as I prefer it; make no doubt about that. 'Amazing Grace' syncopated, for heaven's sakes.' Alice glanced at the clock. 'He's usually home about five. I'll go round and ask him about it then. I'm not having it.'

Harriet began to feel uncomfortable. Alice appeared unnecessarily angry. After all, Gilbert was very experienced musically, and if Alice had heard it she would have been convinced it was a good idea, Harriet was sure. She talked a while longer and then stated that the kitchens at the Old Barn were claiming her attention and she really must go.

Alice, left alone with her thoughts, worked herself up into such a temper she decided to go round to Louise and ask her what had possessed Gilbert to change her plans for 'Amazing Grace'. But she needed to put some work in on her music first and decided to do that and then go round to see Louise immediately before lunch. No, she wouldn't — she'd go now, right now while she was so angry about the whole situation. She told Marcus where she was going and slammed the door behind her.

Louise was ironing a pile of clothes. Alice had never faced a pile so high, but then Louise was ironing for seven, not two.

'Hello, Alice. Feeling better?'

'I was until I heard what Gilbert has done to 'Amazing Grace'.'

Louise had learned to take life very calmly with five children and a busy husband like Gilbert, so the anger in Alice's voice didn't ruffle her. 'Don't you like the idea?'

'No, I do not. Is he at home today?'

'Home about half past five I expect, as usual. But don't come then because we eat when he gets home and our house is hectic from about four thirty until eight, what with homework and music practice. After eight when the younger ones are off to bed is better.'

'Right. Eight o'clock it is. I shall be round, so warn him: I'm so angry about it. It may seem nothing to you, but it is to me. It's my choir, not his.'

Diplomatically Louise gently offered, 'I would have thought that syncopation would jolly it up and make the Turnham Malpas Ladies' Choir stand out from the rest in a competition. Don't you think it's worth a try, surely?'

'No. I don't.' As she watched Louise pick up what appeared to be the hundredth school shirt she'd ironed since Alice arrived she suddenly burst into tears, howling, 'You're so lucky. Did you know? So lucky.'

Very quietly Louise said, 'I know I am. I'm sorry you haven't children, if that's what you want. But . . . believe me, you wouldn't have time for your music like you have now and that in itself is a gift. Children are very time consuming.'

Alice continued to weep. Louise unplugged the iron and went to sit beside her.

'It's not just . . . not having children, is it? It's Johnny perhaps?'

Alice nodded.

'Maybe he's gone home for a family emergency and will be back in no time at all. Have you not heard from him, had no explanation?'

Alice shook her head.

'You know for certain?'

'I told him I wanted to divorce Marcus and then we could be together, and he was horrified and immediately the next day he left. I honestly thought that he felt like I did. He said he did but he didn't, did he, if he's left so abruptly?'

Louise handed her a tissue. 'There are some men, you know, who are scared to death of marriage and the commitment it means. You know, staying with the same woman for life, pushing the pram, loading the car with baby belongings just for an afternoon out when before they'd been as free as air. They panic and it's only when they can't help themselves because they're so much in love that they agree. It could be that.'

'I don't think so.'

'Well, you'll have to wait and see, won't you, and get on with your life, giving singing lessons and piano lessons and making the best of what you have. Does Marcus — ?'

'Oh! No, he doesn't. And he mustn't.'

'So you still care about his feelings then?'

'I only care about the temper he'll be in if he ever finds out. I don't care about him and haven't for a long time.'

'Oh! Alice, I never realised. I'm so sorry.'

'I'm going before I say any more. Sorry for being so ridiculous.'

'You're not, honestly. I'm just sorry it's like that for you.'

Alice stood up. 'I'm going. Thanks. I'll be back tonight later on like you said. Do I look as if I've been crying?'

Louise shook her head.

As Alice left Louise said to her, 'My lips are sealed. Oh! That's Gilbert's car. He's early.'

Alice felt unbelievably silly for having wept, in

fact unbelievably silly for taking such umbrage over 'Amazing Grace' in the first place, and then she did a rapid rethink and thought, no, it was her choir, her choice, so she would tell him right now, as she had said she would.

Gilbert was contrite. 'Sorry, Alice, but I did feel that as it was for a competition maybe doing it differently would be a good idea, make it stand out, you know? Marvellous words, terrific sentiments, but it can come over sugary, can't it? Sorry.'

It was said in the gentlest manner but it still annoyed her. 'Next time I have to ask you to help out with the choir, please remember, it's *my* choir, *my* choice and *I* say how it has to be sung. I know you are excellent at singing, especially when we look at the success your choirboys have, but this choir is *mine*.'

'I never for one moment intended to give offence to you, Alice. Please forgive me.' Gilbert smiled that beguiling smile of his and Alice softened a little.

'All I can say, Gilbert, is don't let it happen again. OK?'

'Right. That it then?'

'Yes.' Alice left without waiting for Gilbert to see her to the door.

When she got home Marcus was clattering about in the kitchen making himself a cup of tea. He was the first to admit he was hopeless at anything to do with cooking, but Alice always suspected that he said that to get out of doing anything not immediately associated with his writing. Alice felt her anger rising again.

'I can't find a thing in this kitchen! Why can't we have it properly organised?'

'It is organised. Here, look! Here's the teapot, the tea canister right beside it. The tap half a metre away and the milk is in the fridge, and that is the kettle. The mugs are in the cupboard to your right where they've always been since we moved in. So what's your problem?'

'Oh! I see. Gilbert's got up your nose has he, so you're taking it out on me.'

'Yes, he did, but he's apologised and we're friends again. It's you that's my trouble: I do all the work, I earn all the money and what do you do? Spend hours up in the attic, writing books that never get published. Hasn't it dawned on you yet that maybe it might be more sensible if you went back to the job you're qualified to do and wrote in your spare time? Maybe that way you might actually join the real world.'

'In my spare time? My God, Alice, you certainly know how to twist the knife.'

'You've spent years obsessed with writing, yearning for the unobtainable, and I'm sick of it. Get real, Marcus.'

Marcus swung round on her and for one appalling moment she thought he was going to hit her. Flashing through her mind was the idea that after all, this house belonged to her, not to him, and if she wanted, she could turn him out. The idea struck her with refreshing enlightenment.

'You're very cruel speaking to me like that. You're my wife, or have you forgotten? After all the hard work I've put in. The hours I've struggled, the endeavour, all the heartbreaking rejection I've had to swallow and you say that to me.' He grew taller with his indignation.

'Ten years! Ten years and you've not earned a penny and you — '

'Just wait till they accept this book, then you won't be talking to me about money; we'll have it by the shed load.'

'When that day comes I shall take back all I've said, but right now, you'll have to put up with it, because I've reached the end of my tether. Made the tea yet? I'll have mine in front of the TV, please.'

She marched out of the kitchen feeling better than she had for years. It had been said and she'd meant every word of it, every single word. From now on if he didn't put money in the kitty then he'd have to do all the gardening, make the occasional meal, and generally help to make her life easier. She'd been a willing doormat for far too long.

When her tea arrived there was no sugar on the tray, though he'd known for the last twelve years she always took sugar in her tea.

Alice pointed out his forgetfulness in a carping tone that was alien to her, but before she'd said more than three words, Marcus picked up his own mug of tea and threw the contents right down the front of her. 'I won't be spoken to in that manner! Get your own tea in future.' He gave her a sneer of a smile and left the sitting room, closing the door with a crash, and as the tea soaked into her clothes Alice heard him tramping angrily up the two flights of stairs to his eyrie.

Dottie, leaving the pub at closing time with Zack and Marie, was witness to the sight of heavy black plastic bags being thrown out of the bedroom window of Alice and Marcus's house. There was no sign of Marcus objecting, and no sign that Alice was in tears about it, for she was throwing them out with deadly intent. The four bags landed in the road and they stepped round them disinclined to protest, because, by the looks of it, Marcus had at last met his just deserts.

# 6

Naturally Dottie reported the event when she went to do her cleaning stint at the Rectory the following morning. 'You see, rector, we've all known for years his idea about getting published was a load of rubbish, just a nonsense to make sure he didn't have to work. They were obviously his belongings being thrown out of the house because a pair of men's trousers fell out from one of 'em. We couldn't believe it! As Marie said, 'No more than he deserves.' Have you heard anything?'

'Nothing at all. Not a word.'

'Question is, where is he now? Did he sleep in the house last night? Or did she make him leave immediately? Perhaps he had to sleep in his car. What's more, what on earth triggered it?'

Peter was looking out of his study window as Dottie asked these questions to which he had no answers. 'Leave it with me. I'll call round.'

'Right. Thanks. Anything special the doctor required doing this morning?'

'No. Nothing.'

'I'll get cracking with my usual then.'

Peter, left alone in his study, only half-listened to the vacuum cleaner and Dottie singing her latest favourite pop song. Oh! Johnny! What a mess you've left behind. Why on earth did you go? Had Alice told you she would never leave Marcus? Yet here she was throwing out his

65

clothes. Peter sighed as he headed over to Alice's. He knocked on Alice and Marcus's door and had to wait a while before he found out if anyone was at home.

Alice was dressed rather carelessly for her, and obviously embarrassed at seeing Peter on the doorstep.

'Sorry! I thought it might be Marcus.'

'You sound relieved.'

'I am.'

'Thought perhaps you might want someone to talk to . . . after . . . last night.'

'You know, then?' Alice was more in control of herself. 'I've just put some coffee on. Will the kitchen do?'

'Of course.'

'Sit down, I won't be a minute.'

After her first sip of coffee Alice opened up. 'I turned him out last night. I don't know where he went and I don't care.'

'What happened?'

'I've got sick of supporting him day in day out, year in year out. He gives me no consideration, just expects me to earn the living, do the shopping, keep the garden going; he does absolutely nothing but writing and being waited on hand and foot. So I decided he had to go.'

'I see. It wasn't because of Johnny, then? Marcus hadn't found out?'

Alice didn't reply and occupied herself by sipping her coffee and staring at the neglected wood-burning stove.

'Everyone knows.' Peter said this so softly she could barely hear his words.

66

'I expect you, with your secure marriage and your exceedingly high standards of morality, consider me a harlot, do you?' The uncharacteristic bitterness in Alice's voice surprised Peter.

'My opinion has nothing to do with it. You are one of my parishioners and I know you wouldn't have done such a thing without serious provocation so I've come to help. If talking to someone impartial and nonjudgemental will help, then here I am.'

'Mmm.'

Peter remained quiet and waited for Alice to speak.

Eventually she looked him directly in the face, saying, 'He's gone, you know. Johnny. For ever, I think. I expected commitment and apparently there wasn't any, despite him saying how much he wanted to be with me. I . . . I'm . . . well, I suppose I'm deeply in love with him, and want to be with him, for always, but . . . ' Alice shrugged.

'I see.'

'No, you don't, Peter. You don't see anything. I've been two-timing Marcus almost from the first day Johnny arrived in the village. It's not his wealth I'm interested in, but believe me he is very wealthy . . . it's him, he's magic. We can't help ourselves. Have you felt like that, ever?'

'Only with Caroline; we met and married inside four months. We both knew the first time we met.'

'It was like that for Johnny and me. All consuming. Inevitable. Him going has made me see what a pointless marriage I have, so at last I have stood up for myself and finished it. Trouble is I've lost Johnny too.' Tears welled in her eyes.

'Has he *said* he won't be back?'

Alice shook her head.

'Then maybe he will, Alice. There's always hope, you know.'

'I don't think so.'

Someone knocked at the door. 'That'll be a pupil I'm expecting. Sorry.'

'I'll let them in. I'm always at home to anyone in trouble. Don't hesitate, will you? Just come and see me?'

Alice nodded her acknowledgement of his kindness and went to greet her pupil, more unfit to teach than she could ever remember.

Peter's phone was ringing when he got back to the Rectory and Dottie was rushing down the stairs to answer it.

'I'll get it, Dottie, thanks. Good morning. Peter Harris speaking. How can I help?'

'It's me.'

'Yes?'

'Marcus March. I don't doubt you know that Alice banned me from the house last night with some story about having had enough of me. I'm certain she doesn't mean it, because she wouldn't. After all, I've done nothing wrong. Not been unfaithful or anything. However, I'm off to London today, to see my publisher.' He paused for effect, expecting to get an admiring response, but none was forthcoming. 'So I'm going to give you my mobile number in case Alice is upset and needs me at home. You're the first person I thought of because I know you won't gossip like the rest of the ill-begotten lot in the village.'

'Right. I have been to see her, and yes she's upset, but determined to carry on. However, if things get worse I will gladly phone you, but only with Alice's permission. On that understanding.'

'With Alice's permission! What does that mean?'

'Exactly what it says. Only at her request. Hasn't she got your mobile number herself? She must have.'

'Yes, but she might not ring. She can be very stubborn and she has no one but me to care for her.'

'I see. Give me the number then.'

'I wouldn't want . . . anyway . . . never mind.' He gave Peter the number and Peter dutifully put it in his phone.

'Hope everything goes well with your publisher. Big opportunity for you.'

'Only what I deserve, you know. Only what I deserve. Thank you. Bye.'

'Bye.'

Peter guessed that Marcus was trying to preserve his marriage as though he were the innocent party and he rather despised him for it. His motives appeared to be self-driven rather than Alice-driven. He'd never liked the man; he was far too concerned with his own ego. Still, if he did get published, financially one hoped they would be better off, but . . . and there was a big but . . .

Had Peter known that as soon as Marcus switched off his mobile he went immediately to the bank and cleaned out his and Alice's joint bank account he might not have been so helpful.

69

★　★　★

In the bar that night there were mixed feelings about Marcus's dramatic departure. Willie was certain it was the best thing that could have happened, but Sylvia wasn't quite so sure. 'Marriage is marriage and just because he doesn't know how to behave within a marriage is no excuse for driving Alice to such drastic action.'

This confusing statement puzzled them all, but it was Dottie who asked for some light to be shed on it. 'Just a minute, Sylvia, I can't make out whose side you're on. Alice or Marcus? Well?'

'To be honest I don't really know, there's faults on both sides isn't there?'

'You name Alice's faults then, because I can't.'

All those seated round the old table waited for Sylvia's reply. 'Well, she hasn't any, but who knows better than Marcus what goes on behind their front door?'

Zack sniggered, Marie gave him a dig with her elbow to shut him up and Dottie roared with laughter. When she finally calmed down Dottie said, 'Well, my word, that opens up a can of worms. What goes on behind *your* front door then, Sylvia?'

Willie was furious and said so immediately. 'Typical of you, Dottie, a remark like that. Nothing untoward goes on behind *our* front door, but what about yours? Eh! A lot too much went on in the past as everyone sitting round this table knows full well, though we don't say

70

anything out of politeness. There were years of it, but none of us ever criticised you for it. And what's more you should be grateful we keep quiet. You were nothing more than a . . . well, anyway.'

A shocked silence ensued. Dottie was horrified. She thought for years that her past life, chequered though it was, was no longer of any interest to anyone at all in the village, except for the older ones who'd known her all her life. And here Willie had broadcast it all round the pub, loud as loud and her whole sad life was out in the open.

Several of them, shocked to the core, said 'Willie!' in horrified tones.

Willie's reply was, 'Have I spoken the truth or what? You all thought the same except it was me that said it. Out loud.'

When Dottie replied her voice was choked with emotion. 'That remark is absolutely unforgivable. A thousand apologies from you will never ever make me forgive you for it, Willie. Never.' Dottie, blinded by tears, stumbled to her feet, pushed her chair out of her way and left the bar. She struggled all the way home down Shepherd's Hill sobbing, staggering in through the door and slumping down on the sofa, at the same time glad but mad that no one had the thoughtfulness to catch her up and offer her comfort.

She'd never denied she been free with her favours, as her mother called it, but unskilled, uneducated, Dottie had found herself in her teens without any means of support and, with the rent to find for the cottage, had taken to the

71

age-old profession of prostitution. Never on the streets, but always available in the old house at the bottom of Shepherd's Hill her mother had rented for years before she was taken into a mental hospital, the horror of which had never left Dottie. She'd given comfort to lots of men in need of kindness and to those who only needed to talk to someone with a sympathetic ear, until eventually she got too old and took to cleaning. For the last fifteen years no one had ever referred to her situation, ever, but there it was coming unbidden out of the woodwork to remind her all over again what a waste of space she was.

She finally managed to make herself a cup of tea, to which she added a drop of whisky to help revive her. How could he? How could Willie remind her when she thought all that part of her life had been well and truly forgotten? Showed what people were like, just waiting for the right moment to stab you in the back. She'd never be able to show her face in the village again.

Then Dottie leaped to her feet at the realisation she simply couldn't go to the Rectory tomorrow to clean, and her heart broke. Nor do the couple of hours at Harriet and Jimbo's like she did every Thursday afternoon, and never again would she help alongside Pat Jones with the events at the Old Barn for Jimbo. But it was not being able to work at the Rectory that really hurt the most, for she loved working there. And here was she thinking all these years that she had finally left her past behind. She'd been deceiving herself. She'd have to write a note. She'd take it up there in the dark when no one would see her.

Then she remembered she wasn't all that good at writing.

It took her three painful tries to construct a note that appeared readable and wouldn't show her up for what she was. She found an envelope and addressed it, glanced at the clock and saw it said nearly ten past eleven and decided to leave there and then to take it up to the Rectory. Then in the morning she'd order a taxi for the station and go to stay with her cousin Irene, whom she knew she could rely on to welcome her with open arms, her always feeling lonely.

★   ★   ★

It was Peter who found the envelope on the hall carpet when he checked the front door was bolted before joining Caroline in bed.

'Darling! There's a letter for you.'

'For me? I wonder who it's from?' She dropped the book she was reading on the duvet and ripped open the envelope.

As she read it she gasped. 'Oh! Peter, it's from Dottie. She says . . . I can't believe this; what on earth can have happened?'

'What do you mean? What's she said?'

'Here, you read it.'

*Dear Doctor Harris,*

*I shall not be coming to clean no more. I should not have had the cheek to start in the first place because I am not a fit person to clean for you and the rector. I'm sorry. Yours sincerely,*

*Dottie Foskett.*
*PS. Please give my love to my dear Beth and to Alex. I shall miss them and you.*

Peter handed it back to her. 'Someone somewhere has said something and here's the result of it. Poor Dottie. I shall go see her first thing.'

'I can't believe this. What on earth has made her say what she's said? No one thinks to mention it nowadays. Poor Dottie.'

'I'm sure she must have misunderstood; people in the village wouldn't dream of bringing the matter up . . . would they?'

'Perhaps someone feeling vicious thought to mention it. She must be heartbroken! No one cleans like Dottie; I could recommend her to absolutely anyone.'

'Like I said I'll call round tomorrow and get to the bottom of it.'

'Yes, please do and make her understand that she's needed here no matter what others have said about her; we want her back a.s.a.p. The hurt she must be feeling . . . people can be so cruel. But who the blazes would confront her with it?'

Peter climbed into bed, grimly remarking, 'Don't fret, I shall find out. Good night and God bless, my darling, it's lonely not having the children to say goodnight to, isn't it?'

'Yes, but they're having a wonderful time; they'll remember it all their lives.'

'True.'

Caroline turned over so she lay behind Peter

with her arm around his waist. 'Good thing Beth isn't home or she'd be round the village interrogating everyone to find out who's been so thoughtless as to hurt Dottie. They are very close.'

'Dottie has a great deal of wisdom; I've always thought so. Good down-to-earth wisdom. I'll be round her house first thing tomorrow, I promise.'

★　★　★

And Peter was. But the house was locked up. He shielded his eyes and peered in through the downstairs windows but there were no signs of life. Everywhere looked tidy with no signs of a hasty departure.

Peter heard someone trying to attract his attention. It was Dottie's next-door neighbour calling to him over the wall.

'She's gone, rector, by eight o'clock this morning. I saw her leave as I was letting the dog out. In a taxi with a suitcase. I spoke to her yesterday morning but she never said a word about going away, so it must be something urgent because we leave each other our keys when we're away just in case, but she hasn't done, not this time.'

'Good morning, Audrey! When I think of you I always remember about when you played the fairy godmother in that pantomime we did once; I thought you were brilliant. So well done.'

Audrey blushed. 'Thank you, didn't think anyone remembered it.'

'Well, I do. Audrey, if you hear anything at all

about Dottie, get a card or anything from her, will you let me know? I feel very concerned about her, you see. We can't understand why she's gone. Look, here's my card with my number. Keep it and let me know, will you?'

'Thanks. Yes, I will. I couldn't have a better neighbour than Dottie. Lovely person, never a wrong word and always a good laugh.'

But the card was propped against the clock on Audrey's mantelpiece and there was still no word from Dottie.

★   ★   ★

The night of the incident that so distressed Dottie, Willie and Sylvia had a terrible argument, the worst they had ever had. It began when Dottie scurried out of the bar looking so distressed. Sylvia stood up calling out, 'Dottie! Take no notice; he didn't mean it.'

But Dottie never looked back. In her fury Sylvia turned on Willie. 'Will you never learn, Willie Biggs, to control that tongue of yours?' Sylvia gave him such a push that he almost fell out of his chair. Her anger made her give him another push and his chair went over backwards and Willie with it.

This incensed him so much that despite his advancing years he rapidly stood upright and managed to proclaim for all the world to hear, 'I only spoke the truth. That's my defence.'

Zack, standing Willie's chair up for him, said, 'There's times to speak and times not.'

'You found it funny. I saw Marie give you a

76

nudge to shut you up.'

'But . . . the difference is I didn't say anything, did I? I'm ashamed of you, Willie, hurting her feelings like that.'

'So all of a sudden the truth is illegal, is it? We all have to tell lies, do we, to be politically correct as they call it?'

Sylvia, breathing hard, said between gritted teeth, 'Home!' pointing dramatically to the door. 'We shall have words when we get in.'

'Honestly, men aren't even masters in their own homes nowadays,' Willie grumbled.

Sylvia loudly retorted, 'Well, you certainly aren't! Out!'

And so it was that Willie slept the night on the sofa while Sylvia luxuriated in having the bed to herself and feeling distinctly self-righteous about it.

So after Peter's fruitless visit to Dottie's he drove home, parked the car in Church Lane and knocked on Willie Biggs's door. Sylvia answered and invited him in. 'I was coming round, rector, but I saw you leave in your car.'

'Ah! Do you have news about Dottie? She's left us a note to say she can't come to clean any more because she's not fit to do so. From the sound of it someone must have — '

Sylvia put a finger to her lips. 'Willie! There's a gentleman to see you.'

The distinct sounds of someone in the kitchen doing the washing up ceased and Willie appeared, looking downtrodden. 'Oh! Good morning, sir. You want to see me?'

'I don't know. Do I?'

'Yes, you do,' said Sylvia, arms akimbo, glaring at Willie.

Willie cleared his throat. 'There was an unfortunate altercation in the Royal Oak last night and unfortunately Dottie took it the wrong way. What I said was the truth but she took offence.'

'I've been to see her this morning because of a note she put through our letter box very late last night. Audrey, her neighbour, says she left first thing this morning in a taxi with a large suitcase.'

Sylvia gasped.

Hesitantly Willie asked if he knew where she'd gone.

'I don't know, because she's disappeared without even telling Audrey where.'

Willie had no reply to this, feeling too shocked to think.

So Sylvia replied on his behalf. 'He can't control his tongue nowadays. He's not as bad as Don, who can say the most out-of-place things and doesn't know he's doing it. Willie knows what he's saying but still he says it.'

Peter turned to Willie. 'What did you say, Willie?'

'Well, it was like this . . . ' So he related the whole conversation to this man for whom he had more respect than any other person on earth and felt deeply mortified as he said it. 'I can't apologise enough. If I could see her now I'd tell her how sorry I am. And I am. Very sorry. I'll get back to the washing up; I've nearly finished, love. It's mopping the floor next you said.'

Peter had to smile at Sylvia when Willie

returned to his domestic duties. 'I see why she is so upset. We never think on those terms, you know, Caroline and I.'

'Neither does anyone else, except Willie. I do hope she comes back. We'll all miss her. I'm so sorry, rector, I really am.'

'So am I. I'll let you know if I hear anything more. Bye, Sylvia.'

With his hand on the door latch, Peter said before he left, 'That's three people gone from the village in one week. What is wrong with everyone?'

'Don't worry too much about Dottie; she's pretty tough is Dottie.'

'Perhaps, Sylvia, but not quite tough enough it would seem.'

'I'm sorry all over again about what Willie said. He simply didn't think.'

Peter nodded his head. 'You see, Dottie is acutely sensitive about her past life, though she may not appear to be.'

# 7

During this first term at Cambridge Beth had chosen to come home for a weekend twice as often as Alex, and she was home again the weekend of the flood victims' coffee morning. She clung to her mother the moment she appeared and Caroline did not need to be told how much Beth missed her home.

'Had a good journey, darling?'

'Lots of traffic but not too bad, no major hold-ups.'

'I can't believe that you passed your test first time. It took me four goes to pass.'

'Mum! Honestly. Four tries! Mmm. Tea, cup of, needed immediately.'

'Kettle's already boiled. In the kitchen?'

'Dad home?'

'Shortly. Sick visiting in Little Derehams; it won't take him long. It's so lovely to see you. Dad was saying only the other night how lonely it was having no one but ourselves to say good night to.'

'It's lonely for me too.'

'But you've made friends, you say.'

'Oh! Yes, plenty, but no one I'm really close to and the temptation to dig out Alex is unbearable sometimes. But I don't. He doesn't want his sister tagging along. He's got his rugby friends, and his science faculty lot and he seems perfectly happy.'

'Here's your tea, darling. I think perhaps he isn't quite as content as you imagine.'

'Well, he's doing a very good impression of being so. I just don't fit in, you know.'

'I'm sorry you feel like that. But it is only your second term.'

'I know. Can I tell you why?'

'You can tell me anything you choose, as you well know.'

Beth sipped her tea, put the mug on the corner of the Aga and then said, 'Don't tell anyone else, not even Dad, but they all like partying and dashing about here there and everywhere and dressing up and it doesn't interest me one little bit, and I don't know why.'

'You used to enjoy parties. What do you prefer to do then?'

'Think about home, and everyone here and wish I was home where I belong and feeling safe. Sometimes it's so bad it hurts.'

'That sounds like bad homesickness and it can be very upsetting, but if you stick at it, it will get better. By the time you go back for your second year you won't be able to wait to get there, believe me.'

'You think so?'

'Yes, I do. Just get stuck in there and give yourself time.'

Beth picked up her mug again. 'Did you know Jake's there?'

'Jake Harding? Really! I thought he'd applied to London.'

'Apparently not. I saw him from a distance the first term; I couldn't believe it.' Beth looked down at her mug of tea and said very softly, 'He's better looking than ever.'

'I see. Is that possible, I ask myself?' Caroline smiled and Beth managed to smile back. 'Beth . . . you don't still have feelings for him?'

'I don't know. Maybe. I think I must have. It's a good thing he left Penny Fawcett when he did to live with his dad. Anyway, he can still turn my knees to jelly.'

The back door opened and in walked Peter. 'Beth, you're home! You've made good time. How's my favourite daughter?'

Beth sprang out of her chair and they hugged. 'All the better for seeing you, Dad.'

'And I am too for seeing you.'

'Tea, Dad?'

'Yes, please.'

Beth got out another mug, poured him his tea and then sat down again in the chair on the other side of the Aga to her mother. 'Everything all right in the village, Dad?'

'Apart from three people leaving in a hurry and we don't know where two of them have gone, yes, I suppose you could say everything's fine.'

'Who's left?'

'Johnny has gone home to Brazil we assume, leaving Alice desperate. Marcus has gone to London to see about his book being published. Before you ask, he has finally got a publisher and I understand from Alice he has taken all the money from their joint bank account. And now Dottie.'

At the mention of the third missing person

Beth's attention was immediately focused. 'Dad! Where's she gone?'

'That's it, we don't know.'

'Why has she gone?'

'All because Willie made an unfortunate remark in the pub the other night and Dottie took serious umbrage and went away very first thing the following morning.'

Beth, who had depended on Dottie right since her first coming to clean at the Rectory said, 'Right! I'll be back for my tea. Don't throw it away.'

'Where are you going?'

'I'm going next door to see Willie, of course. I'm not having this.'

The door to Willie and Sylvia's cottage was propped open so Beth marched in full of anger to get to the bottom of what Willie had said to make Dottie leave the village.

Willie was watching *Countdown* but when he heard Beth's voice he immediately called out, 'You're home, love! Come in, come in.' He found the remote, switched off his programme, delighted that she had called. 'Well, Beth love, how nice to see you. Sit yourself down. I was thinking the other day about how you and Alex used to love to come here for your tea and we'd have a game of Snakes and Ladders or Ludo or something. Didn't we have some fun? Eh?'

'Willie! Dottie's gone. What on earth did you say to her?'

Willie was alarmed by the anger in her voice, he who'd always felt like her substitute grandfather.

'It wasn't anything much, just caught her by surprise.'

'So, what was it? It must have been serious for her to run away; she's not the running away kind. She's strong, and she knows how to talk to people and I need her back, here in Turnham Malpas.'

Willie shuffled about a little, straightened the newspaper and put it in the magazine rack, asked her if she wanted a cup of tea and said Sylvia wouldn't be long, he didn't know what was keeping her.

'Was it about her being a prostitute when she was younger? Because I know all about that.'

Willie had to be truthful to this girl he'd known since the day she was born.

'Well, I'm afraid it was. I shouldn't have said what I said, but I did. It was nothing but the truth and I'm so sorry about it, you've no idea, but she didn't give me the chance to apologise. She went the very next morning before I'd even got up. How do you know about what . . . she was like when she was a younger woman?'

'She told me one day.'

Willie was horrified. 'Told you? She'd no business to.'

'Well, she did. Now all you can do is tell me anything at all that you know about her cousins. I know she has lots of cousins.' Rather threateningly Beth added, 'It's the least you can do. Given the circumstances.'

'There's the one who lives in Little Derehams, but I don't know her name; there's another one called Irene what lives on her own and always wants Dottie to go live with her because she hates being lonely.'

'So where does she live?'

'Somewhere Bristol way, I think.'

'You don't know any more than that? Do you think Sylvia might know?'

'She might, but I doubt it. The Fosketts have always bred like rabbits. Dottie once added up how many cousins she had and when she got to eighteen she had to stop, but she said there were many more.'

'When Sylvia comes home I'll ask her. We've got to find her; I can't bear her to be sad. I'm surprised at you, Willie, saying something about her past life to her. You should be ashamed.' Beth sat down to wait, saddened by her lack of progress, and Willie reluctantly had to decide that she had grown up since she'd gone to Cambridge, and he came to the conclusion she wouldn't be wanting a game of Ludo, not no more. He sighed for past happiness.

Sylvia didn't know where Dottie might have gone either. 'You see, love, it all happened so quick. She just went. I'm real sorry about what Willie said. Will you forgive him? He doesn't want to be at odds with you, nor Alex for that matter.'

'We can't do nothing; we've got to try to find her. You've no idea how she helped me, when I came back from Africa in such a state, more than any other person except Dad. Only Dottie could talk to me without tiptoeing round me as if I was a piece of Royal Worcester; I needed her and it's the least I can do after what she did for me. So, I'll be back.'

'Right, Beth, but remember me and Willie love you no matter what. I sat with you either side of the Aga in your Mum's kitchen feeding you, and your Mum feeding Alex, or vice versa, when you were hardly big enough to have left the hospital and I love you as if you were my own. Don't fall out permanent, will you?'

Beth turned back to smile at her, whispered 'Thanks,' and went home.

It was just as she was getting into bed that night she remembered once Dottie being without her phone at home due to the lines coming down at the bottom end of the village in a storm, so she'd asked Caroline to ring her cousin to tell her she'd no phone. Caroline had put the cousin's number in her phone and promised to ring when she had a minute at the surgery. Beth decided she'd check her mum's phone first thing in the morning. By the time she woke, however, Caroline had already gone to the village hall to help organise the coffee morning so Beth had to wait.

★   ★   ★

The most ecstatic person in the crowd at the coffee morning was Alice, because at eight fifteen that very morning the postman had delivered a letter postmarked Rio de Janeiro through Alice's door.

She thrust the envelope open and began to read, her eyes filling with tears. 'My dear Alice' it began. Her heart missed a beat.

I am a fool to run away from the very beat of my heart and come back to meaningless, stupidly endless, mind-numbing work in an office that revolts me with its plush, excessively expensive furnishings and assistants behaving more like slaves than real people. It is all so sickening to me since I met you. Somehow while living near you my values have undergone an almighty change. I no longer revere the extravagant lifestyle I had before I met you. I long to come back to you. I left because I could not believe that someone wanted me only for myself and not my wealth and position. All my life I have lived amongst moneyed people, and it is hard to find someone so genuine that they love you for yourself and not for your status and what your personal wealth can do for them. I'd heard those very same words of yours before several times, and I didn't believe you meant them. It felt like a well-repeated old story.

But now I know it wasn't. You are the most genuine person I know and realise, with your high principles about marriage and fidelity, what it cost you to say what you did. If you say yes to a proposal of marriage from me I shall come back to Turnham Malpas immediately and make a life for the two of us. To marry in the church where my ancestors were christened, married and buried for generations, and God willing to have our own children christened there, is all I want. To be married to you, Alice March, for I yearn for you every moment.

*It is what I want more than anything in the world and I long for your reply. I know there are hurdles to overcome, namely a divorce from Marcus, but perhaps if his book gets published . . . he won't mind too much.*
*All my love, my dearest,*
*Johnny*

Alice folded the letter, opened it, read it again, folded it and held it pressed to her cheek. So after all the pain she'd gone through and now . . . this. Oh! Johnny, oh! Johnny! I love you! More than life itself. It had taken only one small phrase from Johnny to rid her of Marcus and frankly one small phrase was all he deserved. Alice glanced at the clock; she'd be late for accompanying the dancing group! Help! But her heart sang as she raced upstairs, sang louder when she recollected she'd no need to listen for Marcus tapping away at his computer any more because Johnny would see to that for her. One glance in the bathroom mirror and Alice recognised the face of a woman in love and she rejoiced.

At the dance recital Alice accompanied the group with more vigour and enthusiasm than in any of the many rehearsals they had done. They were Irish and danced with such speed and delight that when she finished playing Alice felt as exhausted as the dancers. The crowd in the church hall clapped and clapped and begged an encore. Luckily they'd got the music for another one that Alice had familiarised herself with just in case. The roof almost lifted off the hall at the end of their exhibition of Irish Dance and Bridget, who'd planned it all, was thrilled. Alice got a hug and a kiss from her. 'Oh! Alice, I've never heard you play so well. Are you sure you haven't got Irish blood in you?'

'Not that I know of. Right! I'll go get us a drink.'

'Sure the drinks are on me; here, take this,' said Bridget, holding out a twenty-pound note.

'I don't want that, I did it for the flood fund!'

'Well, put the whole note in their money box and tell them to keep the change, then.' Alice got another hug, then Bridget dashed off to make some announcements about the raffle and spur everyone on to buy from the stalls. Her rallying tone had the desired effect and everyone who came endeavoured to find *something* to spend their money on. There were plenty of quality things to choose from. Bridget had even got an Irish Tourist Board company to come from miles away and give a percentage of all the money they took for their souvenirs and traditional hand-crafts to the cause. Little Derehams and Penny Fawcett had both had collections to help swell the fund too.

Caroline did well on her nearly new stall, though Sylvia, who had pledged to give her a hand, felt uncomfortable after Beth's difficult visit the previous day. 'I'm so sorry about Willie and Dottie. Heaven alone knows where she's gone.'

'Look, don't worry. Willie shouldn't have reminded her, but he did only say the truth . . . but he still shouldn't have said it. Beth's very

89

close to Dottie, after . . . you know . . . Africa and all that, so I do wish for her sake we could find her.'

'I tell you what; I could go see her cousin in Little Derehams. She might know where she's gone. In fact she might be here. When we have a quiet moment I'll go have a look round.'

'Thank you, Sylvia.'

It was the turn of the village school choir to perform next and their parents had turned up in droves to support their children. A space was cleared for the choir to assemble themselves with Bridget announcing their programme of songs, and the recorder recital too. The next ten minutes were exceedingly special to everyone, not just the parents.

Kate Fitch, the headteacher, was profusely thanked for the children's excellent performance and she said a few words. 'Thank you! Weren't the children wonderful? They've worked so hard to entertain you, and I love them all. My staff and I are delighted to have the children invited to perform and contribute to such a worthy cause.' Caroline noticed that Kate's husband Craddock was there, but not looking his usual bright self. His complexion, always pale at the best of times, appeared drawn as though he had worries he needed to keep to himself, but the smile of appreciation he gave Kate was genuine enough. Business in Turnham Malpas as else-where was going through a bad time and Caroline did wonder if business worries were beginning to affect him. She caught his eye and he came across to speak with her.

'Caroline, my dear, how are you? Looks like you're doing well with the nearly new?' He kissed her on both cheeks. 'Are you keeping well? You look full of life.'

'I am, despite the years going faster and faster.'

He smiled ruefully. 'I know the feeling. Bridget's doing well with this flood victim's fund. She's good at rallying people, isn't she?'

'Yes.' Caroline laughed. 'Has she been rallying you?'

'Just for a donation.'

Caroline got the impression that maybe Craddock Fitch wasn't quite as willing as he usually was to hand out the money that had flowed in all directions in ever increasing amounts since he first came to live here. They'd all benefited in one way or another. She caught him watching Kate behaving in her accustomed efficient headteacher way as she collected together the school recorders; she saw how precious Kate was to him and she was glad. Still there was this surprising underlying feeling that he . . . in a matter of weeks it seemed he suddenly looked his years. How odd.

★   ★   ★

About eleven thirty Beth arrived. Still niggling at the back of Caroline's mind was what Beth had said about not being happy at Cambridge and it worried her. Maybe a gap year would have been better for Beth, whereas Alex appeared to have taken everything in his stride.

Beth came across to her carrying two coffees, one for her and one for Sylvia. 'Mum! Can I check your diary? I remember you putting a telephone number for one of Dottie's cousins in your phone ages ago. Do you think it might still be there?'

'Possibly, darling. My bag's locked in the cupboard in the kitchen. I've got the key.' Caroline delved in her trouser pocket. 'Here we are.'

So Beth stood by the light of the church hall kitchen window trawling through the list of phone numbers on her mother's phone. Eureka! It was there. She'd ring, right away.

'Good morning. Is that Irene, Dottie Foskett's cousin?'

The voice at the other end was hesitant. 'Er! Yes. Who's that?'

'Beth Harris.'

'Beth, did you say?'

'Yes. Your cousin Dottie knows me. It's Beth Harris from the Rectory at Turnham Malpas. Is it possible to speak to her, please?'

'I'm sorry, she's not speaking to anyone. Sorry.'

It sounded as though the line was about to go dead. 'Please, don't hang up. I want her to come back home, straight away. I know why she went but she can't go away for ever and we all want her back. Every one of us. Please, tell her it's me; she may speak to me when she knows who it is.'

'Sorry, she's shaking her head. She's OK staying with me, so not to worry.'

Then the phone went dead.

Beth stood looking at the mobile for a moment, wondering what on earth she could do. She knew it would be pointless ringing back to ask for her address.

★ ★ ★

Caroline had been so busy with the nearly new stall that it wasn't until they were eating a late lunch at home that she got an opportunity to ask Beth what happened about her phone call.

'She was there all right, because her cousin Irene said, to use her exact words, 'she's not speaking to anyone', so though we have her number we don't know the address.'

'Do you remember she had her house renovated and stayed with her cousin in Little Derehams till the worst was over? How about her? Sheila Bissett will know her.'

'Of course she will. I could write a letter and give it to the cousin to address, couldn't I? I'll finish lunch and then — '

'Darling! Maybe she will come back on her own accord; after all, she has the rent to pay for her cottage so she can't go on not living in it.'

'She might give her notice and never come back.'

Peter, slightly alarmed by Beth's persistence about Dottie said, 'I think we should leave Dottie to come home when she's ready.'

Beth retorted, 'Well, I don't. She needs to know that there is someone, *someone* in Turnham Malpas who wants her back. Don't try to stop me, Dad. I'm sorting this or I won't go back.' Having made this declaration Beth realised that she quite simply didn't want to go back anyway and Dottie wasn't her only reason. 'I'm doing nothing for anyone else, just thinking about my academic work every hour of every day and I hate it. What's more . . . I've decided . . . I'm not going back. Ever.' She sprang up from her chair and disappeared upstairs.

Peter and Caroline were staggered. Peter got up and quietly closed the kitchen door so they could talk without being overheard.

'Surely she can't mean it?' Peter said quietly.

'I fear she does, Peter.'

'It's not the end of the world, you know. She could ask to begin again next September, take a year out. You know a lot of them do. She could do a gap year, well, part of one.'

'I did wonder about that myself. She hasn't settled nearly so well as Alex.'

'It wouldn't do her any harm.'

'I don't know how you feel about it, Peter, but I wouldn't want her hanging around the house with nothing to do for months. She'd need some objective. It wouldn't be good for her to fall into a vacuum, would it?'

'Let's wait and see. Perhaps if we solve this Dottie business she'll feel better and go back. If not, I'll go back with her and talk to someone and secure her place for the next academic year. We don't want her feeling as though she's under pressure to go back when she's so unhappy; that would be the worst thing of all.'

'I couldn't bear that.' Caroline was beginning to warm to the idea of Beth being around for six months. In her mind's eye she could see the tiny bundle that was Elizabeth Caroline Harris snug and warm in the hospital cot and the slightly bigger bundle that was Alex and she remembered how grateful she had been to have children, even if they weren't actually her own, but were Peter's. How precious they both were to her, almost more precious than if they had been her very own.

She smiled at him and he reached across the table and took hold of her hand. 'All right?' She nodded. He squeezed her fingers to reassure her. 'We'll sort something out, mustn't let her close the door on Cambridge though. We must keep that option open in case she changes her mind. I feel for her. I remember homesickness myself; it's damned debilitating and makes life hell. I — '

They were interrupted by the sound of Beth clattering down the stairs. The kitchen door was flung open. 'I'm sorry to land such a bombshell, but I can't help it. I really can't. I'm off to Little Derehams to see if Sheila Bissett is in. I've done a letter. Won't be long. I mean it, you know. I'm not going back.'

Peter nodded. 'We understand. Off you go.'

Caroline was relieved to see the gratitude in her eyes for their understanding. Peter always seemed to know the right thing to say in difficult circumstances; she would probably have insisted Beth went back just to give it another try till the end of the Michaelmas term, but in her present mood that could have been disastrous.

When Caroline heard the front door bang shut

she said, 'Jake Harding's turned up at Cambridge.'

Peter raised his eyebrows. 'No!'

'She caught sight of him in the distance at a concert. Beth thought he'd gone to London. More handsome than ever, she says.'

'Right! That definitely is a very good reason for her not going back!'

'I think she still has feelings for him; he is a very striking young man.'

'Not a strictly honest one though, two-timing her like he did.'

'But it was her he put on the pedestal.'

'Indeed.'

They both laughed.

# 8

The morning after the highly successful flood victims' coffee morning Alice was retching over the loo almost the moment she got up. Oh! My God! She felt dreadful. She perched on the edge of the bath and dwelt on her food intake the last couple of days. But she hadn't been actually sick had she, just retched. Maybe if she had some breakfast she might feel better. She threw cold water over her face and hands, dried them off and started down the stairs. But the stairs swam around her feet and she had to clutch the rail to keep herself upright.

The thought of butter made her stomach heave so she tried plain toast. It tasted like wood and she didn't want to eat it, but she forced herself. She couldn't face either tea or coffee, so she drank chilled water from Marcus's American fridge.

The newspaper rattled through the letter box. Alice pulled it through and went to sit in her favourite chair to read it. The world news was depressing as usual, so she turned to the inner pages. She must contact Johnny to tell him how happy she was to have received his letter. She couldn't think why she hadn't immediately got in touch with him. Just exactly why hadn't she?

There was no answer to that. Here she was with his letter on the mantelpiece above the very fireplace she was sitting by, the letter she'd longed to receive because it told her she only had to raise a finger and Johnny would be here and yet she couldn't quite bring herself to make that final earth-moving decision. Why not? Why not indeed? How could she not grab this chance to change her life from something the colour of sludge to something all the colours of the rainbow? She would be an idiot to turn him down. She couldn't turn him down when he was the love of her life, could she?

And where was the other love of her life? He certainly wasn't with her, taking care of her when she'd felt so awful when she first got up. Marcus March had walked away and good riddance to him. She could, she supposed, always ring his mobile, find out where all their money had gone. Why hadn't he been in touch? Where was he? Was he going to be published or had it all fallen through?

She would, she'd ring him. Find out. After all, she was his wife. Even if in name only. Alice rooted in her handbag for her mobile and pressed his number.

A woman with a London accent answered. 'Hello. Marcus March's phone. Who's calling?'

'Alice.'

'Who?'

'Alice March.'

'His sister! I'll hand you over!'

Alice distinctly heard her say, 'It's your sister.'

Completely dazed by this, she didn't immediately speak when she heard Marcus's voice, more clipped and brisk than normal, asking her why she'd rung.

'To find out how you are, of course. You haven't kept in touch.'

'Well, I'm in the office discussing my novel.'

In the office discussing his novel this early on a Sunday morning? That was odd. 'How's it going?' she asked.

'Fine, absolutely fine. Look, can I ring you back? We're rather busy; you know what it's like — every storyline picked apart, every character reshaped a little, and quite right too.' He kind of chuckled in a most un-Marcus-like way. After a pause he added, 'Will you put the money you owe me in the bank account tomorrow? Don't forget. I'll try to ring you back another time. Right. Don't forget the money; I'm running out. Bye.'

'Don't forget the money, I'm running out.' That sounded very Marcus-like. Always seeking the best in people, it took Alice a while to recognise the situation for what it was: he'd found someone else. She was right; she knew she was. She hadn't been married to Marcus for twelve years and learned nothing about him. His voice was so false, so brisk and jerky and . . . the money she owed him? That was the biggest cheat of all. Well, if he had found someone else, and she was sure he had, *she* could fund him like Alice March had been funding him all these years, and good luck to her.

Alice couldn't trust herself to speak coherently over the phone, so she typed Johnny a long email in which she told him how much he meant to her, and how much she was looking forward to seeing him. She was just about to press *send* when something, she didn't know what, held her back. Why had he not believed her when she said she'd divorce Marcus because she loved him, Johnny, so very much? Didn't he recognise that she, the love of his life, was speaking the truth, whereas all the others had been after his money? He'd known her almost but not quite a whole year and yet he couldn't believe her. Had she not sounded sincere? Had she not cast aside her promises to Marcus against her will but for Johnny's sake? He'd claimed he felt guilty about that. She'd believed him when he said he loved her, so why didn't he believe her?

And what about Marcus? She'd trusted him all these years and here he was, only days after leaving home, already with someone else. Who could you trust?

So Alice never pressed the key that would send her message winging its way to her beloved. Instead she walked for miles through the countryside, practised for hours on the piano and got up the next morning to find herself just as sick as she had been the day before.

While she was recovering from her latest painful bout of retching there was a knock at the door. Dragging her feet reluctantly down her little hall, she opened the door to find Bridget Cleary beaming from ear to ear.

'Alice, m'dear. Thought you should be the first to know, seeing you did so much towards our success on Saturday, that, altogether, we made,' with a flourish she held up a piece of paper and written on it was £1,227. 'There now, what do you think? I told you it would be one thousand but it was a bit more. Can I come in?'

'Yes, of course.'

Alice stepped back to make room for Bridget and Bridget's first words were, 'My God and all the saints! You look terrible! I know it's wonderful news but there's no need to go into shock. You are the most peculiar colour. Are you ill?'

'I'm feeling a bit . . . queasy.'

Comprehension dawned on Bridget. 'Oh! Right. Ah!! I didn't know. Dry cream crackers I always found were the best with a cup of tea *before* you get up.'

Alice didn't understand what she meant. 'Dry cream crackers? What are you talking about?'

'Sorry. I've jumped the gun, haven't I? Still, someone with my experience . . . might be able to give you a few tips perhaps.' Bridget looked quizzically at her, but got no response and continued by saying, 'Well then, I'll put the total in the church magazine with a thank you to all who helped, I want everyone to know. It was hard work, but well worth it. Take care! Bye!' and with that she shut the door behind her.

Alice returned to her chair in the kitchen and a terrible truth came over her as she sat down. Bridget must have meant . . . surely to God, as Bridget would have said, she wasn't, was she? She couldn't be. She couldn't be pregnant; they'd always been so careful. It wasn't Marcus's baby — he hadn't been able to for months and months, but Johnny certainly could so . . . obviously . . .

For five wonderful minutes she wallowed in the thought of a baby, of its total dependence on its mother for survival, of the lovely smell of its hair, of the warmth of its head lolling against her neck, of the sweetness of its breath and the joy of its tiny fingers and toes. That was until the matter-of-fact predicament she was in hit her. Marcus would know it wasn't his, so she couldn't pretend it was. She couldn't let Johnny come back because he'd think she only wanted him back because of the baby. She wouldn't cry. Definitely not. A baby was what she wanted and had done for years. Everyone knew that. Well, whatever, she'd bring the baby up herself. It happened so often nowadays and there was no shame in it. People could think it was Marcus's; no one would know it couldn't be. He'd have to come home to make it look genuine. In fact he was the sort of man who would come home and pretend the baby was his to save face. She could bet he wouldn't even question her about it, wouldn't even mention that it couldn't possibly be his and Marcus would proudly claim to everyone he was the baby's father simply to boost his image. What with a book published and a baby on the way he'd be on top of the world.

But was it right not to tell Johnny? To deceive him?

Should she have an abortion? No one need know. Did she want an abortion? After all, it would solve a lot of problems. Yes, that would perhaps be the best route, and the result of that? No Johnny, no Marcus, no baby. How about that for a situation? Only she would carry the aftermath of the guilt.

Later that day she bought a pregnancy test and proved once and for all that Bridget was right.

# 9

In the Rectory, Caroline and Peter were still struggling with Beth's reluctance to return to Cambridge. Getting Dottie's cousin in Little Derehams to address Beth's letter to Dottie for her and post it off had only gone part way to improving her spirits.

On the Monday after Bridget's highly successful coffee morning, Caroline suggested at breakfast that Beth went back to college with her dad to explain her absence and at the very least keep a place open for herself, collect her belongings, take some months off, and then come home for a while and return in October.

Beth didn't reply. She was busy buttering a toasted teacake and after she'd taken her first bite she said, 'Well, I might do that.'

'Have you spoken to Alex about this?'

'No.'

'Why not?'

'Because . . . '

'Because what?'

'I want to stand on my own feet. I've relied on him too much these last years and it has to stop.'

'Yes, but — '

'He has a life to lead too, Mum; he doesn't want me asking for advice over every little thing like I've done since I was about three.'

'Alex doesn't mind.'

'That's not the point, though, is it? Maybe he's

feeling as bad as me and isn't saying anything for fear of looking a fool. But I don't care. I know what I want to do and that's that.'

'Say it all works out and they say you can start all over again next October; what will you do in the meantime?'

Beth sighed. 'I wondered when that was coming.'

'I'm bound to be concerned.'

'You wouldn't be my mum if you weren't. I haven't thought, but I do know Cambridge is not right for me at this moment. Something will come up.'

'In some ways it doesn't matter what it is, so long as you enjoy it.'

'Exactly! I can hear Dad coming. Do you ever get bored with boiling two eggs for him every morning?'

'No, it's about the only boring thing about him.'

Peter arrived in the kitchen, pulled out his chair and said, 'What could be better than breakfast with my two favourite women?'

'Thanks, Dad, for not being cross with me. You've every right to be.'

'You wouldn't be sitting here this morning with your mum and me if you were happy at Cambridge, now would you?'

'No. Quite right.'

The egg timer pinged and Caroline carried his eggs to the table, put them in his double egg cup and kissed the top of his head. 'That's for being a lovely dad.'

'I try my best.' Peter put a sanctimonious look

105

on his face and then grinned at them both.

'As far as I'm concerned you do all right, Dad. Shall we go tomorrow? Will you be free?'

'When I've had breakfast come to my study and we'll discuss it.'

Beth finished her cup of tea. 'I find myself listening for Dottie arriving, but she won't be, will she?'

'No, darling, she won't.'

'I miss her. She's so good to talk to. I don't have to tiptoe around her, you see; she understands all the ordinary things of life and doesn't try to do as she thinks she ought to. She's just *herself*, and that's so rare nowadays.'

'How right you are.' Peter reached across and planted a kiss on Beth's forehead.

'I know she was a prostitute when she was younger and all the wrinklies look down on her, but she's a treasure really.'

'That's important, darling.' Caroline felt as though she'd let Beth down so very badly when she needed her most after they came back from Africa.

'In fact after we've had our talk, Dad, I shall go this very day to see Gilbert, see if he has any use for someone who is willing to work for him, for no pay if necessary. That way I'd find out for definite if archaeology is my thing.'

Peter looked up surprised. 'I thought you knew it was.'

'I do, but just to make absolutely sure. I heard the postman.' Beth leaped to her feet and rushed to the front door. She quickly sifted through the pile of post and found, as she hoped, a letter in

106

an unknown hand addressed to Miss Elizabeth C. Harris.

Dumping the rest of the post on the hall table, Beth tore her letter open.

*Dearest Beth. Thank you for your lovely letter. In view of what you say I shall come home immeediatly because you are home and shuldn't be. You can tell me all about not being at Cambridge and we'll sort it out between the two of us. I shall come on the late train tomorrow, come for a cup of tea the day after about half past ten. That will give me time to dust the house and tidy up.*

*Lots of love, Dottie Foskett.*

Beth tucked the letter in her skirt pocket and took the other post into the kitchen. She didn't tell her mother about Dottie's letter because she knew that her reliance on Dottie caused her mother pain, but the fact remained that her mother *hurt* when things went wrong for her, whereas Dottie took it all in her stride. She kissed her mother's cheek, saying, 'I'm off into Culworth to see Gilbert,' and disappeared upstairs.

'I guess she's had a letter this morning. It'll be from Dottie, I expect,' Caroline said.

'Don't take it to heart, darling. I know it seems odd but . . . '

'Well?

'It's because Dottie doesn't hurt like you do when things go wrong for Beth, and she hates to upset you. All she's doing is shielding you from

107

it, because she loves you so much.'

'It hurts when I come second to a . . . prostitute.'

'Caroline! What a thing to say; that's not like you! You know full well you don't come second with her! Anyway it may not be from Dottie. It could be a school friend or someone; you don't know.'

'If it was she'd have come in here to read it. Oh! my God! look at the time. I'm going to be late.'

Shortly after her mother left for the clinic in Culworth, Beth too went to Culworth, parked in the multi-storey so loathed by everyone, and went to find Gilbert in his office in the archaeology department. She was well aware that every woman in the neighbourhood found Gilbert very attractive and she determined she would not get embarrassed when he greeted her.

As she walked up the steps to his office she was overwhelmed by doubt. What if she realised she didn't like archaeology after all? What would she do then? Still best to find out now, because she'd already wasted enough time at Cambridge.

Beth found a door with Gilbert's name on it and knocked. She heard his voice shouting 'Come!' from inside and opened the door. The delight that spread across his face encouraged her.

'Why, Beth! What a lovely surprise!'

'Are you incredibly busy?'

'Short answer, yes, but always got time for you. How can I help?'

'I'm taking a gap year, I hope. Not done the right thing going straight from school to

108

university. I have to confess to being desperately unhappy there so I've faced facts and postponed my first year. Well at least I hope so — not done the official paperwork yet. So-o-o-o I wondered if you could give me unpaid employment for a while, just being around running errands, going to the post office, generally helping, making the tea, washing up the mugs, anything to bring me in contact with the archaeology world as much as possible.'

The smile on her face was tremulous and Gilbert sensed her underlying unhappiness. He fiddled with his letter opener, straightened a few papers on his chaotic desk and then looked up smiling. 'As you see from my desk I am greatly in need of someone like you. My assistant had a bad fall from her horse last weekend and has to rest because of a cracked vertebra so she won't be back for quite a while. She keeps me neat and tidy and files all these wretched papers for which I have neither the time nor the patience.'

'Really? Would you take me on then? Unpaid like I said.'

'Agreed.' He reached out to shake hands.

'Shall I begin now? I can do today but tomorrow Dad's going with me to Cambridge to sort things out and bring my stuff home, so I shan't be able to come. If that's all right, that is.'

'Of course. The sooner the better, and the odd day missed for very good reasons is no problem to me.' Gilbert had no idea how good she would be at lightening his burden, but for her sake it was worth a try. 'Anything to do with a dig in Chapel Street in Culworth is immediate and needs to stay on my desk; everything else needs putting in the correct file in these cabinets here. I'll be out most of the morning. The kitchen is the second door down the corridor. Charges for coffee etc., are on the notice above the sink and put the money in the tin in the drawer next to the fridge. An hour for lunch — take it when you need — see you about two.'

Gilbert paused by the open door for a moment. 'I'll enjoy your company, Beth. I'm happier out in the field, so to speak, not keen on being tied to a desk. If you're very good — ' he grinned — 'I shall take you out to a dig one day. We're starting over Brocken High Barrow; you'd enjoy that. Walking boots are best, no matter the weather.' He bellowed to someone who must have been at least a mile away, his voice was so loud, and whoever he was came running down the corridor and rushed down the stairs after him, his anorak trailing on the steps behind him as he ran.

Beth laughed and turned to look out of the office window to see Gilbert leap into his four-by-four and race out of the car park with his member of staff still dragging a leg in so he could get the door shut, leaving Beth to spend the best day she'd had in weeks: sorting out Gilbert's office and inspecting a tray of artefacts from a dig.

★  ★  ★

She had a perfectly splendid day and wondered why she had allowed herself to go straight to

110

Cambridge, because being practical and busy in a relatively peaceful atmosphere felt wonderful. Towards the end of the afternoon Gilbert still hadn't returned, which was a mite disappointing, but she overcame that. The telephone rang several times and as she hadn't the faintest idea of the name of the office she was working in she simply replied, 'Gilbert Johns's phone. How may I help?' and made notes for Gilbert when he returned.

She wrote a note reminding him that she wouldn't be there the next day, but would be in later the following day, and she left hugging to herself the thought of seeing Dottie the day after tomorrow, when she'd get her thinking sorted out and get Dottie back housekeeping at the Rectory.

★   ★   ★

Two days later, Beth went down to see Dottie in her lovely old cottage at the bottom of Shepherd's Hill, as requested in Dottie's letter. Inside herself she was in turmoil; outwardly she appeared to be her usual happy self.

She knocked on the door and opened it as she usually did and there stood Dottie in the kitchen: thinner, she thought, but still that same welcoming Dottie as she always had been.

'Shall we have a hug, love?'

'Yes!' and Beth ran straight into her arms and was hugged. 'I'm so glad you're back. Can I ask? Are you back for good?'

'I think so. Go sit yourself down and I'll bring

111

the coffee in. Still the same, milk no sugar?'

Beth nodded.

Dottie followed her into the sitting room carrying two stylish mugs. 'I've lit the fire. The house seemed so cold last night, thought I'd warm it up a bit.' So they sat in front of the huge inglenook fireplace, almost too large for a cottage of this size, but the warmth felt comforting and Beth relaxed.

Dottie explained her new mugs. 'New mugs: me cousin made me buy 'em; she thought they'd suit my cottage.'

'Oh! They do. The roses are just like the ones round the back door. Exactly the same.'

'Now then, what's all this about you home from Cambridge? Eh! I thought we'd seen the back of you for a while.' She grinned as she said it. 'I need to know why. I also need to know what your dad thinks.'

'I'm not ready for it. I'm too lonely, too young and miserable. I haven't made friends very easily and I don't know why, because I was OK at school, lots of friends, you know. It's not the studying; I'm pretty disciplined about that. It's just that I miss home, which seems awfully childish of me, but it's how it is. Dad's all right about it and we went yesterday to collect my things and see Alex and get the whole thing thrashed out. Officially I'm taking a gap year and going back in September next year to start all over again.'

'I see. What does Alex think?'

'He's all right about it. He's been homesick too, but he's met up with a really great set of friends and it's all worked out OK for him. I'm glad for him. But I'm home where I want to be, for now. Do you think I'm being silly?'

Dottie answered her in her own good time. 'Well, I think . . . I think you've done the right thing, except when you go back a second time then you've *got* to *stay* else you will feel *really* stupid, and it'll affect you all your life and you won't half regret not getting that degree, and you don't want to live with regret. That really would be making a mess of things. So spend this year out growing up.'

'You're absolutely right. I've always been so well looked after, with Mum and Dad loving me to bits all my life and Alex fighting my corner for me too. I knew you would talk sense to me. Thanks, Dottie. And you? Are you home where you want to be?'

Dottie placed her mug on the corner of the hearth, but sat, hands clasped, looking anywhere but at Beth.

The silence was a companionable one but Beth was impatient to talk about Dottie's problems and couldn't wait for her to speak. 'Mum wants you back. She says no one cleans her house as well as you do and she can't wait to hear you at the door, saying, 'It's only me.' She misses you; we all do. Well?'

When Dottie looked at her Beth was amazed to see tears in her eyes. 'She means it, doesn't she, your mum?'

'Of course she does, otherwise she wouldn't say it.'

'And your dad? The reverend? What does that

lovely, lovely man have to say about me?'

'The same. He holds no opinion about the past, yours or anyone else's. If coming back to work at the Rectory is all right with you, it certainly is all right with him.' A wicked glint came in Beth's eyes. 'He claims your coffee is better than Mum's anyway.'

'No-o-o . . . is that true?'

'Yes, he's always telling her, but she just laughs.'

'You are so lucky having lovely parents like you've got. I never knew my dad, and my mother was crazy in the head, you know. It wasn't much of a start for me, especially being an only child, and when Willie said what he said, it brought all that back and I felt like dirt. Which I was.'

'Dottie! Don't say that. You're not, not in my eyes. All that is long gone and I want to hear that you've been to the pub tonight and shown them what you're made of. I know for a fact Willie does regret terribly what he said — '

'How do you know that?'

'Because I've been to see him about it and he told me, and he meant it. Sylvia is mortified about it and won't let him forget. He's right in the dog house, believe me.'

They both heard three sharp barks at the front door. 'That'll be Sykes,' Beth said. 'He must have followed me down here. He's a dear little dog, but he is so bossy. Would you mind if he came in to wait?'

'Go let him in. I like Sykes; he's a good friend to me when I'm cleaning.'

So they sat together drinking another mug of

coffee, talking and reminiscing with Sykes comfortably placed first beside Dottie, after giving her a big welcome, and then beside Beth, looking at her expectantly as though saying, 'When are we going home?'

'So do I have your promise about going in the pub tonight and coming to the Rectory to clean tomorrow? I shan't be there — I'm helping Gilbert to keep his office tidy.'

'That won't be easy, I guess.' Dottie laughed when she'd said this and she sounded comfortingly like the old Dottie. 'I'll definitely be at the Rectory tomorrow, but about the pub, I'm none too sure.'

Beth stood up. 'In that case I shall go in there myself, and if you're not there I shall come down here in my car and drag you there. You can't spend the rest of your life not going to the pub, now, can you? You know you love the company, to say nothing of the gossip.'

'No, I don't suppose I can avoid it, but it'll be hard.'

'In any case, the embroidery group is complaining that you're getting behind with your stitching and they say no one does background as beautifully as you do.'

'Have they really said that?'

'Dad said so; he's been to see them. Apparently Sheila Bissett had a go at the background but it wasn't nearly as beautifully done as you do it and Evie had to pull it all out.'

'In that case then I'd better pull myself together and get back to work. Can't have the tapestry for that medieval hall in Abbey Gate

115

held up else we'll get a bad name. I'm that proud we were asked to do it.'

Beth stood up, leaned over Dottie and kissed her. 'I'm off, Dottie. Thanks for the coffee and talking to me; you always do me good.'

'Thanks for my pep talk. Bye, love, bye, Sykes.' Sykes wagged his tail at her as he ran for the front door.

★ ★ ★

The news of Beth helping Gilbert in his office reached the old table in the bar at the Royal Oak in no time at all and as fascinating topics of conversation were few and far between at the moment they were glad to have something to talk about.

Sylvia, her days as housekeeper at the Rectory now long gone, remembered sitting either side of the Aga helping Caroline to bottle feed the twins all those years ago. 'Well, if she isn't enjoying herself then she did right to come back home.'

Willie, however, had a different spin on the matter which he voiced in firm tones. 'Got the chance for a place at Cambridge and throws it away 'cos she's homesick. Plain daft that is. She should have stuck it out and made a go of it.' He slapped down his tankard and looked round for approval.

Surprisingly there were no approving nods.

'Frankly, what's the point of her being miserable?' Vince remarked.

Marie spoke up, saying, 'Maybe she just wasn't ready for it.'

116

Willie scoffed at their sympathy. 'She's got Alex there, hasn't she? Always go see him if she's miserable. Though, why they've gone to different colleges, I'll never know.'

'Sick of relying on each other, I suppose. They've got to grow up some time and manage without each other.'

This remark of Sylvia's angered Willie even more. 'We all know how much the girl relies on Alex; he's a tower of strength, just like the rector. I've known the day when — '

Marie interrupted him. 'So what you're saying is if she ever gets married Alex will have to move in with her and her husband?'

Scathingly Willie replied, 'I'm not that daft. What I am saying is she's given up a marvellous opportunity. Cambridge on your references — what's better than that, eh?' He looked round and saw approval, even on Don's normally expressionless face.

'Mmm,' said Don, 'I just wish Dottie was here. She'd know about it and what's going to happen.'

'She would indeed,' muttered Sylvia, 'wouldn't she, Willie?'

It seemed to Willie that Sylvia could make absolutely any topic of conversation relevant to him being the cause of Dottie's sudden departure.

'Not necessarily; she's always very careful not to let on about what goes on in the Rectory, just like you were.'

Sylvia had to concede that point. They continued on with their gossiping by going

117

round the table so that each one of them related the history of their own education in comparison to Beth's missed opportunities, mostly at the Turnham Malpas village school, of course. Sylvia reminded them all about Dottie when she was at school. 'Poor Dottie, her mother was already crackers when she was born, I'm sure, though we never mentioned it to her. She'd a terrible start in life. Her mother used to keep Dottie from school on her bad days, so if we started long division on a Monday Dottie would be away and by the time she got back we'd most of us got the hang of it, so she got left behind yet again. Pity that. That was why she became a . . . you know what, isn't it, Willie?'

Willie groaned inside but bore it like a man. 'Indeed. Never stood a chance. I miss her, just got that matter-of-fact side to her you can't help but like. 'Nother round anybody?' When they all nodded he got to his feet, picked up the tray and went to the bar.

With his back to the door Willie was unaware of who it was that had walked in. With mouths agape in surprise they silently watched him make his way to the bar, and Willie, busy balancing the tray to avoid spills, turned away from the bar to find himself facing Johnny Templeton.

Eyes wide with surprise he stuttered, 'Come and join us, OK? If you want. Nice to have you back.' Willie walked towards his table, eyes still wide with surprise. Putting the tray down, he began handing out the glasses saying softly, 'Have you seen who's just come in? Sylvia, go warn Alice.'

Sylvia stood up and quietly wandered over towards the ladies', knowing the side door was most probably unlocked. It was. She dashed out, crossed in front of Jimbo's house and Tom and Evie's and tapped on Alice's door. She'd be sure to be in. It was too late for piano lessons or singing lessons.

She heard Alice's footsteps on the stone-flagged floor of the hall, heard the bolts being pulled back, and there stood Alice. Too late, Sylvia knew she should have worked out what to say before she knocked.

'Hello! Sylvia, do come in.'

'I wasn't going to.'

'Oh! I see.' Alice couldn't remember Sylvia ever knocking on her door before and was at a loss to know what on earth to say to fill the silence. 'Can I help?'

'There's a message.'

'Yes?'

When Sylvia remained silent Alice asked what the message was.

'It's just that someone's come back.'

The blood drained from Alice's face. 'Who?'

Sylvia's tongue stuck to the roof of her mouth. 'I thought you should be warned.'

'It's not Marcus, is it?'

'No-o-o. It's the other one.' That sounded terrible, as though she had a string of men.

Alice's knees began to buckle and Sylvia caught hold of her elbow. 'Now, now, don't you faint on me; it's not that awful, is it? Him coming back — isn't that what you want?'

Alice said, 'Are you sure?'

'I've seen him. He's having a drink in the pub with the others, and we thought it best to warn you, then you couldn't get a shock. Well, I don't mean a shock, I mean a surprise, in case he's come back a bit unexpected.'

Alice visibly pulled herself together, saying, 'Thank you for telling me.'

Sylvia nodded and then headed back to the pub.

Unbeknown to Sylvia and Alice he'd already been asking about Alice, claiming he'd had to go back to Brazil in a hurry on important business. Then with no more ado he asked to their horror about Marcus.

Don, unfazed by his question, plunged in with, 'Well, he's up in London having got someone interested in buying his book, and hasn't been seen since. Poor Alice; it's just not fair leaving her all on her own. He hasn't even got in touch. Mind you, she did turn him out one night, lock, stock and barrel, so there's no wonder.'

At this point Sylvia slipped back into her chair as though returning from the ladies'. Under the table she pressed the palm of her hand on Willie's knee and squeezed it to let him know her mission was completed, then smiled a greeting to Johnny. He acknowledged it and then said, 'So she's on her own now?'

'Seems like it, but she's lost her sparkle,' said Marie.

Johnny appeared to clutch at this idea. 'Has she now? I think I'd better go see how she is.' He left immediately, his pint of home brew abandoned only half drunk.

'I mean, let's face it: like it or not, they were lovers.' Sylvia gazed soulfully into her glass and Don reached across to pat her hand. In a loud voice he said, 'Living in sin, more like.'

A gasp of embarrassment went round the table but Don remained oblivious. He drained his glass and got to his feet. 'Come on then, our Vera, let's be off.'

Without waiting for Vera to struggle out from the settle he set off, just in time to see Alice talking to Johnny at her front door.

'Alice, please let me in. I need to explain.'

'Why should I?'

'Because I love you, as you well know.'

'Then if you love me, why did you leave without a word of explanation?'

'Because I misunderstood.'

Alice opened the door a little wider, and then reluctantly let him in. She didn't intend telling him her news. Or was it *his* news?

What Alice needed at the moment was a cup of tea, so as it gave her something to do other than being flustered by Johnny being back, she filled the kettle and got out the tea cups.

He stood close to her, drinking in the beauty of her, the smell of her perfume, the sway of her body as she hurried to find a tray and a plate of biscuits.

'Alice! What is the matter? Will you let me explain? Please stop rushing about and let me tell you.'

They sat together on the sofa in the kitchen. Alice, conscious this was the first time he'd been

121

in her house, knew it felt good, but she'd have to wait for his explanation before she could begin to enjoy him being there. 'Well?'

'Well.' He took her hand and though she tried to pull it away he wouldn't allow it. Instead he kissed each one of her fingers, then turned her hand over and kissed the palm and the joy of his touch took her from being furiously angry to longing to hear his reasons.

He caught sight of her half smile and knew she was ready to listen. Johnny began by telling her of the women who pursued him back home in Brazil. 'They said exactly the kind of thing you said, but unlike you they were not wanting me, not the real Johnny Templeton; they wanted the social position and the lifestyle that the wealth of my family could promise them. I'm not boasting; I'm simply telling it how it is out there. When you said about loving me, you were using words I'd heard before from women who didn't care what kind of a man I was. They would have put up with any behaviour on my part just to get at the money. I can't pretend I'm not well off — I am — but it counts for nothing compared to how I feel about you. I'll give it all away if you'll have me.'

'You forget I'm not free.'

'You could be.'

'But I'm not. I don't even know where Marcus is. I know he's in London but that's all. He's changed his mobile so I can't even phone him. I've tried calling it over and over, but it's dead.'

'What's he doing in London?'

'He's got a publisher interested. You can

imagine what that's done for him.'

'Has he? He must be over the moon, I expect. In that case you can get in touch with him through his publisher.'

'At the moment it pleases me not to be in touch with him. At least he's stopped asking me for money, but I don't want him coming home. I think he's found another woman.'

Johnny wasn't quite sure how to take this news. Surely this was the moment for asking about a divorce? Alice seemed distant from him, which Johnny couldn't understand. Didn't she want him? Had he got it all wrong?

'I've come because I didn't hear from you, and because I know for certain I can't live without you. You do acknowledge that, don't you? I want you and I would be married tomorrow if we could; even tomorrow isn't soon enough. I've lost all enthusiasm for the hotel business — there's no pleasure in it any more. I want the here and now with you in my house, in this village that eighteen months ago I didn't even know existed and I want to take up a life like Great-Great-Uncle Ralph had. I want to be Sir Jonathan Templeton of this parish and go to church with you, and go to the races and the county show, and do things that country people do. I'm a good shot and I ride so I'm halfway there.'

Alice smiled properly for the first time. 'It sounds lovely. Just right for an English country gentleman.' She held his hand against her cheek and he felt her welcome him at last.

'Alice! I want the children you've longed for.

123

The eldest boy would inherit the title, wouldn't he? I have need of a son and heir.' He smiled at his own foolishness but Alice looked the other way and didn't reply.

'I can afford a dozen if you like.' Johnny placed a finger under her chin and turned her face towards him, but his heart chilled when he saw her expression. The welcome had begun to melt away and he didn't know what to say next to paint the picture that would finally entice her into his arms, and they ached for her. 'I'll pour the tea,' he said softly.

She accepted the tea and drank almost the whole cupful, scalding hot though it was. 'Darling! Be careful! A biscuit?' What had happened to the suave, talkative, polished socialite he had been all his adult life? He'd never been at a loss for words before. He felt so tender towards her, so caring, yet he couldn't put his feelings into words.

Alice accepted a biscuit and rapidly devoured it. She helped herself to another.

But still she didn't explain how she felt. Johnny stood up and made as though he was about to leave.

'Should have come to see you earlier today, but I needed a long sleep. You know how it is. Jet lag. I know it must be a shock to have me come back so unexpectedly. I'll go now, give you space, time to think. I mean every word I said about living here in the village. If you don't want me any more I shall still be here to delight in seeing you, even if it's only a glimpse, to hear you play, to listen to your heavenly voice singing something wonderful as only you can. Any time you want me you know where I am, when you're ready. Dearest heart.' Johnny bent over her, kissed her forehead with genuine tenderness, squeezed her hand and left.

Alice sat alone sipping tea, eating biscuits, torn apart by longing and indecision.

Johnny returned to the bar, but Dottie had turned up in his absence, and they were all preoccupied with her arrival, so silently he picked up his glass and went to sit by himself, deep in thought, at the small table by the big open fireplace.

Dottie had quietly bought herself a drink at the bar and then, taking a deep breath, approached the table with the long settle down one side. Busy speculating about what might be going on between Alice and Johnny, they hadn't noticed her come in and were surprised when she said, 'Hello, I'm back. Anyone sitting here?'

Willie pulled the chair out for her. 'If there is, they're not any more, because it's yours and you're welcome, Dottie. We've missed you, haven't we? All of us. And I'm dead sorry about what I said. It was uncalled for and I can't apologise enough.'

Sylvia, grateful for Willie apologising so sincerely said, 'And if you hadn't come back we'd have had to cancel the embroidery group next week. Sheila Bissett tried doing your filling in but made a hopeless mess of it, so believe me you'll be welcomed with open arms on Monday.'

Dottie acknowledged the compliment by patting Sylvia's hand. 'Right, don't panic,

Dottie's back and ready for work. I'm back at the Rectory tomorrow and Pat Jones has left a note to say I'm booked for helping her at a big do at the Old Barn this Saturday, so it's a good job I'm back. This village can't function without me, apparently.' She grinned at them all and they raised their glasses to her and said 'Amen to that!' And Dottie sighed with relief.

# 10

Johnny's invitation to dinner, promised weeks ago when Alice's world was not nearly so complicated as it was now, plopped through the letter box late one night. Hers was addressed only to her, no Marcus of course, and tearing the envelope open she felt tears rising. So here it was, Friday night next week, seven for seven thirty. Alice read the fancy card again, re-read the envelope and couldn't decide what she should do. When Marcus told her Johnny had been that time to ask which was the best night for her and after that he'd gone back home, she'd dismissed the whole idea from her mind, but obviously Johnny hadn't.

What a totally impossible situation this created. If she didn't go, what would her excuse be? She'd find one, that was for sure. Only Johnny would know it wasn't true; the others wouldn't. Before she knew it the baby would be showing, and then the cat would be out of the bag, so to speak. Johnny had not troubled her since that first time. She'd seen him passing the house once or twice but they hadn't actually met face to face. After that tense arrival of him at her door, flowers had arrived the following day from the most expensive florist in Turnham Malpas with a card that declared her his own Alice, the love of his life and at the bottom the single word 'waiting'. But that was all.

She put the invitation card on the mantelpiece and stood back to admire it. The idea that ran through her mind was if she got Marcus to come back, his ego would make him accept the baby was his, rather than face the truth, even though he knew it was impossible. If she knew nothing else about him she knew he was totally capable of deceiving himself. Then she'd never have to tell Johnny. Thank God for that. Why was she glad? Because it meant he wouldn't have to marry her out of guilt, nor obligation, nor pity. That was it, yes. She'd get Marcus back.

The very second she had made her decision she knew what a fool she was. She would be the deceiver, not Marcus, nor Johnny . . . only Alice, with the whole of her life lived in a never-ending fog of guilt. With a jolt it also occurred to her the wrong she would be doing to her baby; it too would be deceived all its life. How could the wonderful loving time she'd had with Johnny become such a sullied, complicated affair?

She was already seven or eight weeks gone, she guessed, so the day for the big revelation was fast approaching. Decision time had arrived and the honest truth, when looked at from all angles, was what had to be declared.

★   ★   ★

The following night, after the last of her piano pupils had left, she combed her hair, checked her face, made sure she had her house key and set off round Stocks Row to Johnny's house, her heart all of a flutter remembering the last time

128

she'd told him the truth and the hair-raising result of that.

When she rang the doorbell it had a new sound. Mmm, new doorbell. I wish I felt as jolly as it sounds. She heard his beloved positive footsteps coming down the hall and there he stood. Looking wonderful. Absolutely wonderful. Her heart seemed to leap to her throat. 'I've come.'

Johnny's face shone with love for her. He reached towards her, took her hand and drew her in over the step with the intention of kissing her.

'No! Not yet! You have to hear what I have to say first.'

He looked shocked as he asked, 'Have you come to say no?'

'Can we go in and sit down?'

'Of course.' He opened the sitting room door and she followed him in and chose to sit in a chair where her face was in a slight shadow. He sat down too.

'You said you want children?'

'Yes, I do.'

'Well . . . ' Her news came out in a rush. 'I'm already expecting a baby and it's yours. There, I've said it and it's the truth; it is yours. I'm about seven or eight weeks. No doubt about it. That's what I came to say. If you want me to go I will. I just thought you ought to know; it's only right and fair you should.'

The emotions, the conflicting emotions that crossed Johnny's face told her nothing. First his face lit with joy, then it changed to sadness, and she dreaded what he was going to say, then it softened into tenderness, then he drew a great breath and he asked, 'How do you know it isn't Marcus's?'

'Because for almost eighteen months now Marcus has not been able to . . . well . . . perform . . . Not at all. He never discussed the problem but then he's like that; he avoids talking about things and hopes they'll go away. Thoughts have been charging round my head ever since I knew I was pregnant. You'd gone back to Brazil so I thought, no, I won't tell him — he obviously isn't interested in hearing news like this. If Marcus comes back I'll say nothing and when it's obvious he'll take it on board and he'll persuade himself it's his because it boosts his ego and admitting the truth wouldn't. Boost his ego, that is.' There was nothing more she could say. His forearms were resting on his thighs, his hands were twisting together, over and over again and his head was bowed, so Alice couldn't even see his face to guess his reaction.

'I'm thrilled to bits, Johnny. It's what I've wanted for years, but daren't because we'd have had no income for a while and Marcus was writing and hoping . . . and Marcus . . . well, I don't know what he'll think . . . '

'Do we have to go on talking about that damned Marcus? On and on?'

The suddenness of his outburst shocked Alice. He was so very angry.

Still looking down at his hands Johnny said through clenched teeth, 'The man is a damned waste of space and not worth one single moment

130

of consideration from you. He's treated you like dirt all these years and still you are concerned for him. I don't want his name mentioned in my presence ever again. As far as you and I are concerned we'll wipe him off the face of the earth. Do you hear me? Mmm?'

'I heard you. Yes.' Alice still didn't know how he felt.

His hands relaxed and he looked up at her. 'Sorry for shouting; you don't deserve it. Come and sit with me.'

Still hesitant, she stood up, but before she reached him she asked, 'How do you feel about it? It is the truth and I'm wonderfully happy and will be even more so if you are, but if not, I've decided I cannot and will not have an abortion, not your baby, so I'll bring the baby up myself, and . . . I will do my best by her . . . or him.'

This then was the brave sweet woman he'd loved from the first moment he'd met her, and she was so tenderly concerned for his feelings. A courageous, loving, thoughtful, honest woman any man would be blessed to have for himself. She sat awkwardly on his knee till he pulled her closer and hugged her in a way that made her feel cherished, which was what she needed right now.

But still he hadn't said.

After a silence that Alice didn't feel able to interrupt with her chattering, which tonight had turned into nonsense for some reason, Johnny stirred, kissed her cheek and said, 'Dear heart, of course I want this baby; it's mine. It's yours.' He held her more securely, as though taking

131

possession of what was his.

'Never again will you want for anything you need, never. I swear. You'll have all my support and I shall be proud to be looking forward to a child of ours.'

'And what about me?'

Johnny looked puzzled. 'What about you?'

'I mean, is it just the baby you want? Not me.'

'Of course it's you. It's all about you. I love you no matter what. I shall wait for you till you're free and then we'll have a lovely village wedding, or just have the two of us there if you prefer and we'll do the thing they say in fairy tales, live happily ever after. And we shall, I'm determined.'

'So you've asked me to marry you then?'

'You're teasing me! What else? Isn't it what you want?' He laughed when she nodded her head in agreement, kissed her, kissed her again and then tipped her off his knee.

'We'll drink to our future lives together. I'm never without champagne in the fridge, so we'll drink a toast to ourselves and the future and the baby right now.'

'Johnny, I'm not drinking alcohol at the moment.'

Surprised by her firmness he paused in the kitchen doorway to look at her face, thinking there must be something she still had to tell him, which maybe he didn't want to hear, but he saw the earnestness there and light dawned. 'Of course, you won't want to. You mustn't. Then I shan't either.'

So they drank to their future with lemonade.

# 11

Dottie arrived at half past eight as usual. She announced her arrival by calling out, 'It's only me!' and Caroline rejoiced at the sound of her voice.

'Good morning, doctor, good morning, sir! Good morning, Beth! Beautiful morning. Sun's shining, what more could we ask?'

'Good morning, Dottie. Come in, and close the door.'

When the kitchen door was safely shut Caroline explained, 'Marcus March has spent the night with us in Alex's room. He arrived last night looking for Alice and eventually Peter had to tell him the truth that Alice wasn't in because she'd gone out with Johnny for a meal, and then the truth came out and he had a terrible shock as he'd no idea they'd . . . got together, so he's spent the night with us in Alex's room. He came home expecting to pick up his life with Alice, you see. I don't know when he'll be getting up but leave him be, will you, Dottie? If he gets up and wants breakfast would you get it for him, because Beth and Peter and I are all out for most of the day. In fact, we should be out of the house already.'

'Leave him to me. I'll give him breakfast and a cold lunch, shall I? Or not, doctor?'

'Yes, give him breakfast and then see how things work out. He's very low in spirits, Dottie, so he needs careful handling, but I know I can rely on you for that.'

Dottie nodded. 'You most certainly can.' She turned to Peter. 'Will you be home, sir, before I go? Just wondering what to do with him when I'm ready to leave, you know. Leave him in the house?'

'In the circumstances, I'll change my plans and make sure to be back before you leave, Dottie. Thanks for being so helpful.'

'Don't want to do the wrong thing, that's all.'

Caroline smiled at her, grateful she was back and looking so happy. 'The usual today but there is rather a lot of ironing. I'm afraid it's kind of mounted up.'

'I don't mind in the slightest; leave everything to me.' She began clearing the breakfast table.

Beth came in to say goodbye before she left for Culworth. 'I'm off now. Is there anything you need in Culworth, Dottie? I can easily shop during my lunch hour.'

Dottie looked up to smile at her. 'You look bonnie this morning. Enjoying your job?'

'It's like paradise in Gilbert's office. I honestly feel as though I belong.'

'Good, better than being unhappy at Cambridge. There's nothing I need, thanks.'

'OK then. Bye!'

It was ten o'clock before Dottie heard Marcus stirring upstairs. She was getting close to the end of the ironing and she hoped he'd dillydally in the shower room while she finished the last few bits. She'd laid the table, and the kettle had been boiled so it wouldn't take her a minute to get his toast done and sit him down. But what do you

134

say to a chap when you're not supposed to know what his problem is? You can't come straight out with, *So you've found out she's got a lover, have you? Are you surprised, because you shouldn't be.*

The door burst open and there he stood.

'Good morning, Mr March. Lovely day, isn't it?'

All she got for her cheerfulness was Marcus glowering at her.

'The doctor said I should make you breakfast. How about it?'

'Tea and toast, that's all. Two slices, brown if possible.' He slumped down on the reverend's chair looking defeated and shrunken, his clothes roughly thrown on, and unshaven. At least he'd showered, so that was a plus.

'Did you sleep well?' She felt she had to say something.

'No.'

'Sorry about that. Glad you're home? I expect Alice will be. It gets lonely on your own and I should know.' Then she wished she'd never said it.

He looked at her, trying to assess how much she knew. 'I expected Caroline would have told you.'

'No, she doesn't tell me anything about the lame dogs that end up here. It's none of my business. I only clean. My one other qualification is that I am a good listener, but that's about all.'

She put down the teapot and covered it with the cosy, handed him a fresh jug of milk, pressed the lever on the toaster and got herself a cup and saucer so she could share the teapot with him. 'Mind if I sit down? I won't talk. It's just that it's time for my break, you see.'

They sat in silence while he struggled to eat a bowl of Beth's muesli. He was halfway through it when he gave up trying. She poured him a cup of tea and offered him the sugar.

'No, thanks. Toast ready?'

'Oh! Yes. Here we are look. Lovely and brown and straight from the toaster; what more can a man ask?' She smiled and got a snarl in return.

Dottie decided to speak out. 'Whatever your problem is, ignoring it won't help. I'm the soul of discretion; that's why I can work here at the Rectory. I hear all sorts of tales but never a word passes my lips. Believe me. I'd be out on my ear if I told tales.'

Dottie waited and eventually when he'd eaten his toast and drunk a second cup of tea he looked directly at her and said, 'Did you know about Alice and Johnny?'

'Yes.'

'Does everyone, absolutely everyone, know?'

'Yes.'

'I didn't.'

'That tells you something then.'

'What exactly?'

'That you didn't care enough to realise things between you were going wrong.'

'Of course I cared. She's *my wife*.'

'Not no more she isn't.' Dottie would have taken every single one of those words straight back, she should never have said it, but it was as plain as the nose on her face to her.

'*She still is.*'

'Well, on paper she is. But that's all.'

Marcus shot her an angry look.

'You've got to face a few facts. What you think isn't so no more.'

He didn't reply.

'She's found someone else and if you'd been a wonderfully satisfying husband she'd never have looked anywhere else. The idea would never have crossed her mind.'

'I don't think it was her *mind* it crossed.' He leered at her and Dottie took offence.

'If you're going to talk like that you'll have to leave. We don't talk like that in this house.' She stood and rolled up her sleeves as though about to manhandle him out of the house.

Marcus stared in disbelief. 'I think you've misunderstood your position in this house. You're the paid help; you don't *live* here.'

Just in time Dottie remembered how hurt he must feel and that she just happened to be handy for him to lash out at.

'Sorry if I've provoked you, Marcus, but a bit of straight talking wouldn't go amiss this morning. You've spent the last ten years thinking day in and day out about writing and being a success and that poor wife of yours has worked all hours teaching music to keep a roof over your head, when what she wanted above everything was to have your babies. Not anyone's, yours, but she couldn't because you'd have had no food on the table and no roof over your head. But I don't think you cared one teeny little bit about that. Finally, you, not anyone else, killed her love

137

for you. She tried but she couldn't try any longer and there came Johnny walking down her street. I don't suppose either of them deliberately made it happen but happen it did.'

Marcus sat with his fists clenched on the table, rhythmically beating a slow tattoo. 'I'm going to sit in Peter's study out of your way.'

'Sorry, but you're not. It's not my day for cleaning in the sitting room so you can go sit in there undisturbed till the Rector gets back.'

Tempted to get his own way about where he sat, Marcus almost challenged her about it, but changed his mind, because so much of what she said was true; he had in part brought it all on himself. But admitting that didn't ease the dreadful loss he felt. His home, his refuge in the attic, his computer, his writing, to say nothing of his very soul. He had in fact lost everything essential to his existence and fallen to the very bottom of the ladder of life. Had he joined the great unwashed army of the homeless? Because that was what he was right now. Homeless.

Peter came home at twelve. Dottie and he had a quiet talk in his study about the morning's events. He didn't inform Dottie about what he'd been up to, but at least he did have a plan. 'Make Marcus and me some lunch, would you? Then you go. I know today should be one of your long days, but it hasn't been easy for you this morning and I think you've done your bit. He and I will have lunch together and I will outline my plan to him.'

'Very well, I'll do that. Thank you. Soup and fresh salmon sandwiches be all right? Piece of

138

that cherry tart to finish?'

'Sounds wonderful! Serve it in the kitchen, Dottie; don't go to a lot of trouble.'

★   ★   ★

So Marcus ate lunch with a man for whom he'd never had much respect and found himself the recipient of a temporary solution to his problem.

'So you see, Marcus, if you choose to go along with it for a week or two, Greta and Vince Jones have agreed to let you have Paddy Cleary's old room, just till you get your life sorted. Greta will cook for you and you can have the use of her washing machine, if you decide to take up their offer. It would give you time to clear your mind and make some decisions.'

Marcus shook his head. 'I can't. I've no money, not till I get my advance for my book.'

'I've taken care of all that. You don't need to find the money. It's just temporary till your advance comes.'

To accept money from this man whose way of life was anathema to him? Absolutely not. He damn well wouldn't eat humble pie; he'd been through enough. He, Marcus March, the author, would go back to London, use an overdraft facility he knew he still had to live on and go live with that other member of staff who'd been as sick as a dog that he'd chosen to go live with what's-er-name instead of her. Lauren, that's right, that was her name. She wasn't too awful, quite pleasant in fact, though not a patch on Alice; no one would ever come up to her standard. Marcus paused for a moment to think about Alice and briefly, but only briefly, he regretted his neglect of her. He remembered the good years, the laughter and the happiness and the togetherness before he got the writing bug and wished . . . but it was too painful and he quickly turned his back on it, knowing he'd had to choose a different path. *Here I come, Lauren, just hope you still feel the same about me.*

Marcus stood up. 'That's what I'll do, shake the dust of Turnham Malpas off my shoes and make a new start.' His ego needing a boost, he added, 'You might see news about me in the press or see me on TV once I get published. A whole new life I'll make.'

'You'll divorce Alice then?' Peter asked.

Marcus sat, thought for a moment. *Maybe she deserved for him to be difficult about it, make life hard for her, maybe not.* 'Of course.' *This blasted man brought out the best in him. The sooner he left the better.* 'I'll go, right away. Collect all my gear and go. Thanks for all your help. I think, perhaps, I didn't deserve it. I'll go back to London. I know someone who'll greet me with open arms. I might as well say goodbye to Turnham Malpas now I haven't even got a wife here any more.'

Suddenly he lost his appetite. He pushed his bowl away saying, 'Sorry. Nice soup, but no appetite for it.'

'Don't worry. Dottie will never know.'

'Don't know why you should bother about her feelings; she only does your cleaning, for heaven's sake.'

'The contribution she makes to the smooth running of our lives means we have respect for her. She's also been instrumental in helping our daughter Beth through a very troubled time in her life and for that we are eternally grateful. What about a sandwich? Fresh salmon.'

'Thanks.' Better eat something, especially seeing as he didn't know where his next meal would be coming from.

They ate in silence, deliberately so on Peter's part. As for Marcus, he was silent out of desperation until the words, 'What the hell am I going to do?' burst unexpectedly from his mouth. 'Without Alice?'

'I rather imagined, from what you said just now, you weren't interested.'

'I am. I am. I know she's left me for Johnny. This mess is entirely my fault. I'm to blame. I can't face everyone in the village. They've always despised me. But I've won out, haven't I? I've got a publisher and they never expected that, did they? Oh! No. Marcus March was too stupid to get a book published, they thought, but I've won out in the end.' He punched the air in triumph, got to his feet, picked up his hold-all from the kitchen floor and left. The front door banged shut.

Then after a moment's silence it opened again and Marcus appeared back in the kitchen. 'Thank you for your help, and the bed for the night. You're the one who's come out of this mess the best, and I rather imagine you always will come out best, you're that kind of chap.'

But as he drove away hatred took possession of

141

his soul. Somehow, some way he'd get his own back for what had happened to him. None of it was his fault; it was that moneybags smart alec of a Johnny who was entirely to blame. Alice would never have left him if he hadn't tempted her. Well, watch out Johnny, one day I shall have my revenge . . .

# 12

Everyone knew by the following day that Marcus March had gone for good. But one prominent person in the village had more catastrophic matters to occupy his mind, for Jimbo, opening his morning post, had received a letter from Craddock Fitch on company notepaper. 'Craddock Fitch Enterprises' it said at the top in eye-blasting lettering. Its contents made Jimbo break out in a sweat.

Words leapt from the page: *due to the credit crunch . . . money draining away . . . new building coming to a standstill . . .* God, what next? Jimbo turned to the second page and there was the point of the whole letter. *In view of this I am looking for a buyer for Turnham House estate . . . therefore your contract for the catering for the students will regrettably . . .*

Jimbo sat down, pained beyond belief by what he read. This contract was his bread and butter that solidly supported the shop and the Old Barn events. On their own they would be shaky and surely if a company the size of Craddock Fitch's was being affected by the credit crunch what about him? What about the Old Barn? Maybe a new owner wouldn't want people tramping up and down their drive, so that would be yet another blow.

His mouth went dry, his tongue stuck to his teeth and he began to shrink from within. He wasn't, common sense told him that, but it was how it felt. At least he was now only supporting Fran — the other three were well away with their careers, and wouldn't need financial support unless something drastic occurred.

Harriet! Of course, he'd find Harriet: she'd make him pull himself together.

He shouted down the phone, 'Harriet? You there?'

'Where else at this time in the morning?'

'I'm coming home.'

'Home? Are you ill?'

'No, but I'm about to be.' He banged down the receiver, shouted to Tom he was going home for half an hour and fled.

Harriet was waiting for him at the door.

'Darling! You look dreadful! Whatever is it?'

Over a coffee into which he'd poured a shot of medicinal whisky, Jimbo told Harriet his news.

Harriet held out her hands to him. 'Show me the letter, please.'

Jimbo passed it to her, noticing how his hands shook, but Harriet's were steady.

His first words after Harriet had read the letter through to the end were, 'We're done for, you know. Absolutely done for.'

'Have you studied your calendar for the Old Barn lately? It's chock-a-block with bookings. For the next nine months there's at least one if not three or four events every week. Weddings, parties, and don't forget those trade fairs you're hosting.'

'He could get a buyer within a few short months. Then where would we be?'

144

'If whoever buys it hasn't the sense to see what a money spinner the Old Barn is then they're a fool . . . you've panicked, that's your trouble. It could be years in the present climate before he got a buyer. We'll pull our horns in a bit and before we know where we are you'll be top side of everything in no time at all.'

Harriet stood up and, leaning over Jimbo, kissed the middle of his bald head, put her arms around his shoulders and gave him a squeeze.

'Harriet! What would I do without you?'

Grinning, Harriet asked had he never realised before that she was the power behind the throne?

Momentarily his spirits lifted and he smiled. 'There, you see, I never knew before it was all due to you!'

'I hope that's not you being sarcastic. I've backed you all the way, even if I haven't always been certain you were right.'

'You're right. Very right. You have always supported me. With the mail order and the website too, we should be OK, shouldn't we?'

Harriet smiled. 'Of course we shall. I wonder who will buy the big house?'

'Certainly no one who wants to buy it to *live* in. I mean, who would? There's no one flush with that kind of money nowadays; it would have to earn its keep.'

'A hotel perhaps, do you think?'

'Might be, might be. I'm off up to see the man himself and ask when he wants to stop the contract. I hate having to lay people off; it's so upsetting.' Jimbo got to his feet. 'Remember, not a word! To anyone. Not even Mother. In fact,

145

definitely not to her.'

'Of course not. The news will get round fast enough without her assistance.'

Harriet watched him leave the house and wished he didn't have to tell his staff at the big house they were without a job. He'd keep them on if he could, but of course he couldn't — there'd be nothing to pay them with. She saw him brace his shoulders, walk towards his car, pause and then carry on walking and she knew he was going to go all the way up to see Craddock Fitch on foot instead of driving. Obviously he needed time to think.

And think he did. Halfway up the drive to the big house he concluded that the one he should be feeling sorry for was Craddock Fitch, not Jimbo Charter-Plackett. Standing on the gravel driveway gazing up at the beautiful Tudor house he remembered what a proud man Craddock was, how he thrived on the cut and thrust of the business world and how much he would hate any kind of sympathy, no matter how sincere.

His receptionist/secretary looked distraught. Obviously it was not the right moment for the usual jolly banter she and Jimbo frequently exchanged. 'Is your boss in?'

His reply was a nod of the head, and another tear beginning to roll down her cheek.

Jimbo tapped briskly on Craddock's office door and without waiting for his permission to enter he walked straight in.

Craddock was standing at the window lost in thought. He turned to see who'd entered and Jimbo saw he had a whisky glass in his hand.

'Join me?' Craddock asked.

Jimbo nodded. Craddock refilled his own glass and then handed one to Jimbo. They both stood side by side looking out of the window at the green rolling fields and hills of Turnham House grounds. The lake between the house and the hills shimmered in the morning sun. Their eyes followed a lone swimmer crossing the lake, both envying he who had the time to enjoy a swim on a morning of such shattering disappointment.

Craddock Fitch cleared his throat. 'Love this view. Always have. Damn it! To lose it will break my heart.'

Jimbo had never heard Craddock make such an emotional statement in all the years he'd known him.

Jimbo muttered, 'I had an almighty shock when I opened my post. At a loss to know what to say right now. So sudden.'

'These things always are. I've an office building project in Sweden standing half-finished because the owner has run out of money and big bills still owed, then a succession of smaller failures, a couple of rogue bankrupts running scared, and before I knew where I was the bank, damn 'em, were calling in my loans. I've opened quite a few nasty letters lately from the bank and now this is the end. The time comes when you know that you have to shut the lot down and stand back watching all your hard work come to nothing. Thank God I've got Kate.'

'I'm damned sorry. Twenty years it must be you've been here in this village; that's a long time in any man's life. Of course you'll miss it. If

. . . there's . . . we could always put you up now we've none of the children permanently at home. Tide you over until — '

Craddock raised his hand to silence him. 'Kind offer, but no thanks. Kate and I will move to Glebe House . . . '

'I thought you'd rented it to that peculiar couple we never see?'

'I did. But no longer; I've given them notice to quit. They were always late with their rent so they might possibly be glad. So that's more people I've given a shock to this morning.' Ruefully Craddock smiled at Jimbo. 'At least I shall have a roof over my head, but that's about all. I've grown to love this old place.' He looked round his office, gazed soulfully at the beautiful fireplace and the ancient panelling covering the walls, the ages-old bookshelves, and sighed. 'So your contract ends as of now. Sorry, we've been good friends, you and I.'

Jimbo nodded.

'The students in training have all been told and by the sounds of the bumping and banging I can hear they're busy packing this very minute. My head office in London will cause a problem. Who the blazes wants to buy first-class offices on a prime site in London in this financial climate?'

'No one. I shall say this and then not mention it again. I'm deeply sorry about it all. Deeply sorry.' Jimbo hesitated about bringing up his own rather desperate situation — it felt to be a small matter compared to Craddock Fitch's multiple problems. But he had to. 'About the Old Barn. I have events booked months ahead.'

'I don't expect I shall find a buyer this week or even next month, so keep going until we can't.' Craddock returned to staring out of the window. He was silent for a moment and then he spoke with a bitter tone in his voice. 'There'll be people in the village laughing their heads off; that'll be the hardest thing to bear. I've been too scornful of them in the past for them to feel sorry for me.'

'I wouldn't be too sure about that. They've really got to like you since you married Kate. She'll be a comfort to you, I've no doubt. I'll go gather my catering staff together and tell them the news. Something I don't like doing, but there it is.'

'I've always appreciated your high standards. That's why it's been such a money spinner for you, because of your high standards. Shows you've a good head for business.'

Jimbo realised that Craddock Fitch was looking at him, this time with a smile on his face. Then he turned away and Jimbo left him where he'd found him, gazing sadly at his land.

Jimbo pushed open the green baize door to the kitchens and found his catering staff preparing lunch. 'Chef!' he bellowed.

His chef appeared, buttoning his whites. 'Yes? You're early.' Not liking the look on Jimbo's face he asked, 'What's up? Summat wrong?'

'Have a word, your office.'

Dave the chef was a big man and it was a squash in there for the two of them.

'Tell me straight out, no messing. It's true, isn't it?'

Jimbo raised questioning eyebrows. 'What have you heard?'

'That the glory days are over. Craddock's fallen flat on 'is face.'

'What makes you think that?'

'I've a cousin works in the city, rumours and all that.'

'Yes, that's exactly it. He's heartbroken.'

'Heartbroken? Never realized he 'ad one.'

'Now, Dave!'

'He's a b — never mind, ignore me. So we're all out of a job then. As of now?' Dave began taking his whites off.

'Well, yes. I'm so sorry. I didn't have a hint of it. Then this morning I got the letter. I'll tell the others.'

Dave studied Jimbo's shocked face. 'No, it's got to be me. You can stay if you prefer but they are *my* staff, trained to *my* standards and *I* should tell them. OK?'

'Thanks. I'll never get used to sacking people. I'll sort out the redundancy money for them; it'll be on the salary slip, end of the month. Right?'

Dave looked Jimbo straight in the eye. 'No need to worry about me. I've a job waiting for me in London should I ever decide to take it up, so I'm OK. As for the rest of them,' he shrugged his shoulders, 'having worked for you and been trained by me they'll all get good jobs. Everyone in the business knows you don't employ fools, and I don't train idiots, so they won't be unemployed for long. There'll be cafés and restaurants in Culworth waiting to snap them up, believe me.'

'Thanks, Dave. Always been glad of your straight-out-with-it Northern talk.' He turned to go, and then came back to say with a grin on his face, 'Don't be too outspoken in London; it might not go down too well with them.'

Dave slapped him on the back and roared with laughter. 'Just go!'

But Jimbo stayed to hear him tell the others about their bad luck, and then shook hands with them all, thanked them for their hard work and left before he lost his cool and broke down.

★   ★   ★

The villagers who worked on the estate had heard the news from the catering people when they saw them leaving so early in the day and naturally the collapse of Craddock Fitch's empire was all round the three villages before teatime, and nowhere buzzed with the news quite so much as the bar at the Royal Oak.

Earlier than usual the regulars were assembling for a good gossip about the man who had been at the hub of village life for so long.

'Well,' said Willie, 'it's a real shame.'

'Real shame? It blinking isn't a shame; he deserves it. He deserves to be in the gutter for the way he's treated us villagers.' Don, still subject to outbursts of the truth, slapped his glass of orange juice down on the table, daring anyone to contradict him.

'Have you forgotten the times he's held parties for us all? What about the education scholarships he's awarded, to our Dean for a start. He'd never

151

'ave gone to Oxford if it had been left to us. Now would he?' This was Pat, having a free evening from organising Jimbo's events. 'He's made it, 'as our Dean. He has a wonderful life and I've the nicest daughter-in-law any mother could hope to have. Old Fitch doesn't deserve this.'

'What about that time your Barry nearly got sacked over them paving stones and them urns that mysteriously appeared in Vera's garden, eh?' asked Don.

'What about the champagne race meeting up at the big house when we made all that money for the mission in Africa?' challenged Willie.

Don remembered another matter he could hold against Mr Fitch. 'I'll give yer that, but what about the houses in Little Derehams what he bought? Eh! Winders letting the draughts in, and the paths bad enough to break yer leg.'

'What about all the years they've had rent free? Yer forget about that, oh yes! Living rent free all these years and they won't mend their own winders. Then they blame him!' This from Willie, who'd recently paid for new windows in his own house and still cringed at the thought of how much it had cost him.

Before the two of them came to blows Vera interrupted their tirade. 'Calm down or you'll be getting turned out; Georgie's on tonight an' she's not as tolerant as Dicky.'

Don opened his mouth but Vera banged her hand down on the table and said, 'Another word and *I'll* turn you out, and believe me I will, make no mistake!'

'Me! Turn me out?'

'Yes.' She gave his shoulder an affectionate punch, laughing but meaning it. 'See if I don't.'

'You wouldn't dare, woman. Not me, your dearly beloved.'

Sylvia spoke up. 'Shut up, Don, you've said enough. We've been mighty glad of Mr Fitch in years gone past. What about the cricket pavilion, and like Pat said the education sponsorships he's given? Lynn Patterson wouldn't be dancing with the Royal Ballet if it hadn't been for Mr Fitch and his education scholarships.' There were murmurings of approval from quite a few people round their table and Don knew his moment to shut up had come, but still pursued his point. 'I still say — '

'No, you don't. You get dafter the older you are, Don.' Vera gave him another punch on his shoulder and this time he retaliated by hitting her across her face, hard. That did it.

Georgie appeared as if by magic. 'I will not have this kind of behaviour in my pub. Out you go, and I mean it, Don Wright. Out!' She pointed to the outer door and glared ferociously at him.

'My!' Don said, excited by her temper. 'I like you when you're angry. Your eyes blaze, you don't half cut a tempting figure; that Dicky must have some fun with you.'

Angered by Don's comments, Georgie said loudly, 'You're banned! For a week. Don't you dare set a foot in here until then. Right?'

Willie and Alan nodded in agreement to indicate they were on her side. To Don this provided a further challenge, so he purposely sat tight and ignored them. It was fun being annoying to people; at least they took notice of him.

Willie gave Alan a wink and the two of them stepped forward, one either side of Don. They each took hold of an arm, heaved him to his feet and frogmarched him out of the door with Don protesting all the way. Georgie ran after them with Don's stick and they all sat back, relieved that he'd been turned out, though they were horrified by him hitting Vera.

But Vera wasn't. He'd hit her before for much less; the difference was this time he'd done it in public.

Sylvia caught her eye and saw for herself what was written there.

'Vera! Love!'

Vera burst into tears.

Sylvia put an arm around her shoulders, at a loss for words, patting her comfortingly.

She got no reply because Vera was too ashamed. Keeping it all to herself these last . . . was it two whole years it had been going on? She couldn't bear to admit it. He didn't mean it, she was sure, but . . .

Willie leaned across the table to say, 'Vera, it's not right.'

Vera nodded. Of course it wasn't, but what could she do? Bring shame on them both by letting on?

Sylvia, deeply sorry for Vera's plight, said, 'I'm so sorry, love. It must be dreadful for you.'

Vera shook her head, and wiped her eyes saying, 'Got to go. He won't remember where he

154

left the car.' She hastened out, leaving the others feeling full of sympathy for her.

Pat and Barry came to their table. 'Can we join you?'

Willie and Sylvia hurriedly agreed, glad of a diversion. Barry pulled up a couple of chairs and they toasted everyone round the table and immediately asked if they'd heard the news about Mr Fitch.

'We have,' said Sylvia, 'but I bet you know a lot more than we do.'

'Well . . . ' Barry paused for maximum effect, 'his business has collapsed. That's why he wants to sell up. Everything.'

Willie hadn't realised the magnitude of Mr Fitch's decision. 'The whole estate? All of it? Never! Thought it was just the Turnham Malpas bits.'

'All of it. Every stick and stone. The house, the grounds, the lake, the Old Barn and . . . everything in Sweden and the big offices in London.'

'London, too?'

'The lot, Willie, the whole blinking lot, and he's going to live in Glebe House.'

'He can't,' Sylvia declared. 'There's people live in there, not that we see them much, well hardly ever.'

'He's given them notice.'

'I can't believe it. It's a right come down for 'im, isn't it? The poor chap.' There was a small element of glee in Willie's voice as he said this.

'All of us out of a job, I expect,' Pat added rather bitterly. 'But maybe not yet; they'll need someone to supervise the gardens and that. He won't sell an estate the size of his in a moment. It could take some time. My dad's a favourite of Mr Fitch but he's far too old now to do a day's work. He's all right supervising but someone new wouldn't want him, and with Michelle not here no more I rather think we'd be out on our ear. I've loved that house, I really have loved it.' Pat sighed. 'I shall be sorry to say goodbye to it. Still, it might be a while yet.'

'Of course it will,' Sylvia said sympathetically. 'Heaven's above, the money it'll cost to buy that lot! He'll have to break it up. His London side in one lot. The Swedish stuff in another . . . how much *is* he asking, do you know, Barry?'

Barry couldn't resist teasing her. 'Fancy being lady of the manor do yer, Sylvia? How are you placed with the bank, Willie?'

Sylvia snorted her annoyance at his teasing. 'Don't be daft. Of course not. I just wondered if you knew, kind of, you being at the hub of things on the estate.'

'I don't think he'll be advertising any of it in the *Culworth Gazette*, do you?'

They had to laugh at the idea and they all cheered up enormously, but despite all their speculation, they still hadn't got the answer, had they? Who would buy it and what difference would it make to the village and more important, what would happen to them?

# 13

Johnny had overheard them talking about Craddock Fitch and the collapse of his business in the pub a couple of nights ago but he'd kept a straight face and said not a word. So his opportunity to buy Turnham House, the big house as they all called it, had come. He was standing in the shade of the Old Barn gazing with joy at the house he longed to own. The longing for it surged through him and he knew that no matter what, no matter the price, it was going to be his. In fact, no point in hanging about dreaming; he'd go right now and do something about it straight away. He'd tried Alice out about living there in a teasing tone and she'd just laughed, thinking he was making a joke, but she hadn't outright objected, so that was something.

As he walked towards the house, he saw Craddock's car parked outside.

Good! Craddock was home. His driver was giving the car a polish with a huge piece of chamois leather, slowly, almost lovingly, caressing the chrome on the bonnet.

'Good morning, Ian, nice day for it.'

'Morning. It is. Love of my life, this car, and it's going today. Selling it, he is. If it's him you're wanting to see, watch your step; he's not in a good mood. Anyway, it's going and I'm reduced to driving a four-by-four from the farm.'

'Whoops! That's a bit of a come down.'

'Too right.' Ian turned back to the car to hide his feelings from Johnny. 'Then it'll be me being sold off, so to speak: driving himself, he says he is. Rotten driver, too. Thinks he owns the road and everyone should move out of his way. No patience, you see, none at all, worse since . . . well . . . yer know . . . 'aving to sell.'

'I'll watch my step. Thanks for the advice.'

His secretary was still there, her face lighting up like a Catherine wheel when she saw who it was.

'Good morning, Sir Johnny, lovely morning.'

'Good morning.' He nodded his head towards Craddock Fitch's office door. 'Is he free?'

'I feel really sorry for him this morning. It's all getting him down, but yes he's free. I'll tell him you're here.'

'Thanks.'

She came back into the hall holding the office door open for him. 'Please go in.'

Johnny tried hard to disguise the shock he experienced when he saw Mr Fitch. He seemed to have lost weight. Normally bristling with energy, he was sitting lost in thought, slumped in his big leather chair, his eyes downcast, fiddling aimlessly with a ruler.

'Good morning, Mr Fitch.'

There was no response.

'It's Johnny Templeton.'

'I'm not blind.' Even his voice had lost its vibrancy.

'Come to see you on business.'

'Come to gloat, then.'

158

'No, not gloat; that wouldn't be gentlemanly.' Instantly Johnny regretted using that word. It implied . . .

'You'll know all about that, being an up and coming fly-by-night from the seamier side of South American business life.'

Johnny was furious. 'Not up and coming; we've *arrived*, my brothers and I. We own the largest and the best hotel chain in South America.' He found he was trembling at the slur on his character, but his business brain controlled any further outburst.

'So what are you doing here in this village, then?'

'Taking up my inheritance. That's why I've come to see you on business matters.'

'You're very like him. Same aristocratic nose from which to look down on everybody, same fair hair, same nut-brown eyes. God! I hated that uncle of yours. Got his own way about everything because of his title, and never needed to hand over a sweetener.' Somewhat wryly he expanded on his statement. 'Oh! No, not Sir Ralph! It would be beneath him. Not the action of a true gentleman. I expect your family persuaded you to come and take up your inheritance, did they? I bet their eyes glistened at the thought of a title in the family. Must have been very tempting.'

Johnny pulled out a chair and sat down, ignoring Mr Fitch's anger at his familiarity. 'They tried hard to dissuade me. Why go to a third-rate country; stay here where it's all happening, they said!'

He thought Mr Fitch was going to explode.

159

'Third-rate country! England! A third-rate country! How dare they. Us? A third-rate country! My God! What arrogance.'

'From where we stand, it is.'

'You'll be saying next that you want to buy the estate!' He peered at Johnny through screwed up angry eyes and realisation dawned. 'My God! I'm right, you damn well do! That's why you're here. Blast you for your temerity!'

'Yes, you are right, I am.'

'I wouldn't sell it to you if you were the last man on earth. I wouldn't soil this hallowed place with a jumped up . . . with a jumped up . . . ' Lost for words he got to his feet and shouted, 'Get out. Go on, out!'

Johnny calmly stood up and leaning his hands on Mr Fitch's impressive desk he said softly, 'You know where I live when you've reached the end and need my money. I'll pay whatever price you ask, but don't go to excess. I'm not a fool.'

Johnny went out, closing the door softly behind him. He'd seen desperation before in a strong man's face and he'd seen it again this morning. His heart went out to the man. He sensed the shame of the collapse and that it was killing him from the inside and he sensed the fear. Poor old Fitch, now no longer the generous benefactor. Johnny clenched his fist and shook it at the sky. 'Yes! Yes!!' he said quietly so Ian wouldn't hear. 'See you around, Ian. It's rather good fun driving a four-by-four. You might find you enjoy it.'

'Not the same as driving the finest car in the district.'

Johnny stopped for a moment. 'No, you're right,

it isn't. Treat him with care. It's a stupendous blow for him.'

'You're a gentleman, just like Sir Ralph. Did you ever meet him?'

'Never. I wish I had.'

'Lovely man, gracious you could call him. Yes, that's right, he was gracious was Sir Ralph. No one has a wrong word to say about him. He'd have liked you, and you'd have liked him. I remember once he gave — '

Mr Fitch shouted from the front door as he emerged from the house, 'I'm ready to set off, Ian. Right now. This minute.'

They left in a swirl of gravel and squealing tyres, leaving Johnny to stand alone admiring the house he hoped, no *knew*, would soon be his. That modern extension that housed the swimming pool would have to come down; how he'd ever got permission for it Johnny couldn't begin to imagine — it was so ugly, so out of character. It must have been a sizeable sweetener to achieve that. The temptation to go back inside and persuade the secretary to take him on a tour of inspection was so great his feet took him inside again before he knew it.

'I can't show you his flat, you know. His wife is at home today. Half term.'

'You mean he has young children?' The surprise in Johnny's voice amused the secretary and she giggled.

'No! She's the headteacher at the village school.'

'Oh! Right, of course, I'd forgotten. I just want to see the historic parts.'

'The whole building is historic.'

161

'Of course yes, but the best bits, if you know what I mean.'

'My name's Anne.'

He offered his hand. 'Call me Johnny, everyone else does. I haven't got used to the Sir bit yet.'

'You will, given time.'

The next ten minutes he spent filled with awe at the wonderful Tudor stairs, the splendid panelling, the lovely, gracious sitting room, kept just as it had been for hundreds of years with some of the original chairs and sofas still in situ.

'These of course are priceless, literally. Mr Fitch had the upholstery renewed using the same design as the original, specially woven for the job. No expense spared.'

'A house like this deserves that level of care.' Johnny was overwhelmed with the beauty of the house and if anything he was even more determined to own it. A door opened somewhere. He heard quick footsteps and then a woman appeared. She had a kind of sparky determination about her and he knew she'd be straightforward, that there'd be no pretence with her.

'Anne! Will you introduce me to your visitor, please?' She must have been in her fifties, but you never would have thought it.

Johnny stepped in to explain. 'It's Johnny Templeton, we've met before, at the youth club. I've been to see Mr Fitch on business, and before I left asked if I could look round and Anne agreed. Sony if we're intruding.'

Anne began to apologise but was interrupted by Mrs Fitch.

'How do you do!' Her handshake was strong. 'I remember you, of course.'

'I've just been speaking to your husband. He — '

'What do you think of the house?'

'It's truly magnificent.'

'It is, isn't it? We shall be very sorry to leave it. Architecturally the one we are moving to is a horror, but beggars can't be choosers.'

'You appear more philosophical about the move than your husband.'

'Anne, could you organise a tray of tea for Sir Johnny and me? Would that suit? We'll have it in the flat.'

So Johnny saw the private sitting room and listened quietly to Kate Fitch's explanation of the situation they found themselves in, while he sipped his tea.

'Frankly not a single buyer in the whole world will please him. He pulled himself up by his shoe laces from nothing, literally nothing, every penny hard earned, and this house is his reward. He adores it. Who wouldn't? Having to leave it is killing him. Eating him away from the inside, but it has to be done. It has to be sold to whoever. If it's not to be ours then I don't care what kind of Philistine buys it; at least they can't pull it down or change it too much because it's a Grade II listed house and there are rules.' Every fibre of Kate Fitch's body pleaded with him to answer 'Yes' when she asked after a pause, 'Do you really like it?'

Johnny couldn't frame the words to tell her how much he wanted it, couldn't describe the deep yearning in his heart. All he could do was nod his head in agreement.

Kate Fitch said, 'I can see your passion for it in your face. Don't give up hope. He'll fight you, but it'll be so very right for you to own it; the house coming back to its rightful owner would be wonderful. I'm sure it would sigh with relief.' She reached across and patted his hand. 'Not a word to anyone about this. It'll be our secret. Got to go, I'm needed elsewhere. What this house needs is children, then it really would come alive and be a real home, and it hasn't seen one since Sir Ralph was born here, something like eighty or ninety years ago.'

Johnny stood up to say goodbye. 'Thank you for finding time to talk to me. I love this house and there's nothing I'd like better than to live here. I have the money to buy it; you have my word on that. If he'll let me.'

'Good, I'm glad. I'm sure I'll see you again sometime.' Kate Fitch saw him down the stairs and out of the door. Johnny loved that big front door; he loved it all. Every brick, every room, everything about the house and in his heart he made a vow that no matter how long he had to wait it would one day be his and Alice's.

Johnny strode off down the drive, his head full of what he'd seen, imagining his brothers coming to visit, thinking about swimming in the lake, owning a dog or two, but most importantly about how Alice would feel living up at the big house.

She'd just got in from teaching when he got back. She looked strained and weary.

'Sit down. What would you like, a cup of tea or

proper coffee?' Johnny asked.

'Tea, please.' She sat on the sofa in front of her log-burning stove and welcomed the warmth of it. They still hadn't settled on which house they would live in. Johnny favoured his own that had once belonged to his uncle, but Alice preferred living in her own house, so Johnny was playing it cool and leaving her to make the final decision.

Johnny handed her a cup of tea, and sat down opposite her on the old chair that had been left in the house by the previous owners. 'About where we live. I know you find it hard to believe, but I have pots of money. A disgraceful amount of money, which when we marry will be jointly yours and mine.'

'Johnny! I've said before I don't want loads of money; it's too much responsibility. You keep it. You've earned it and — '

Johnny placed a finger on her lips to silence her. 'Hush just for a moment and let me finish. Turnham House. I want to own what is rightly mine and I intend to live there.' He was interrupted by a howl of displeasure from Alice. 'Hush! Hush! I've spoken to Craddock Fitch this morning and he refuses to sell to me, turned me out in fact.'

'Oh! Good, I'm glad he did. I'm a cottage person, not a lady of the manor person. I love my cottage!'

'But that house is where I belong; I need to be there. I'm the rightful owner and he's just an interloper.'

'He paid for it and as far as I'm concerned he can keep it.'

165

'We shan't move there until after the baby has arrived. Alice, when the baby is here . . .

'Just a minute! He's refused to sell it to you, so that's that.'

'Yes, I know he has, but . . . '

'But what?'

'Someway or another I am buying it back.'

'You can't just snatch it back; he has to agree.'

'Which he will in a while, when things get even more desperate than they are now.'

'You don't know Mr Fitch if you can say that. He's a very determined man.'

Johnny laughed. Alice pouted, which made him laugh even louder. 'Not nearly as determined as I am. I have the money; he hasn't. His whole world has collapsed and whilst I'm not willing to take advantage of that and pay much less than the market price, I am prepared to put pressure on him to sell.'

Alice drank the last drop of her tea and as she placed her cup on the kitchen table she said, 'Well, you'll move in there by yourself then, because I'm most definitely not.' She laid her head against the back of the sofa. 'I'm so tired; please don't mention it again. In any case, you can't possibly have enough money to buy the estate. He'll want millions.'

'Actually I have enough and more.'

Alice's eyes sprang wide open. 'You haven't! Have you really?'

Johnny nodded.

'I knew you were wealthy, but I had no idea. Not that it matters to me, just so long as I have enough to feel secure . . . have you really got

166

enough to buy the estate? Actually buy it?'

'Yes, and to pull down that dreadful eyesore of a swimming pool extension. That has to go; it's an abomination.'

Alice sat silently for a moment and then said with a smile on her face, 'That big room with a fireplace at each end . . . '

'Yes?'

'That would be lovely with a grand piano in it.'

'Yes, it would,' Johnny answered, thinking she was warming to his idea.

'But I still don't want to live there. I've imagined feeding our baby sitting here,' she patted the sofa cushion next to her, 'on a cold winter's night. Right here, with the warmth of the fire wrapping round us. Wouldn't that be lovely? With you sitting where you are now, watching me and talking about your day.'

'Considering Craddock Fitch's hatred of me and my uncle Ralph, you probably will be, because it could take that long to get the finance sorted with him, even when he's agreed to it. He's a hard nut to crack is Craddock Fitch, but one plus is that his wife is on my side.'

Alice went on the alert. 'His wife? Kate?'

Johnny was amused by her interest. 'We had a cup of tea in their flat.'

'In their flat? No one gets invited up there.'

'I did. She wants me to buy it. The whole house, that is.'

'She does? Has she said so?'

'She has. Now look, you've not to get upset about it right now; you've enough on your mind

167

without worrying about moving house. That'll all come in time, when you're ready for it.'

'Johnny, what have I just said?'

'Yes, I know, darling, but it won't be for months yet, possibly even years, so there's no need to worry about it right now.'

'You are not listening to me. I don't want to be the lady at the manor.'

'Fine, fine. I shan't mention it again. Honestly.' Johnny, deep inside, was bitterly disappointed.

'I'm all right as I am.'

'More tea, Alice?' he asked, as though he'd put the whole idea out of his mind. Which he hadn't and didn't intend doing. Somehow or other when the baby had arrived and she was more like her usual self he would bring her round to his way of thinking, because Turnham House was going to be his and his children's. All he had to do was play the waiting game. He glanced across at Alice and saw she was almost asleep. He studied the beauty of her face in repose, loved her delicate, sensitive hands locked together over her bump and thought about the splendid music they created when she played the piano. His eyes lingered on her throat while he recollected her sweet singing voice. What a lucky man he was — lucky because all that rare passionate beauty belonged with him for the rest of his life.

Well, it would once the divorce had gone through. That damned Marcus with his over-bearing ego, convinced the publishing world should be grateful that he had decided to grace their corridors. Johnny had looked up the

168

publisher who'd taken him on and found it a very minor player and he'd laughed. He'd said nothing to anyone of what he'd discovered; he couldn't be so cruel but . . . he smiled again at the thought.

Alice stirred and shuffled about on the sofa and then slipped into a heavier sleep. She slept for a whole hour, leaving Johnny to sit thinking about his beloved house and how he could persuade Mr Fitch to sell it to him. The man had all his sympathy, losing everything like he had. He knew how he'd feel if it was the hotel business about to sink into oblivion, everything he and his two brothers had worked for all their adult lives.

He became aware that Alice was waking up. 'Feel better?'

'Yes, thanks.' Alice stretched elegantly. 'You're still thinking about Turnham House, aren't you? I can see it in your face.'

'I was thinking about Craddock Fitch and how I would be feeling if everything I'd worked for was swirling down the pan at this very moment. For a proud man like him that's hard.'

'You're proud too, aren't you?'

'Regrettably, that's something I suffer from just like him.' Johnny smiled at her, knowing as he did so he hadn't yet won her round to his way of thinking. And there was still Craddock Fitch to persuade.

But he would win. Eventually.

★   ★   ★

Craddock Fitch returned home at the same time Alice had woken up. He hadn't the heart for the office today. He needed to talk to Kate, but she was out so he went into his office and sat in his leather chair that in happier days had always fitted him beautifully. But now it felt like there were lumps and bumps in it right where there never had been before. He couldn't remember a time when he felt worse than this, not since he was sixteen and had just left home to escape his father's brutality.

Craddock Fitch rested his head back and closed his eyes. Those had been the worst days: lonely, penniless, homeless. Well, that was until he stole that wheelbarrow and shovel and offered his services on a building site and since that event had never looked back. Out of the blue he thought about his two sons. They'd been three and five when Faye left him and he'd never seen them since. Never heard their laughter again and they'd been a happy pair of boys. He wished as never before that he'd been able to keep in touch; they'd have helped him out of this mess. He opened his eyes and, staring out of the window at his favourite view, he reflected on which would have been the more precious: being the owner of that view or watching his two boys growing up. They'd be in their forties by now. God! That made him old. He wished they would be coming to see him. Right now. He glanced at the clock. They'd be just in time for a cup of tea.

He heard his secretary tap on the door, saw her come in with a tray of tea just as he liked it. Silver teapot, silver sugar bowl and milk jug, *three* china cups and saucers . . . three! Were his boys actually coming for tea then, just as he'd wished?

Anne put down the tray. 'Mrs Fitch and the reverend are taking tea with you, Mr Fitch.'

'The reverend? Coming to tea?'

'Yes, Mrs Fitch found him walking up the drive to visit you.'

'I'm in no mood for the reverend.'

'Too late, he's here. I've forgotten the biscuits. Back in a tick.'

When Anne came back with the biscuits Kate was pouring the tea. 'You don't take sugar, do you, Peter?'

'No, thanks.' Just like Johnny, Peter had had a shock when he saw Craddock Fitch. The man was a mere shadow of what he used to be. He was glad he'd come.

'How are things, Craddock? I know life must be difficult at the moment,' Peter said, wishing he'd never come; it was so obviously the wrong moment.

'It is. Yes.' Craddock shuffled himself straighter in his chair to put on an appearance of good health. He should have joined the other two in the easy chairs over by the fireplace, but the desk gave him security and he didn't want to leave its safety.

'If you need any help please feel free. I'm not a business person but I might be able to throw a different light on things, should you ask me.'

As if . . . Craddock thought. 'Thanks all the same, but I'm managing very well indeed, always been the man in charge. How are things with you?'

171

'Excellent, thank you. Kate tells me you're thinking of moving to Glebe House.'

Craddock Fitch, who loathed the idea but had no alternative, answered briskly, 'Might sell it instead and find somewhere more compatible. Not to my taste, nor Kate's. But house selling at the moment is in a slump like everything else, so it may be better to wait and see.'

'Of course. Very sensible.'

'If it's a donation you're wanting . . . '

Peter hastily interrupted. 'I'm not here to ask for money. I wouldn't be so insensitive. In fact I don't think I ever have *asked* you for money for the church; you've always offered it so generously.'

'Well, I can tell you right now, those days have come to an end.'

'So I understand. And I'm sorry about all your business troubles; it must be tremendously hard for you.'

His sympathy made Craddock Fitch stiffen up. 'I don't need your sympathy, thank you very much. In fact I don't need you at all and I don't know why on earth you've come. Finished your cup of tea, have you?'

Peter put his empty cup on the tray.

'Good. Bye then.'

'Should you need me . . . '

'Well, to be honest I shan't, unless you have a few million going spare?'

Peter, surprised by Craddock's attack, apologised, thanked Kate for the tea and left.

Kate was appalled. 'Darling, you'll have to apologise. That was unforgivable. How could you?'

172

'Very easily, and I shan't apologise. He's very safe, isn't he? Regular salary, a roof over his head. What more can a man ask? Children, too.'

The bitterness in his voice when he said 'children' went straight to Kate's heart. 'You knew children weren't on the menu when we married. I was already too old to begin a family.'

He got to his feet and went to look out of the window. He made a comment in a voice so low Kate couldn't hear what he said and had to ask him to repeat it. He drew in a great breath and said it again. 'I was thinking about my two sons before you came in. Perhaps if I'd known where they were, been able to speak to them, things could have been different.'

'You never mention them.'

'What's the point? I can barely remember their names.'

'I can, you told me once. Graham and Michael. Graham was the older one.'

'That's right. Yes. Graham and Michael. Fancy forgetting their names! How could I? Goes to show.'

'Goes to show what?'

'How self-absorbed I've been all these years. Money. Money. Money. Except when I wanted you. Best day's work I ever did, marrying you.' Craddock turned from looking out of the window and she noticed he was showing his age more than he'd ever done. He said harshly, 'Will you want to leave me, now the money's gone?'

Kate leapt to her feet and flung her arms round him. 'Leave you? How can I, when I love you so much? You don't want me to, do you?'

173

He wrapped his arms around her and muttered, 'Of course not. Like you said 'How can I when I love you so much?'' They stood together, hugging each other by the window that looked out on his view of the lake and Kate decided she should try to persuade him to sell out to Johnny Templeton.

He released her and went back to sit at his desk. 'You know that Johnny Templeton? I've investigated his hotel company.'

Kate held her breath.

'He's right; he has the millions to buy this place.'

Kate feigned surprise. 'Oh! Has he?'

'Yes, but he's not having it. Under no circumstances. I'd set fire to it and collect the insurance money rather than him buy it.'

Kate, very carefully assuming disinterest, though she knew she would hang on every word he said, asked, 'Why?'

'Mainly because I knew Ralph was superior to me and always would be no matter what I did or said. Breeding, you know, he had breeding and I had none. Public school stuff, I expect.'

'Darling, nowadays that doesn't matter. Not any more.'

'It mattered to me.'

'Well, you shouldn't have let it.'

'But he knew he was superior to me.'

'Did he ever say so?'

'No, of course he didn't; he was a gentleman, you see, so he wouldn't, would he?'

Kate could hear a sneering tone in his voice. 'But . . . '

174

'He'd more respect for that dog Sykes, because Sykes never tries to be something he isn't and Ralph thought I did, and he was right.' Craddock leaned his elbows on his desk. Irritably he inquired, 'How old is that dog? He seems to have been here for years.'

'He has, he can't live much longer, surely.'

'Like me then.' Craddock smiled ruefully at Kate.

Kate picked up the tea tray saying, 'No more of that, if you please. That's defeatist talk and I won't have it. Be positive! Nothing, and I mean *nothing*, comes from being defeatist. You do what you have to do and so will I. I refuse to give in.' Kate marched determinedly out of the office, knowing exactly what she must do.

# 14

The uncertainty about the big house and their jobs and who would buy it and what were they all going to do when they'd no benefactor caused everyone in the village to feel unsettled. Even those whose livelihood didn't depend on Craddock Fitch's whim felt restless and wished it could all get sorted.

No one more so than Jimbo. Should he or shouldn't he book more events for the Old Barn? The weeks rolled on and he couldn't in all conscience keep on booking into the future hoping Craddock Fitch wouldn't find a buyer.

He stood one morning, when Tom had a day off and Jimbo was therefore in charge, looking out over the village, thinking hard. At the moment the only movement was Sykes on his morning trip round his favourite calling points. Jimbo glanced at the clock and saw Sykes was running late this morning. Jimbo watched him as he went up the church path as usual. Strange that, for a dog, liking to sit in the church. Briefly Jimbo wondered if he might get some inspiration of what to do about the Old Barn if he sat in there each morning like Sykes did.

If he turned his head slightly he could just glimpse Sykes changing his mind and not going in to church as he always did. In winter when the main door was kept shut to keep the heat in he'd trained Zack the verger to open it by barking sharply three times so Zack would know he was waiting to be admitted. But this morning Sykes didn't bark for admittance; instead he paused as though having a deep think and then trotted round the back of the church and disappeared from Jimbo's view. A customer! It was one of the mothers from the school.

'Good morning! Lovely winter's day, isn't it?' Jimbo called out.

'Is it? I hadn't noticed.'

Jimbo knew her husband was helping out temporarily in the gardens at the big house, seeing as two of the workers there had found permanent employment with the council in view of the pending sale.

She sounded too disgruntled for Jimbo's chirpy chat so he went to sort the greetings cards and fill in any gaps with new stock. He forgot she was there and had to be alerted by her asking if he wanted paying this morning or not.

'Sorry! Sorry! Got absorbed in sorting the cards out. I mean, how can someone return a card for a six-year-old's birthday by slotting it on to the Deepest Sympathy section? Some people!'

'If that's all you've got to worry about, you're lucky. My husband's just been given his notice. Six weeks he's slaved up in those gardens in all weathers and out of the blue he's been told his work isn't satisfactory, he says, so that's him unemployed again. But I know different.'

'You do?'

'Yes, that so and so up there is fast running out of money, that's why.'

'Are you sure?'

'Never been surer.'

'Oh, dear,' said Jimbo with as much sympathy as he could muster.

'It isn't fair. I've had to *sell* my car; he just swaps his beautiful car for a four-by-four he *happens* to have hanging about at the farm. No skin off his nose, is it? I can't afford to run mine so I'm shopping here instead of in that cheap supermarket on the bypass. Your prices!'

'But my food isn't rubbish like it is there; mine's best quality, and trade isn't all that good I can tell you at the moment.'

She glanced rather scathingly at his rounded stomach, which made Jimbo pull it in as best he could.

She unzipped her purse. 'Yes. I can see you're starving to death. Right. Eight pounds twenty you say.'

'That's right. If you haven't the change we'll call it eight pounds exactly; I'm a bit short of change today. Should have gone to the bank yesterday but I forgot.'

The customer dropped her shopping into her own carrier bag saying, 'That'll be a big help, I must say. Twenty pence!' and left.

When customers complained about his prices Jimbo always took it badly. He'd introduced his economy lines and that did appear to have helped people but obviously it hadn't been enough. He should never have opened up again; that had been a bad decision. What was worse was not knowing whether he would still have the facility of the Old Barn when the big house changed hands. Wild ideas flew around his head.

178

Could he borrow enough money to buy the estate himself? No. Would Craddock sell off the bit where the Old Barn stood? No. Should he cancel all future events immediately? No point in people booking weddings and parties and things and then him having to cancel at the last minute. Jimbo shuddered at the damage that would do to his business. He could get a letter tomorrow, or even today to say his Old Barn business was over forthwith. He reminisced about the wonderful events he'd held there: Ford and Mercedes' Tudor Banquet, the rotary club charity ball — now that had been fantastic; the euphoria from that had lasted weeks — the rugby club bash, now that had really been something; he'd kept control of it by the skin of his teeth. It could so easily have tipped over into a riot.

Jimbo opened the door and stood out in front of the store straightening the advertising boards he had out there and enjoying the surprising warmth of the sun. He loved living here, he loved the people, he loved the countryside, he loved the gossip, the feuds, the fun they had. What would it be like without their benefactor? There'd be no more big bonfire-night parties with the refreshment tent and the drinks tent and the jacket potatoes eaten standing by the bonfire. His children had all grown up here and loved coming home to the village. But was it time for him to be moving on? Fran only had one more year at school and then he and Harriet were free as birds to move where they chose. He'd miss being at the heart of the village, the chief recipient of all the gossip, and did he love the gossip! Pathetic really when he remembered his standing at the merchant bank and how they'd all thought he must be mad, with a future like he had, to bury himself in the country. But he'd done the right thing.

Sykes came trotting past, paused long enough to greet Jimbo and receive a pat on his head for his thoughtfulness and then he strode on full of purpose down Shepherd's Hill. Change of routine then, this morning. Strange little dog. He seemed to consider that it didn't matter who fed and housed him, so long as he lived in Turnham Malpas. Everyone knew him and he knew everyone. Not unlike himself, thought Jimbo: he knew everyone and everyone knew him. He was interrupted by the phone ringing, and reluctantly Jimbo left the sunshine to go inside to answer it.

It was Craddock Fitch's secretary. Could he come up asap?

'I'm on my own at the moment, but I'll come as soon as I can. Bye!'

He rang Harriet. 'Darling! I need someone to look after the store for half an hour. Craddock Fitch wants to see me. I expect it's about the Old Barn . . . and things. Can you come?'

'Won't be a moment.'

So Jimbo left the store a few minutes later and drove up to the big house with a sinking feeling in the pit of his stomach and a powerful feeling of regret that the money spinner he adored was about to be given the chop. He loved the drama of the events held there and couldn't cope with the idea that there would be no more.

His mind was so taken up with the bad news

he expected to hear that he didn't register how ill Craddock Fitch looked. He accepted the delicious coffee the secretary made for them both and sat back to hear why he'd been summoned, because that was how it felt.

'I do believe I've found a buyer. A cash buyer for the estate, and I thought you should be the first to know, because of the Old Barn bookings.'

'Ah! I thought perhaps that was it. A cash buyer! My word, what amazing luck.'

'He and his board members are very keen, just what they've been looking for. Unfortunately they will be making use of the Old Barn, so won't want you to carry on as you are. I had hoped to find someone who would let you do that very thing, but unfortunately they don't. But I can't turn down their offer in the circumstances.'

'Of course not. I wouldn't expect you to. May I inquire who they are and what they'll be doing with the Old Barn? Just out of interest of course.' Jimbo took another sip of his coffee and hoped his grave disappointment didn't show. It was then he noticed how unlike his normal self Craddock Fitch appeared to be. God! The man looked completely drained.

'They're an entertainment company and will be holding events of all kinds in the Old Barn three nights a week: Thursday, Friday and Saturday. They haven't a Sunday licence as yet but they are hoping to get one. I doubt they will, but there we are. It's a heaven-sent opportunity for me.'

'So someone will be living here.' Jimbo spread

his hands to indicate he meant the big house.

'The owner will.'

'And he is?'

'Freedom Blade, whoever he might be. Obviously a made up name. I haven't met him, just his agent's been round and loves the place: just what they've been looking for.' There was a smidgen of sadness in Craddock's voice and Jimbo's heart went out to him, but he had to be warned.

'You do know what he's about? Read about him in the press or seen him on TV? That he's not quite . . . '

Craddock looked up listlessly as though he didn't care a hoot how degenerate the man was so long as he solved his problem.

'No. Does it matter?'

'He's into drugs, he's an alcoholic, he abuses women, loud parties, you name it. He most certainly is not what this village needs or wants.'

'Since when have they ever thought about me? Mmm? They've accepted the parties and the scholarships, the money I've given to the church, whatever I've offered and then laughed behind my back. I owe them nothing. Absolutely nothing.' He picked up his morning post and sifted through it, ignoring Jimbo.

There had to be something he could hit back with, thought Jimbo. What was his soft spot? 'Would you really want this magnificent house, which you love, to be abused by a man like him?'

Craddock looked as though he'd been stabbed clean through the heart. He put down his post and looked directly at Jimbo. 'If you were in the financial position I find myself in, you wouldn't care if it was the devil himself moving in so long as you were free of the responsibility. Every day it gets me deeper into debt. Now, off you go and let me get on with rescuing myself.'

But Jimbo didn't go. 'For God's sake don't do it, man, he's a wrong 'un. A dreadful man, not fit to own a dog, let alone a house like this. Think of the village. Please.'

Craddock sat back in his chair, closing his eyes briefly as though trying to shut out the inevitable. 'I've got to do it; he's the only one who's offered the money with any certainty. The only one. I can't wait any longer. My situation is dire.' He dismissed Jimbo with a tired wave of his hand.

'Is there nothing else you could sell, like Glebe House, perhaps?'

'A drop in the ocean that is, a drop in the ocean.'

Jimbo said, 'I'm so sorry. I wish I could help, wish I could buy the whole estate outright but I can't. Think twice about this Freedom Blade because within a year this beloved house of yours will be a wreck, believe me. None of us could bear that. I know it doesn't belong to the village but it *feels* as though it does. Just a pity it had to be sold after the Second World War, then there'd have been a Templeton here and we'd all feel safe. Tradition and all that jazz, you know. Anytime you need someone to talk to, a sounding board, please feel free to ring me.'

Jimbo left Craddock sitting with his eyes closed again, head resting back as though the last ounce of his strength had been taken from him.

The news got round the village faster than the speed of light. Jimbo wasn't to blame — the only person he told was Harriet when he took over the reins again on his return.

'Not a word, darling. It may all fall through, you never know, so there's no point in alarming the village unnecessarily. If a customer comes in, mum's the word.'

'But Freedom Blade! My God! That's terrible. We'll be invaded.'

'Exactly, once the fans find out. Could be good for business though. Could we rig up a pizza oven and serve . . . or, I know, we could always . . . ' Jimbo's business mind began exploring the different possibilities of making money.

'Don't you dare. The man is a beast, but we can't stop Craddock selling it to him.'

'He's desperate and I mean *desperate* . . . I don't want to profit by Old Fitch's misfortune, but when it's someone like Freedom Blade, there's a limit. He's foul, if you believe everything they say about him in the papers.'

But the subject was the very first to be discussed that night at the table in the bar with the old bench down the side. Willie got the drinks in for Sylvia, Dottie, Maggie, Vera, Don, Barry and Pat and when they'd all taken their first reviving sip conversation broke out.

'So, Barry, reveal all. We're all waiting,' said Sylvia, who'd seen Freedom Blade on TV and thought that despite all the stories about him he really was a very appealing if misguided young

184

man. Her mother would have described him as in need of mothering. 'What does he look like in real life?'

Barry dashed her hopes immediately. 'He's not been to see the house; it was his agent or manager or someone. Quite by chance,' he grinned, and they all acknowledged what he meant, 'when he was looking round, I happened to be attending to a window at the front of the house that had jammed shut. Been meaning to do it for weeks and thought this morning was my moment.'

'So what did you hear?'

'Apparently . . . ' the saloon bar wasn't all that big and Barry was well aware that half the patrons were paying him close attention, 'it's this Freedom Blade; he's sent his manager to take a look and take lots of photos, which he did, and this Freedom fellow is wanting to make the house his permanent home and use the Old Barn for parties and regular events, three nights a week.'

Dottie drew in her breath sharply. 'Surely not, not the Old Barn. Well, I'm not working for someone like him. Not likely.'

They were horrified by the prospect.

'All those crazy fans turning up!'

'The noise. The traffic. All-night parties.'

'Surely we can stop him.'

Willie gathered all their comments into one succinct sentence. 'This spells disaster. Village life as we know it will be gone. For ever.'

Willie said, 'We've stopped Fitch's antics before; maybe we could do it again.'

There was a short silence while they

185

contemplated this statement and then Maggie said, 'Remember the effigy of him we hung up.'

Sylvia added her penny's worth. 'The central heating needing a spare part from Germany that took weeks to get here. Thumping big lie that was, Barry.'

'Don't blame me, I only did what I was told. It all worked though, didn't it? He didn't sell the church silver he'd found, did he?'

'We'll have to protest again,' Don suggested.

But Barry didn't appear to be keen. 'I see more of him than you do, being his maintenance man, and to be honest I feel sorry for 'im.'

Vera couldn't believe what she'd just heard. 'What's there to feel sorry about then?'

'He's taking it very badly.'

'Who wouldn't, when his business has collapsed like it has? I don't feel sorry for 'im, not one jot.' Willie picked up his glass and relished the taste of Dicky's home brew with delight.

'I mean really badly. He loves that house and it's killing him having to sell. He's grabbed at the first buyer with the money to pay cash and who can blame him?'

'Are you being sarcastic?' Don asked.

'No, I mean it; I feel sorry for him. He's always been a fit-looking man, you know, no extra weight, but he's lost weight and he looks something terrible. Kate's out of her mind about him.'

'But Freedom Blade! We all know from the telly what he's like. Does Jimbo know all this?'

Barry nodded.

Maggie asked Dottie if the rector could do

186

something about it. 'Has he said anything?'

'Not to me,' Dottie replied, privately thinking she wouldn't tell them if he had.

Discussion of the matter lasted most of the evening till they had to cheer themselves up with speculation about Johnny and Alice, but there were no conclusions drawn about either of them. She was pregnant. They lived in Alice and Marcus's house mostly. Johnny was so well off he didn't need to earn a living. The entire village was about to be taken over by Freedom Blade's teenage fans and should they sell their houses before all hell was let loose on Turnham Malpas?

But the next day there was something else much more significant to think about.

# 15

Poor old Sykes hadn't come home all night. He was usually back home in the Rectory just before Dottie left at lunchtime, but she had to lock the door with him still wandering about.

She anxiously tut tutted for a while, stood outside and called his name, checked the church, and generally wandered about outside hoping to catch sight of him, but he was nowhere to be found. So Dottie left a note on Peter's desk and had to leave.

He still hadn't returned by bedtime and Beth began to worry.

'But, Mum, where can he be? Do you think he's been run over?'

'He'll probably come home during the night and one of us will have to go down to let him in. I expect he's got locked in someone's house by mistake. You know what he's like.'

'But if he was he'd bark like he does and they'd let him out. I mean, he's missed his dinner and he loves his food.'

'Considering what an independent dog he is he's not going to go missing by mistake, now is he? Go to bed, darling, and don't worry, he'll turn up. You wait and see.'

'I'll go out with a torch right round the green and call him, see if I can hear him barking.' Seeing Caroline was about to object she hurriedly grabbed the torch they always kept in the hall table drawer and left.

While Beth went round the green, in vain as it turned out, Caroline went out of the back door to call him and Peter went into church to check if he'd got locked in there, but all three drew a blank and had to go to bed hoping for the best.

★   ★   ★

There was no sign of him the whole of the next day. Peter did some posters about him being missing and put them up outside the church, in the village store and one nailed to a tree in the churchyard. Then he made smaller ones and took those to Little Derehams and to Penny Fawcett and nailed those to prominent trees by the bus stops.

Though Peter wasn't all that fond of dogs he'd grown to value Sykes's companionship since they'd taken him in. They'd enjoyed some happy afternoons when Peter was working in his study and Sykes curled up on the sofa asleep, tired by his morning perambulations, or when he reminded Peter it was time for their joint tea and biscuit break about half past three. In fact Peter had come to the conclusion that Sykes must have a private alarm clock, he was so accurate with his timings. Whether a saucer of hot tea with milk and sugar was good for a dog Peter didn't know, but that was their secret, and he felt extraordinarily lonely when he took only one biscuit from the tin in the kitchen that afternoon.

Consternation consumed the whole of Turnham Malpas. They all remembered how Sykes had mysteriously appeared the afternoon of that massive pile-up on the bypass all those years ago and everyone had been convinced he was Jimmy's dog reincarnated after his agonising death in the rabbit trap. So in their own way they all felt an attachment to Sykes and searched every nook and cranny in case he'd got shut in their shed or in the old stable where they kept their gardening tools in the winter.

When after two weeks he was still missing it was suggested that a memorial service for him might be held in the church. Or at the very least a word of prayer. After all, he'd belonged to the whole village, hadn't he? Briefly Peter was tempted — it seemed such a good idea until common sense reasserted itself and he gently refused, still holding out hope that Sykes might show up.

There were quite a few people who were grievously hurt by his refusal, others who knew it wasn't quite right to ask God's blessing on a dog, and the upshot of it all was that those who wished could come to the Royal Oak next Saturday night and at nine p.m. precisely they'd all raise their glasses to Sykes.

Dicky and Georgie thought they might be a bit extra busy but never imagined for one moment that so many people would turn up. By eight forty-five it appeared the entire village was crammed shoulder to shoulder in the saloon bar and in the dining room serving food became next to impossible.

Grandmama Charter-Plackett asked to be the one to speak about Sykes — after all she had

190

been one of his owners, so, as no one else volunteered, she was the one standing at the bar facing the crowd, glass in hand. Dicky announced her in his big megaphone voice and silence fell.

'Thank you, Dicky. We all loved Sykes; he was a dog of dogs. He knew every house and everybody in Turnham Malpas, right the way down Shepherd's Hill and the new houses along the Culworth Road, and right the way down Royal Oak Road. But best of all he loved the old centre of the village and as we all know he had his own spot on the old Templeton tomb in the church where he loved to take a nap mid-morning. In our hearts, that spot will always belong to him.

'He was never bad tempered, never once did he nip anyone, though I'm sure if I'd had a burglar in my cottage he'd have made a good try at defending me. Yes, we all know he was naughty for wandering about on his own — he liked nothing better — and I'm sure we all have our own tales to tell about him, but tonight we are saying 'Goodbye' to Sykes.' Grandmama had to pause here to regain control of her trembling lips. 'Let's hope he's happy, and being well cared for, because he deserves nothing less. For some reason, deep inside of me, I'm certain he won't come back to us, somehow I know . . . his time has run out, therefore I say, raise your glasses in memory of Sykes. To Sykes, everyone, to our well-beloved Sykes, wherever he may be.'

By this time there was scarcely a dry eye in the pub, but the toast was drunk and gradually the silence there'd been while they listened to Grandmama's eulogy was broken by them recalling their own memories of him and then other subjects cropped up and everyone began to relax.

Jimbo kissed his mother's cheek. 'Thanks for that, Mother. He deserved every word you said.'

Someone, trying to lighten the atmosphere, said loudly, 'Knowing Sykes, he'll probably turn up tomorrow bright as a button just to prove us all wrong, wondering what all the fuss is about.' But the man who spoke didn't believe a word he'd said. Like Grandmama had reminded them all, Sykes's time had run out.

# 16

Days went by, but the answers they were all breathlessly waiting for about the future of the big house never came. Speculation, yes, hours of it, but no answers, and slowly the main subject of conversation turned to other more important matters. Such as who had been invited to which Christmas party and would Alice, in view of her rapidly increasing size, be conducting the ladies' choir for much longer? They'd done well in the BBC *Women Singing* competition, reaching the last five in the village section — a triumph when you thought about it, their village beating choirs with populations twice and three times the size of Turnham Malpas. But then they had not only Alice but Gilbert helping out too. They made a dynamic duo, did Alice and Gilbert.

Beth was still working for Gilbert in his office and thoroughly enjoying her life, though it had taken a while for her to get over Sykes's disappearance. She found herself listening for his bark, missed secretly feeding him cake, which he loved. But being home and helping Gilbert was far better than Cambridge and living in halls, especially as she was now getting paid to work for him, and secretly she intended never going back. Peter and Caroline, blithely unaware of her intentions, were glad she was in such good spirits. Which she was — she'd made friends with people from the county archaeology office

193

and often socialised with them, and everything was going well for her until she went to the twenty-first birthday party of a girl called Rosie she'd been mildly friendly with at school.

Beth had pulled out all the stops with the dress she bought for it, with money she had earned herself and therefore felt justified in spending absolutely every spare penny she could. It was scarlet, and clinging and shining and didn't have her mother's approval. 'It is rather daring for you, Beth, don't you think?'

'Yes. But it's a posh hotel and I need to look good. Rosie says it'll be her last big event before she gets a job in one of the big fashion houses, when it will be hard grind all the way with no time for fun as she calls it. She won't go far, because she's no good at it, but she's convinced she is. So that's why her parents are pulling out all the stops for her twenty-first. So we'll wait and see.'

Caroline was still surveying the dress with disapproval. 'I can't say I approve.'

'Well, that must be a first. I love it and I did buy it with my own money, so . . . you should see what some of the others are wearing. I understand this is discreet by comparison.'

'Well, I'm glad you're enjoying the social life again.'

Beth gave her mother a kiss in gratitude and Caroline was enveloped in a powerful perfume. 'What's that perfume? It's awfully strong.'

'Oh! Mum! You are old-fashioned. I'm off.'

'Have you the money for the taxi to come home?'

Beth patted her red beaded handbag. 'I have. Is Dad taking me or you?'

'He is. Have a good time.'

'I will.'

When Beth got inside the hotel the thought did cross her mind that Rosie was overindulged. The whole of the reception area was filled with flowers, music poured from every speaker and the guests were dressed in the absolute pinnacle of fashion. Rosie's parents were there to greet their guests, smiling and dramatically kissing everyone as though each was a long-lost friend. The whole event felt seriously overdone.

Rosie whispered in her ear, 'Wait till they see the surprise entertainer I've booked! Little do they know!' She nodded her head in the direction of her parents and when they noticed her she twinkled her fingers at them and blew them a kiss.

Beth couldn't believe what she saw. There he was! Shaking hands with Rosie's parents. Larger than life and twice as wonderful. Oh, God! Jake! Beth's heart exploded. Since he'd gone to live with his father in Culworth she'd seen him once in Cambridge from a distance but never spoken to him, and here he was looking absolutely splendid in a dinner jacket and bow tie, greeting Mr and Mrs Baker-Smythe. He smiled at Rosie and Beth realised he'd caught sight of her standing beside Rosie. For one long moment Beth's heart pounded against her rib cage till she thought her ribs would crack. How on earth could anyone have such a powerful effect on her? Surely the pounding must be audible to Rosie, who stood so close? But Rosie was too busy making a good impression on Jake. Still admiring him she breathed to Beth, 'I never thought he'd come! Gorgeous Jake Harding's come. What a man! Isn't he sexy! In every way!' She nudged Beth. 'He's looking at you. Do you two know each other?'

Beth stirred herself. 'Vaguely, from school. He knows my brother.' Mercifully she could still speak with a modicum of intelligence.

Jake turned to Rosie, who flung herself into greeting him so enthusiastically she might have been welcoming an Arctic explorer who'd been missing for months in its icy wastes.

'How lovely you could come! You know Beth Harris, do you? Her father's the rector in Turnham Malpas.' Rosie's statement put Beth into a kind of untouchable category at a time when Beth felt completely the opposite.

'Yes. I know. Lovely to see you again, Beth.' Jake shook her hand and, just as she'd read about in Mills and Boon novels, her world stood still. The smell of him. The look of him. The style and confidence his time at Cambridge had given him. The sheer animal magnetism of him. So this was Jake Harding, now a man, and she couldn't get enough of him.

'It's been a long time. What are you getting up to these days?' Jake asked.

They moved away from Rosie, leaving her standing open-mouthed by their abrupt abandonment of her. Even totally self-absorbed Rosie could recognise their togetherness. That stuck-up Beth Harris! She should never have invited her.

196

She'd purposely mentioned her father's job to warn Jake that Beth was not available, so to speak, but much good that had done. Rosie covertly watched them standing close, completely absorbed by each other and wondered what they were talking about. Beth looked mesmerised. Jake looked as though it was his birthday and Christmas all rolled into one, while Rosie was consumed by jealousy.

'I'm taking a year off. Couldn't stand it and got homesick, then I got flu.'

'I got that too; it was evil.'

'Well, I wouldn't say evil.'

'It was. I've never been so ill in my life.'

'But you're still at Cambridge. You haven't . . .' Words failed her.

Jake nodded. 'Your dad OK, is he?'

Beth smiled. 'He is. Absolutely fine.'

'Frightens the hell out of me.'

'He's a pussy cat really.'

Jake laughed. 'He's intimidating, in the nicest possible way! Your mum is lovely. You're so like her, not in looks, but in temperament.'

Beth almost explained the situation with Caroline, which she never normally did, but changed her mind, Jake meant nothing to her so he didn't need to know. But maybe one day she'd confide in him.

To fill her silence Jake suggested they find something to drink, so the two of them moved through into the party room and danced and ate and grew more comfortable with each other till the time apart fell away and it was wonderful just to be together, to dance, to talk, to laugh. The evening spun by on gilded wings and suddenly the party was winding down.

'I have a taxi booked for a quarter to twelve; he'll be here soon,' Beth said.

'Five minutes to go. I'll come with you and if it doesn't come I'll drive you home.'

'He will come, he's very reliable.'

Jake took her arm and went to stand outside with her on the steps of the hotel.

Out of the blue he said, 'I'm home with my dad for Christmas.'

'That'll be nice for you.'

'I was meaning we could meet and I could write in the meantime.'

Beth said, 'No, text me please or email. Don't write.'

His grip on her arm tightened. 'Am I still persona non grata then at the Rectory?'

'Here's my taxi. Here, look, this is my mobile number.' She scribbled it on an old receipt she found in her bag.

'OK. Goodnight, Beth.' She looked up at him, sensing a kiss coming and she wasn't sure. Suddenly Beth turned away to get into her taxi, so he missed kissing her mouth but kissed her shining, sweet-smelling hair instead, and felt privileged.

Jake carefully stored the old receipt in his top pocket.

Beth fell into bed exhausted, but couldn't sleep because her mind was filled with the memories of the evening. How he'd looked, how he'd danced, the feel of his hand on hers, his arm round her waist, his attention to her and no one else, the embarrassment they shared about the excesses of the food, the music, the entertainment, the take-home goody bags.

'My God!' Jake had said. 'Is there no end to it? No one will dare hold a party after this. What could better it?'

'Best enjoy it while we can then.'

Beth giggled helplessly. She heard her mother's footsteps coming along the landing and decided to be asleep because she felt she needed to be on her guard about Jake. He'd been right when he asked if he was still persona non grata in the Rectory.

Her mother bent over her to kiss her goodnight, but Beth couldn't resist her kisses. 'Night, night, Mum.'

'Night, night, love. Home safe and sound. Had a good time?'

Beth nodded.

'Goodnight, then. Tell me all about it in the morning.'

Not likely, thought Beth.

★   ★   ★

But she did; she couldn't help herself because she'd hardly spoken to anyone else but Jake and eventually his name popped up so the cat was out of the bag.

'Jake was there! Did you know he was going?'

'No. Rosie thinks he's absolutely fabulous.'

Caroline poured her some tea. 'And what did Beth Harris think about him?'

Beth shrugged. She tried hard to appear nonchalant. 'He's OK. Handsome as ever.'

Caroline cast a sceptical look at Beth and her heart sank. All Beth needed in her present state of not knowing which way her life should go was the added complication of Jake 'I know I'm wonderful' Harding. 'Right. So what's he doing when he finishes next summer?'

'I don't know, actually.'

'The subject never came up? Toast?'

'No. Yes, to some toast.'

'Who else was there?'

'Mum! What's this? The Spanish Inquisition? All I did was go to a birthday party of a girl I only know because of being in the drama club with her at school. She's an overindulged egotistical idiot.'

'Sorry. Sorry. Just interested.' Caroline backed off, but in her heart she knew something very significant had taken place last night and she had a dread of Beth being embroiled with Jake. He was too charismatic for his own good and certainly not the kind of young man she would like for Beth. Her ambition for Beth was a good career first and then marriage, just like she'd had herself.

The front door banged shut and Peter came in the kitchen, back from eight o'clock communion.

'Morning, Beth. Did you have a good time last night?'

'Don't you start another cross examination, please.'

Peter knew immediately, just as Caroline had done, that something important had happened to Beth last night. 'OK, OK. Just asking.'

Caroline asked him, 'How many this morning?'

'Twenty-one.'

'That's heartening!'

'It is indeed.' The two of them carried on a conversation about numbers and village matters until Beth said, 'Sorry. I'm tired. I'm going back to bed. I won't make it to the eleven o'clock, Dad.'

'Don't worry, it's not often you miss.'

Beth paused at the kitchen door. 'You know, don't you, I only go for your sake, not because I want to. It's always been like that. Going for your sake, so's not to let you down. The time will come, perhaps, when I won't go at all.'

Beth left behind a stunned silence.

Upstairs under her duvet, she deeply regretted what she'd said. If only she'd kept that bit about church to herself. But her dad preferred the truth and the truth was what he'd got. She had to stand up and be counted as her own person and somehow this felt the moment to do it. They wouldn't like how she felt about Jake . . . how *did* she feel about Jake? Beth pulled the duvet right over her head just as she'd done when she was small and had been naughty, and stared hard at the milky whiteness of her duvet cover. Jake's face joined her, then her Dad's sad face superseded it and she felt bad telling him how she viewed the entire purpose of his life. She should never have said what she said. It could have been her secret for years once she'd left home.

Downstairs she could hear Mum clearing the

table and Dad shutting his study door with a bang. But she meant it. She had to make a stand about her life; after all, it was her life and no one else's and she had a right to lead her life as she wanted. If they didn't like Jake, well, too bad, she did. She recollected the kiss that missed her mouth and landed on her hair, and rejoiced.

They both left for church together and didn't even call upstairs to say they were leaving. Beth felt abandoned, neglected, left out of things. But wasn't this how she wanted it? To be independent, not included? Doing her own thing? Even so she felt uneasy. After last night she'd thought her life would flow with unadulterated delight, but already she felt both miserable and elated all mixed up together. Blast it. She struggled out hot and sweaty from under the duvet and sat up. Out of the window she saw the view she loved best in the world; at least that view was still hers. Thing was her parents were the one reliable stable factor in her life. Whatever she did they'd still love her, whereas Jake could be calling round at that awful Janey's in Penny Fawcett right this minute. But she stopped there, because she somehow sensed that he wouldn't, not any more. Jake had changed. And so had she. Beth sprang out of bed determined to make amends for her forthrightness earlier. She showered and dressed, then went down to begin putting the Sunday lunch together, at the back of her mind shaping an apology to Dad as she worked.

During a lull in the preparations she checked her mobile and found Jake had already left a message for her. *Going back to Cambridge tonight. Want to see you before I go — the George? Pick you up from Rectory at 3?*

Her reply simply said, *Three o'clock at the George. Beth.* So it said nothing at all about her pounding heart or the excitement of reading his almost too casual invitation. Didn't mention how her eyes lit up, nor how she was already planning what to wear. Nor her dilemma; she had planned to spend the afternoon making amends to her mum and dad, but that was out of the window now. There was no way she was missing out on this invitation. She did wonder about ringing Rosie to thank her for the party last night and at the same time mentioning about seeing Jake this afternoon.

She changed her mind three times before she rang Rosie, finally deciding not to mention her afternoon tea with the so-called gorgeous Jake Harding. No point in upsetting people unnecessarily; it wouldn't be fair. But Rosie sounded thoroughly out of sorts about the party and accused Beth of telling fibs — well, she called it lies — about Jake. 'You obviously knew him rather well, seeing as you spent the entire evening with him. Do you?'

'I met him about two years ago, but since then I haven't seen him.'

'You must have; he's at Cambridge too, you know.'

'I never met him there and was amazed to find he hadn't gone to London after all. I'm sorry, Rosie, it wasn't intentional.'

'Anyway I'm in serious bother this morning

for that entertainer.'

'Well, he was a bit dodgy.'

'Dodgy? He was downright vulgar. I'd no idea
— he'd been recommended by a friend. Just
shows how useless one's supposed friends can
be.'

From the tone of Rosie's voice Beth knew she
was included in *one's supposed friends* and
she felt guilty for keeping Jake to herself at the
party. But it was too late now. They finished their
conversation with Beth promising to go out with
her one evening after work, which was definitely
not what she wanted.

The front door opened and her mother walked
in.

'Hi! OK?' But Beth got no reply. 'Mum?'

'How could you? Mmm? Your own dad. You've
a right to your own opinions but . . . you've
really upset him. Everything he stands for just
thrown in the bin in a couple of sentences.'

'I didn't think.'

'That's pretty obvious, Beth. I've never heard
you speak in that way before. What's happened
to you?'

'I don't know.'

'Has Jake been talking like that to you about
him?'

'No, he most definitely hasn't; he has the
greatest respect for Dad, has Jake. Honestly. He's
even a bit scared of him.'

'Good, I'm glad to hear it.'

'It's Dad's absolute honesty that alarms him.'

'Oh! I see. However, when your dad gets back,
and he won't be long, you'd better explain

yourself. Above all be truthful; he'll know if you're insincere.'

Caroline walked into the kitchen and realised that Beth had done the Sunday lunch. She sighed. 'Thank you for this. That's lovely. But it doesn't square things with your dad, you know. Although it does help, I suppose.'

Peter came home and went straight to his study. They were used to that as he nearly always had notes to make about things he needed to attend to first thing on Monday morning. Beth gave him five minutes and then knocked on his door and put her head round it, saying, 'It's me, Dad. Will you talk to me? Please.'

He was seated at his desk writing and nodded his agreement. Beth went to sit on the big squashy sofa, a recipient of many long tales of woe uttered by his parishioners, which had once caused Beth to call the sofa *the village confessional*. She hadn't the faintest idea of how she was going to put things right between them. But she had to.

He put the top back on his pen, closed his parish diary and sat back. After an awkward silence, when it was clear Beth didn't know what to say, he gave her one of his lovely compassionate smiles and she stood up filled with love for his generous forgiveness and rushed to sit on his knee. So with her arms round his neck and her cheek against his, just like she used to do as a little girl, she apologised.

'I'm so sorry, Dad. What I said was unforgivable. I meant it when I said it, but not any more. Not now. You are the loveliest dad

205

anyone could hope to have and I'm glad I'm yours. I wouldn't want anyone else at all for my dad.'

He kissed her forehead and then said, 'Let's forget it, shall we?'

Beth nodded.

'Do you still feel like that? That my life is a waste?'

'No, I don't. It's not a waste. Not when you can smile like that at me despite the grievous harm I caused you. That in its own way is power. Jake's frightened of you.'

'In that case then — '

'He's changed, you know. He's got standards and I'm one of them.'

'Has he indeed.' He looked at her and at such close quarters she saw the sadness in his eyes.

'You're sad. I thought we'd made up.'

'We have, but when you talk about Jake there's a light in your eyes I haven't seen before and I reckon you've grown up since this time yesterday.'

'But I have to grow up. I can't be a child for ever, can I?' She got up from his knee and stood beside him. 'You don't need to worry about Jake; he's changed. Before, when I knew him, the girls all thought him gorgeous and he knew it and took advantage of them if he chose to, but not now. In fact, to be honest he's asked me for afternoon tea today at the George before he goes back to Cambridge, and there's nothing more reliable than that, is there?'

Peter laughed. 'That sounds very reliable. Keep your feet well grounded, my darling. Take things slowly. Right. I have some reading to do.

Give me a shout when lunch is ready.'

But when Beth turned back at the door to thank him for his understanding he wasn't reading. He was praying.

★  ★  ★

They began serving afternoon tea at three thirty and it annoyed Jake that he'd got the wrong time. Beth couldn't bear for him to be upset. 'Don't worry, we can go look at the river while we wait.' So they wandered out onto the terrace. 'I think this is my second-favourite view. Isn't it lovely?'

'What's your favourite view then?'

'The view from my bedroom window at home. In the winter I can just see the big house through the trees but once the leaves are out I can't. The owner's trying to sell it, you know.'

'Why?'

'Because his construction business has collapsed and he has to sell. Do you know Freedom Blade?'

'Yes. He's not wanting to buy it, is he?'

Beth nodded.

'Surely he won't sell it to him?'

'We all hope not, but Mr Fitch is desperate. The whole problem is making him ill. My dad's very concerned about him.'

'Oh! Right. This place wouldn't be my first choice, but there's nowhere else to go in Culworth on Sundays. I'm sorry.'

'Don't worry, you've gone up in my dad's estimation, bringing me here.'

'He knows, then? You've come out with me.'
'Yes.'
'And he didn't object?'
'No.'
Jake leaned his hands on top of the wall and studied the swans now rushing towards them hoping to be fed. 'You're so lucky having a family that cares. I just have Dad and no brothers or sisters and no mother. Well, I have but she's a waste of space. She should never have had even one child.'

Beth didn't know how to reply. 'I can't begin to imagine how that feels. I've been cared about all my life.'

They stood silently, side by side, watching the swans until Jake said, 'And it shows. Right, let's claim a table.'

He took her elbow and guided her to a table. He ordered afternoon tea and charmed the waitress, and charmed Beth too, entertaining her as they ate with tales about his tutors and the friends he'd made. 'Next September will you please go back to Cambridge?'

'I don't know about that.'

'I am. It's what you should do, Beth.'

'I was thinking of not going back and staying here and helping Gilbert. I'm so much happier doing that.'

'Beth, believe me, for someone like you that will not be fulfilling for ever; you need more than that. Alex will still be there. In ten years' time you would be full of regrets for not having taken up your place again.' Jake glanced at his watch. 'I should go.'

He stood up, caught the waitress's attention, paid the bill, helped Beth to put on her coat and set off with Beth trailing along behind him still buttoning it.

Out in the car park he settled her in his car and drove in silence far too fast to Turnham Malpas. They sat outside the Rectory, not knowing what to say.

Jake abruptly declared, 'Remember what I said about going back. See you at Christmas.' He then whipped round the back of the car, opened her door for her and then stood beside her while she put her key in the lock. 'Kiss? Till I see you at Christmas?'

'Yes, I thought maybe — '

He kissed her very gently and this time managed to kiss her lips.

'Jake, thanks for the tea. I — '

But Jake had gone, roaring out of the village like someone possessed. Beth closed the door behind her and went straight upstairs to her room to think about her curious afternoon and to make sense of him.

# 17

The village was entirely unaware of the financial affairs of Johnny Templeton. They'd realised he was wealthy but never guessed a young man like him would be rich enough to buy the estate outright. But it would be nice — he was such a lovely man — with him up at the big house. Things would be *right*, yes, very right. Only Mr Fitch knew that he was able to buy the whole estate and all Johnny needed was a nod from him to put the wheels in motion. Whether Mr Fitch fully understood how much money he had available or indeed his passionate need for buying the estate, Johnny had no idea.

But on the Monday morning after Jake had gone back to Cambridge, Johnny rang up the big house and asked to see Mr Fitch. 'It's imperative I see him.'

His secretary, Anne, still hanging on to a job she loved and also out of sympathy for Mr Fitch, whom she'd grown to like, answered him by saying, 'Hold the line a moment, Sir Johnny, I'll ask.'

Mr Fitch's answer was a begrudging, 'Very well, then.' Which Anne translated into 'He'd be delighted to see you. Are you coming right now?'

'I'll walk up.'

'Good! I'll get the coffee on.'

For some reason Johnny had not heard about the impending sale of the estate to Freedom

Blade. Somehow he'd been out of the loop of village gossip, mainly because Alice had not been well — nothing specific, but the pregnancy was taking its toll on her vitality and Johnny was endeavouring to ease her burden of driving here and there to give piano lessons by driving himself and then sitting listening to the radio while she did the teaching in people's houses. He'd discussed with her several times about taking life easier, but she would not listen. 'I have rates to pay, food to buy, car insurance due, road fund tax due; I have to have money, Johnny.'

'But I have explained, I can pay those for you.'

'I know you can.'

'In fact, I'd love to pay them because I love you, you see. I don't want you to have worries.'

Then she'd burst into tears and the whole argument was put back on the shelf still unresolved. He couldn't understand about her need for independence. 'Are you afraid I shan't go through with the wedding? Is that it? Even if I have to drag you up the aisle by your beautiful hair I *will* marry you.'

'Why doesn't Marcus get on with the divorce? Every letter he gets takes him ages to deal with.'

'Alice! Don't you see? He doesn't want to lose you. That's why.'

'I'm sorry Johnny, but if you'd seen the way he treated me when he was here you wouldn't say that.'

Johnny had shot to his feet when she said that. 'You don't mean he used to *hit* you? Do you?'

'No, no. Not Marcus. He wasn't like that. He was neglectful because he thought his writing

211

was so important, much more important than me.'

Johnny had knelt beside her and put his arms around her. 'I'd never think that. Ever. You are the first woman in the world I have ever wanted to marry, and I will. Believe me.'

Alice had put a hand either side of his loving face and kissed his lips. 'Thank you for saying that, and you're the only man in all the world I wish to marry. If only fate had brought us together earlier. If only.'

'Well, fate has now, and we will marry. I know we will.'

'You've given up on buying the estate, have you?'

'Not really.'

'I understand someone is interested, but I can't for the life of me remember his name. Somebody really odd and unexpected.'

That statement was what had triggered him off into marching up the drive of Turnham House and tackling Mr Fitch. Despite having a perfectly good car, Johnny walked all the way up the drive because of the thrill he got when the house came into view. He liked it to come steadily into view like it must have done for generations before cars were invented. He wondered if Alice had realised where he had gone.

If it were possible Mr Fitch looked even worse this morning. Johnny offered to shake hands but he refused to make the effort. All he did in greeting was nod towards the chair opposite his own. Anne came in with coffee and placed it close to Johnny as though inviting him to pour.

'Shall I?' asked Johnny. Anne nodded and left the office, leaving the door very slightly open so she could hear from her own desk what was being said, for Anne knew things were critical today.

As Johnny passed him his coffee, Mr Fitch asked, 'You've heard then?'

'Heard what?'

'About my buyer.'

'No.'

'I thought that was why you were here in such good time. If all goes well I shall have it signed and sealed by five o'clock tonight. That's the deadline and he's keen.'

'Well,' Johnny said, 'you don't look too chipper about it. You should be dancing on the rooftops.'

'I am, except I'm doing it from down here.'

'In that case you won't mind telling me who's the lucky man.'

Craddock Fitch glared at him. Twice he opened his mouth to say it and twice changed his mind, and then he came out with it. 'Freedom Blade.'

Anne, listening hard from behind her desk, could hear the proverbial pin drop, then Johnny's chair fall over as he stood up, and then his harsh voice saying, 'My God, man! It's sacrilege! How could you?' Then Johnny burst out into peals of laughter. 'You've caught me out. Now stop pulling my leg, and tell me the truth. Who's buying it?'

'Freedom Blade! Like I said.'

Anne heard Johnny pull his chair up from the floor and by the sound of it he'd sat down again.

She could only just hear him whisper, 'So, you're not joking.'

She heard Mr Fitch give a kind of cracked laugh and say, 'No. He's got the cash; he's signing it. It's his once he's done that. Five o'clock tonight. Thank heavens. I've signed, he's signing, job done and I shall move out. One fewer problem.'

'But you knew I wanted to buy it. You knew. I told you so.'

Mr Fitch leant across the desk, and thumping his fist so hard on it he made his pen bounce, he said viciously, 'I'd put a match to it rather than have you living in this house.'

'Why? What have I done? I have the money, clean money too, I might add.' If Anne could have seen Johnny's face she would have been horrified by the bitter expression on it. She held her breath while waiting for Mr Fitch to reply.

'Your Uncle Ralph, or should we pronounce it *Rafe*, eh? Him being who he was.' Anne could sense the sneer on his face. 'Always considered himself better than me, blue blood, public school, alma mater and all that jazz, then Oxford, then the diplomatic service, always the gentleman. Me! I pulled myself up out of the mire by my boot laces.'

'I see.' Johnny couldn't resist pointing out that things were not so rosy now. 'And look where it's got you. You've lost everything. Every stick, every stone.'

Mr Fitch leaped to his feet. 'Get out! Go on! Get out.'

Standing at the door ready to leave, Johnny

214

said, 'As God is my judge, I shall buy this house. It may not be this week or this month or this year even, but one day it will be mine.' He made a fist of his right hand and held it up for Mr Fitch to see. 'Mine!'

Johnny went home to Alice and when she saw him she said, 'Where've you been? You look upset.'

'To see Mr Fitch.'

'Not about buying the big house?'

'What else?'

'Oh! Johnny.'

'I'm too late anyway.'

'Well, darling, I'm glad you're too late. You know I don't want to live there.'

'Not even for me?'

'No, not even for you. I'll live in your uncle Ralph's house but not the big house. Please don't ask it of me. Well, you can't now, can you? And I'm sorry I feel like this but I do. That house is just not me.'

'But it's what I want.'

'We can't always have what we want. Money doesn't buy everything.'

At that Johnny wept inside and sat brooding for most of the day. He always got his own way, because money did that for you. He'd so wanted that house, because that was where he belonged, where his ancestors had lived their lives for generations and it was within his grasp if only . . .

At five o'clock he looked at his watch and thought, that's that then. He had some photographs going back to the early twentieth

215

century that the solicitor had given him. He got them out for the thousandth time and looked through them, feeling he'd let them all down by not buying their ancestral home.

Here was his great-uncle Ralph dressed for cricket; he must have been about twelve years old. The other boys must have been cousins or friends from the village. There was definitely a likeness; it couldn't be denied. Ralph's cousins, the nose, the stature, the way they held themselves. Here were some girls who must have been their contemporaries, and a very old photo of a man who looked rakish and unreliable; was that his own grandfather or great-grandfather even? He looked the sort who'd have to take a risk and go out to South America to escape bother at home. Johnny had to smile. Should he go back to Brazil too? Take Alice with him. Did she love him enough to go all that way when she wouldn't even move as far as the big house to be with him? But he was consumed by love for her and she for him so he'd have to content himself with living in Uncle Ralph's own house and bringing up what they now knew to be his *son* in the village of his ancestors.

★   ★   ★

Instead of sitting all evening studying his company's end-of-year accounts to a background of Alice's pupils coming for piano lessons, Johnny should have gone to the Royal Oak and heard the news that was buzzing at every table.

'Well, come on then, Barry, tell all.'

216

'Where's my drink then? I need some lubrication.'

Maggie agreed she'd get him his drink on the understanding that she sat next to him so she didn't miss a word of his news. So they all shuffled up and left a space on the settle for her. She came back to the table and squeezed herself in; she really would have to lose weight. She put Barry's drink in front of him, appropriately placed by chance on a mat with a picture of Turnham House on it from a set Dicky had made for the pub's five hundredth anniversary celebrations, and waited to hear the events of the afternoon.

'As it happens,' said Barry, 'I was in the hall, making a start on the Christmas decorations. Anne gets more ambitious as the years go by. She'd just gone to make me my mid-morning coffee — well, the second of the morning — very good she is at getting my coffee just right; she — '

Maggie interrupted him. 'It's not your coffee we want to hear-about, it's what's happened about the big house. Has old Fitch sold it? Yes or no.'

'Anyway, I was in the hall by myself working away, when the phone rang. She didn't come to answer it so eventually I put on my best voice, picked it up and said, Fitch Construction, how may I help?'

'Well, they wanted to speak to Mr Fitch, but I didn't know how to put the phone through so I asked them to hold, knocked on Mr Fitch's door opened it and said, 'It's the phone, Mr Fitch.

217

They want to speak to you.' 'Who is it?' he asked. 'Ah! I don't know,' I said. He waved me away and pressed buttons on his own phone. So I shut the door and could hear as plain as day what he was saying on the phone, 'cos I still had the receiver in my hand.' Barry, pausing for maximum effect, sipped his home brew.

Scandalised by the thought of Barry deliberately listening in, Sylvia said, 'Shouldn't you have put the receiver down?'

Willie, less moral on such matters, asked, 'Well, what was he saying?'

'I can't repeat it. He used such foul language. One word I didn't even *know*.'

'Be a Cockney swearword I expect,' Don remarked.

'Anyway, turns out it was the solicitor, letting him know that there was some doubt about that Freedom chap coming through with the cash, and he thought Mr Fitch ought to know, apparently five o'clock today's the deadline.'

There was a chorus of 'No-o-o-o' from all over the bar, a noisy mixture of relief and disappointment.

It was a few moments before Barry could continue his report. 'The phone went dead, then Anne came back, gave me my coffee and rather sharply put the receiver back on. She gave me a filthy look and headed for his nibs' office. 'Anne,' I said, 'he's just had a phone call, sounds like bad news, so watch it.' She paused a minute to collect herself like and then went in and I could hear him exploding with temper. So altogether it's been a terrible day.'

'But what's happened?' they all asked.

'Well, I'd finished everything in the hall by half past one so I left, but I called in before I went home to see if Anne was satisfied I'd done the Christmas things as she wanted, and believe me she'd aged and not half. I asked her straight out what the news was about the sale.' He irritatingly took another sip of his home brew.

'Well?'

'Mr Fitch 'as given him another twenty-four hours and then, if no money's transferred . . . ' Barry concluded triumphantly with a chopping gesture to his throat and an appropriate gurgling sound.

'It all sounds dodgy, doesn't it? I mean, we don't want someone like that Freedom chap here. It's the fans and the all-night parties we don't want either . . . but you have to feel a bit sorry for old Fitch, him being in such a fix.' Willie swallowed the last of his home brew and sat silently gripping his empty glass, lost in thought.

'We'll have to hope he doesn't hand the money over. Who'd want to welcome that horrible lot to our beautiful village? We've trained Mr Fitch to our way of thinking, haven't we? Took a while but we did,' Maggie reflected. 'Well, more or less.'

# 18

Craddock Fitch stormed about his office the following day in desperation. 'I can't believe it! He was so enthusiastic, loves the idea, seen the photos, can't wait to move in and now he's changed his mind. Kate, I'm really desperate now. Really desperate.'

'Here's a whisky to calm your nerves.'

'I'm not supposed to.'

'Well, just this once. Sit down, relax and let's have a good think.'

'You have a whisky too; not much fun on your own. Just wish I'd never said a word to anyone. I must look a right fool. A whisker away from selling and at five minutes to five he won't sign. I wonder if there's a law against that — taking someone right to the wire and then refusing.' He rubbed his face to refresh himself, and groaned. 'Kate, what the hell am I going to do? Financially I mean.' He looked up at her, his face so close to hers as she leaned over to kiss him. After she'd kissed his cheek she said, 'Well, at least you've still got me! If that's any comfort.'

'It is. How I would have managed without you I do not know. What shall we do, darling?'

'Run away? Drown our sorrows? Go into hiding?'

'That's not us though, is it?'

Kate laughed. 'No, it isn't. I know someone who'd buy it right now. This minute and all this worry would stop. Just like that.' She clicked her fingers and waited his response.

'That Johnny Templeton, you mean. Over my dead body.'

'That wouldn't be much use now, would it? And I certainly wouldn't like it, believe me.'

'I can't bear the thought of that moneyed so and so living here.'

'So you're prepared to tear your guts out rather than snap his hand off for the money.'

'Yes, that's exactly right.'

'It's not right though, is it? What would be right is to allow a Templeton with *clean* money to come back into this house. It's so right, and it's in your hands to make it happen.'

'Well, it won't. I'm damned if I'll allow it. That Ralph never liked me and I hated his ability to get his own way with his accent, and his reasonableness, and his paternalistic Lord of the Manor attitude. That council, who over the years had thousands of pounds from me slipped into their own pockets, were putty in his hands. *Putty!* And there was nothing I could do about it. Nothing.'

Kate stood beside him and slipped her hand into his. 'Which is better, total financial ruin or selling to a Templeton whose money has nothing to do with Sir Ralph, absolutely nothing at all? He's fabulously wealthy in his own right. If that Freedom Blade did come up with the money imagine what damage he'd do to this village, that, let's face it, we both love. And remember we'll be living in it too, at Glebe House.'

'He may not use Ralph's own money to buy it,

but he has Ralph's blood in his veins.' He got up and walked to the window to stare silently out across the land. Glebe House! Huh! How he hated the idea of living there. So modern, so brash, so glitzy. His hand trailed along the window frame, tenderly caressing it. How he loved this place! He brushed away the tears that unexpectedly trickled down his cheeks. Was he really going to have to be grateful to Sir Johnny for his salvation? Damn it. No, he wouldn't: anyone but him. He'd start up a new advertising campaign, different angle, new photos, different publications, he'd show 'em.

Kate's sweet attempt to make Johnny Templeton more acceptable to him had had an effect — not enough to make him change his mind, but enough to make him at least contemplate the possibility of Johnny living here; it would after all be the right thing to do. Better than that maniac Blade whose face was plastered across the tabloids this morning, him having been arrested for something or other . . . what on earth for? Something revolting, no doubt. He gripped Kate's hand tightly, saying, 'What a comfort you are to me.'

'Will you think about letting him buy it, then?'
'Absolutely not.'

★   ★   ★

Johnny Templeton had other things on his mind this morning. Alice was not at all well. She kept getting sharp pains, not exactly contractions but almost. 'But there's five weeks to go; they can't

222

be real contractions, can they?'

Alice shook her head. 'I've no more experience than you about babies. I just don't know. But if they're not, what are they?'

'I'm going to get Caroline. She'll know.'

'She's never had one of her own and she isn't an obstetrician.'

'Look, Alice, let's stay calm about this. OK. It may be the early stages of labour but if it is we're only . . . what is it? Six miles from the hospital, so it won't take five minutes to get there in the car. So you make sure you have a bag packed and I'll get you there in time if things get . . . ' he was going to say 'worse' but changed his mind, 'more advanced?' Inside he was terrified. Being the eldest of the three brothers didn't mean he knew anything about babies, because he was only four when his youngest brother was born and though he loved the idea of his son being born and holding him in his arms bathed and fresh-smelling and presentable, the actuality of the whole event was more than he could bear.

Alice in pain. The threat of things going wrong and no one realising, the sweat, and the screaming. Would Alice scream? Perhaps not, and the slimy newborn sliding out, the most primitive experience any human being faces, was horrifying for him. If only his mother were there. But she wasn't. So he had to be a man and face up to it. His hands shook as he struggled with making Alice a cup of tea. She loved tea at the moment, and it had to be in a delicate china cup. As he carried it to her, for she'd retired to the sitting room as the sofa was more comfortable in

223

there, he braced himself to be cheerful and in charge.

'Here we are, darling, your favourite cup of tea. If it isn't right I'll make another.' He sat on the other end of the sofa and admired her. With him as its father and Alice its mother how could their expected child be anything other than beautiful?

Alice experienced another of those strange pains, but it didn't upset her quite so much as the others, so maybe they were fading. Johnny felt relieved.

Someone rattled the knocker on the front door, the door opened and footsteps could be heard in the hall. Alice sensed something very familiar about the footsteps. They sounded like . . . but they couldn't be . . . Marcus! Oh! God! She struggled upright, fearful of meeting him at a disadvantage. Why had he come? Not to stay! Please God not to stay; she didn't feel strong enough to face that.

The sitting room door opened and there stood Marcus March, smiling. Smiling? Marcus? They were both shocked: all Marcus had become to them was letters from a solicitor about Alice's divorce. Nothing more; they never contemplated how he fared nor what it would be like seeing him again, because they never expected to. But there he stood, smiling, holding himself with unaccustomed confidence, which was a surprise in itself.

Hand outstretched, he went to shake hands with Johnny. 'Nice to see you again, Johnny. How are you?'

'I'm very well thank you, Marcus. You look to be in fine fettle.'

Marcus didn't reply. He turned to bend over Alice and kiss her forehead. 'Nearly time for you, isn't it, Alice?' He turned again to Johnny, saying, 'You're a lucky man, but I expect you know that.'

'Indeed I do. Tea or something stronger, or lunch even?'

'I think lunch would be taking things too far in the circumstances . . . but a cup of tea would be more than welcome. I've driven down from London. Took an age, so much traffic.' He went to look out of the window. Johnny flicked a look at Alice and winked. She smiled back, nervous of this invasion, worrying something nasty would come out of Marcus's mouth and her whole world would fall apart.

While Johnny made a cup of tea for them Marcus sat on the other end of the sofa. 'I thought I'd come myself to say I'm so sorry I caused our marriage to fall apart. Sins of omission rather than anything deliberate. I've found someone who thinks the sun shines out of me. I've become aware it doesn't, but she thinks it does. It makes for a very happy life. It does me good. I think the world of her, and she of me. I don't deserve to be so happy, I know that, but I can see you're happy too so that makes it all right, doesn't it?'

Alice was struck speechless by his understanding.

'I can see Johnny's good for you. I went up to the big house to find you, thinking he'd have

225

bought it by now. Seen all the furore in the news about old Fitch's collapse. I can just see you as Lady of the Manor.'

'I'm not moving there.'

'And what does Johnny think to that?'

'He's disappointed.'

Marcus leaned over and took her hand in his. 'You should encourage him, if it's what he wants. It's only right if you love him.'

Alice almost laughed in his face. Marcus discussing love! What did he know about it? Then she looked into his eyes and saw compassion there. She wriggled free, uncomfortable at seeing emotion like that in Marcus's eyes, of all people.

'I mean it, Alice. I've learned a lot about loving and giving from Laura; it was her that helped me to survive when I was in pieces about you. She's built me up, given me a new start. I've got a few copies of my very first novel in the car; can I give you one? I've already signed it to you both. Only if you want it, though.'

'Well, yes, all right then.' She got up to go out with him to the car, but he insisted she stayed where she was. 'You've done enough running about after me in the past. It's my turn now.'

The novel was in hardback, with a very attractive cover.

Alice was impressed. 'Why, it looks great. Love the title: *Sky Spies*. The illustration is excellent. So appropriate.'

'You sound surprised.'

'Not surprised, no, of course not.'

'Laura thought up the title. Brilliant jacket,

226

isn't it? You should have had more confidence in me.'

Johnny came in with the tray of tea and relieved Alice of having to find a sincere reply.

The three of them chatted politely whilst drinking their tea, then suddenly Alice felt deeply tired and it showed in her face. Marcus recognised her fatigue and said he must go. 'You look tired, Alice. Look after her, Johnny. She's very precious, but then you know that. My trouble was I never realised how precious she really was until it was all in ruins. Don't make the same mistake, will you?' He took hold of Alice's two hands and bent over her; as he kissed her cheek he squeezed her hands affectionately. 'Hope very much that all goes well with the baby. Let Laura and me know when it all happens. Remember what I advised, Alice. Thanks for the tea, Johnny.'

And then he was gone.

Johnny broke the silence. 'Well, that was a surprise! He's so much more approachable. So what did dear Marcus advise?'

'He didn't.'

'I heard him say it. *Remember what I advised,* he said.'

Alice, emotionally exhausted by keeping her cool while Marcus was there, declared she couldn't remember his advice, but Johnny knew she was being evasive. 'The pains, have they stopped now, darling?'

'Just about.' Alice paused as though she had something else to say but couldn't quite find the words. 'Johnny.'

'Yes?'

'I've got to be truthful. He said if you wanted the big house I should go along with it if I loved you. I do love you, but I can't go along with it. It isn't in my nature to live in a house like that and all it entails.'

'It entails whatever you want, no more, no less. You would make your own style of Lady of the Manor, just as Kate has done. I mean, headteacher of a village school and Lady of the Manor.' He grinned. 'That's a funny combination if ever there was one.'

Alice smiled.

'Besides, think of your son, our son. Think of his heritage. The big house should be his by right, don't you think? But anyway, this Freedom Blade no doubt will buy it, so don't worry.' Johnny hoped to goodness not, but he didn't want to worry Alice right now. His determination to be the owner hadn't diminished. It was all a question of timing. He turned to speak to Alice again but she was asleep. How beautiful she looked, fair-haired, fair-skinned, sweet-faced, long eyelashes fluttering slightly, as though she dreamed a dream, elegant hands gently holding the bump that was their son. How he longed for his arrival. He had to buy the house for his son, for all the future generations of Templetons, of that he was certain. Somehow Alice had to be persuaded.

# 19

Gilbert had taken over the training of the Ladies' Choir, both for the competitions they were pledged to undertake in the New Year and the performance they were giving during the Christmas services in the church, which was a new departure for them. Some had queried whether or not it was the right thing to be doing, but Gilbert with his charm and his underlying sexy personality had won them over. Beth had been allocated the task of organising the music for the church performance and also for the competition. So she had two sets of music to print out and covers to design for them for each and every member of the choir.

She loved helping Gilbert. He was such an enthusiastic person to work for, always so ready with genuine praise that working for him became a privilege. But the sexy side of him touched her not one bit. It was Jake who provided that for her, even though he was away in Cambridge and she hadn't seen him since he'd treated her to tea in the George. They communicated by texting almost every day, and Beth had not told her parents that they were regularly in touch. She knew she should, but at the same time things were so delicate between them that she felt she mustn't tell anyone at all. But five days before Christmas Beth did tell them both.

Alex was now home and the four of them were

just finishing breakfast when Beth said, 'Jake will be home for Christmas tomorrow.'

'Will he? How do you know?' Caroline asked.

'He texted me yesterday.'

Caroline had no inhibitions about asking for further explanation of this surprising news. 'Does he text often?'

'Every day. Well, nearly every day.'

Alex laughed. 'The crafty beggar. He said he was, but I didn't believe him.'

It was Beth's turn to be surprised. 'When did you see him?'

'At a party just before I came home.'

'You never said.' This was Caroline, trying to keep cool about the matter.

Peter smiled. 'He must be besotted.'

'Dad! We're just good friends.'

'OK, sorry. Will you be seeing him then?'

'Of course. He's spending Christmas Day with his dad and coming to see us on Boxing Day. Just for an hour, not for a meal or anything. Like I said it's all very casual.'

Caroline, keeping a smile well hidden said, 'Oh! Right. Your granny and grandad will be delighted to meet him.'

'I'd forgotten they're coming for Christmas. Oh! Well, he'll have to put up with the inquisition.' Beth was delighted she'd got away with her news without too much opposition, but the thought of her granny meeting Jake was almost too much to bear. Granny would be like some kind of high executioner, interrogating him about his pedigree, his attachment to Beth and a very in-depth discussion about his future plans and most especially his earning potential.

'Can you ask her to soft pedal her inquisition, Mum? She could frighten him off.'

Alex intervened. 'No such luck, sister dear. She won't frighten him off; from the way he was talking to me he's too devoted to you.' Alex pretended to be sick, which made Beth slap him. He just laughed and Beth flung herself out of her chair and went upstairs to avoid any more leg pulling. *I could kill him, I could, the stupid boy. Who wants a brother like Alex? Certainly not me* . . . then she stopped on the top step wondering what Jake had said about her. She raced back down the stairs, burst into the kitchen and asked, 'What did he say to make you think he was devoted to me?'

'Look! I hardly said a word; it was just the way he so delicately asked questions to confirm you weren't seeing anyone else. As I said at the time, I am not my sister's keeper so I can't say for certain,' he grinned, 'but she is very captivated by the chap she's working for at the moment, so maybe . . . '

Beth was furious. 'I am not.'

'I said he's married and has five children and he's acknowledged to be the sexiest man in the village but — '

Beth was about to slap him again.

But Alex reassured her. 'I didn't really, but he is thrilled to bits with you, though; I could tell by the way he tried to be casual but wasn't, if you know what I mean.'

'Huh!' Beth stormed out, leaving her astonished parents cringing as the kitchen door slammed shut.

Alex drank the last of his tea, stood up and said he was going back to bed, which he did.

Peter took Caroline's hand in his and kissed the back of it. 'Darling, it had to happen. He's not a bad chap. We'll just have to get used to the idea.'

'He's leaving Cambridge in the summer, so you know what that means: she'll give up her place at Cambridge and go to live with him wherever he goes. Heavens above, this isn't what I wanted for her.'

'It isn't what I wanted, but it's her life and she has to live it as she sees fit.'

Caroline swung round on him, her eyes angry. 'Let her do that without a fight? Just let it happen when we know it isn't for the best?'

Peter sighed. 'It isn't what *we* want, is it? We can advise, but we can't make her do what we think fit. Now can we?'

Caroline collapsed back on to her chair, her face grim with concern. 'She's worth more than just being a prop to a man with an ego the size of . . . I don't know, whatever. All that charm.'

'We'll have to hope her own good sense will prevail; after all, they are very young.'

'Exactly, too young to have good sense. Peter, please, have a word with her. She'd listen to you.'

The doorbell rang and Peter went to answer it.

The man in question was standing on the doorstep. He held a beautiful bouquet in his hand.

'Hope you don't mind me calling early, sir. I wonder, can I see Beth? Is she in? If it's inconvenient I'll come back.'

232

'Jake! Of course, please come in. I'll give her a shout.'

Peter stepped back to allow him room.

'Is Doctor Harris in? These are for her, as a thank you for the meals I've had here in the past.'

'Yes, she is; she's in the kitchen. Go through. I'll tell Beth you're here.'

Beth came down, her face glowing with pleasure.

Jake couldn't help it, he bent his head to kiss her cheek, but she avoided him, suddenly embarrassed in front of her parents and worried by the feeling of fear she experienced as he leaned towards her.

There was an awkward silence so Caroline found something to say about her flowers. 'Look, Beth, Jake's brought me these flowers! Aren't they beautifully Christmassy?'

Beth dragged her eyes away from Jake and admired the blooms. My word, they were beautiful, magnificent even. Flowers for her mother? Why?

Jake smiled at her, and it worked its magic as usual. 'I thought we might have lunch out.' It wasn't a suggestion, more a decision.

'That would be lovely. It's still early though. Shall we have a coffee first?'

'Yes, thanks.'

The two of them sat in the sitting room drinking coffee, feeling self-conscious and not quite knowing what to say. But Jake appeared happy just to be with her. Beth, with so many weeks of not seeing him, felt uncomfortable.

Together they both said, 'It's — ' and laughter broke the ice. Then Alex came in carrying a coffee and before they knew it conversation flowed. It turned out that Jake was hoping to do research when he'd got his degree.

'Where?' asked Alex.

It was then the bombshell landed.

'At an American university, I hope.'

Alex and Jake discussed it and what it would mean, leaving Beth confused and upset. American? Then I'd never see him. Is he going there on purpose to avoid me? How could he? She cautioned herself to be grown up about his news. After all, they'd no mutual arrangements, no talk of living together or marriage — they simply knew each other and he was free as she was to live anywhere in the world without obligations or breaking promises. But it was hard.

'Thing is,' Alex was saying, 'now's the time to do it, when you're completely free to do whatever you want, and it's a marvellous opportunity. I envy you.'

Jake warmed to his theme and by the time he turned to her for her response he'd painted a very convincing argument for going.

Poor Beth muttered that it seemed a long way to go, which wasn't what she'd determined to say. She'd meant to be sensible like Alex, but instead she'd been feeble and she could have kicked herself for it. 'But if that's what you want, it does sound a brilliant opportunity.' And somewhere deep down Beth was relieved.

'You'd approve?'

'It's not for me to approve or disapprove.'

'I'd still like to know how you feel about it.'

'Like Alex; it's a wonderful chance, if that's what you want and you get the offer . . . I-I-I'll take the mugs out.'

In the kitchen, emptying the dregs of the coffee and stacking the mugs in the dishwasher, Beth wanted to weep. Great big tears of disappointment welled in her eyes, but she wouldn't cry; she was tough. The real Beth Harris didn't cry. But somehow . . . she was terribly mixed up. Part of her felt glad for him and relieved he was going away.

Footsteps sounded in the kitchen. It was Jake. 'I wanted your approval. It's only for a year. That's no time at all.'

Beth turned to face him. 'No, it isn't. It's a good opportunity for you, and just think of your CV. It will look good.'

All Jake did was kiss her forehead and squeeze her hand. 'Dad tells me a new restaurant has opened in Culworth, so I've been to see it and booked a table — they're like gold, it being near Christmas, but I persuaded them we wouldn't take up much room. Shall we try it? For lunch? It's much less pompous than the George.'

The expression on his face was that of a little boy pleading for approval and she couldn't resist him. 'It sounds lovely. I'll go upstairs and change.'

'America may be far away, Beth, but it won't separate you and me. Believe me. We've time on our side and we mustn't rush things. While I'm away, make a go of it at Cambridge, get your

235

degree; you'll never regret it.' Then he kissed her, properly, and she almost drowned in the waves of passion that rolled over her. Shaken to the core, she raced upstairs to change.

Peter came in.

'Sir . . . '

'Peter, please; no one calls me sir.'

Jake cleared his throat. 'Peter. Can I take Beth out for lunch, or will it upset your plans for today?'

'Of course you can, and there's no need to ask my permission. If Beth wants to go that's OK by me. I know I can trust you to take care of her.'

'Yes, you can. Between you and me I'm trying to persuade her to take up her offer at Cambridge. I may have a chance of research at Harvard, so I shall be well out of the way. I've told her she'll always regret it if she doesn't make a go of it. Which she will, regret it I mean; you and I both know that.'

'Thank you for saying that. She'll listen to you.'

Jake smiled. 'She'll listen to you more than me. So if we both try to — '

Peter put a finger to his lips to hush Jake as he'd heard Beth coming down the stairs.

'Have a good lunch. If you've time to spare, have supper with us, Jake.'

'Sorry, but I've promised Dad I'll be home. Beth, I could take you to see my Dad — he'd be delighted if you came. He's a good cook.'

But Beth shrank back from that. She wasn't ready for it. Officially meeting Jake's dad. No. She wouldn't go. 'I've things to do, sorry.'

236

Mustn't get too involved, not when Jake was hoping to go to the States, gladly, willingly leaving her as though afraid to make a commitment. No way. 'Perhaps another time.' The feeling of relief that Jake would be in America and not crowding her surfaced again. What on earth was the matter with her? Beth couldn't reconcile the Jake she liked and the Jake she didn't.

★ ★ ★

In the middle of that night Beth woke up. She was right under the duvet and dripping sweat all over her body. She pushed the duvet down to her waist and lay there terrified by the images that were teeming through her head. She was somewhere hot, and huge moist green leaves were touching her face; she pushed them away and still the leaves kept covering her face, and then it was branches crowding in on her, then it was the smell of someone else's sweat — rank unwashed sweat, that suffocated her. There was no escape. Somewhere Alex was shouting as though he was raving mad. She began screaming and screaming but whoever it was kept coming closer. She was somewhere tropical surely, and she couldn't get her breath.

Then her mother's voice cut through the fear. 'Darling! Whatever's the matter? Calm down, love — you're safe at home.' Caroline took hold of her, flung the duvet off her completely and sat on the bed.

'Come on, love, it's Mum.' She hugged Beth to calm her nerves, saying, 'These jimjams are soaking. Let's change them; there'll be a fresh pair in the drawer.'

Caroline found some and went back to the bed to help Beth pull the sweaty ones off.

'No! No! Leave me alone. Go away! Please, just go away!'

'Please, Beth, let me take them off.'

But Beth began screaming again. Peter came in and in a moment they could hear Alex stumbling down the stairs from his attic bedroom. 'It's the nightmares again, Dad. Come on, Beth, you're all right; it's me. Alex.' He took hold of her hand and shouted, 'You're home, you're safe.'

'Beth! It's Dad here. It's Mum and Alex holding your hands, darling. You're absolutely safe.'

Peter's reassuring voice brought a small measure of calm to Beth, but she was still shaking and fighting to escape. 'Let me go. I've got to get away. Alex! Alex!'

'I'm here, Beth. He's dead. Absolutely dead. I'll bury him.'

'Not here, not here.'

'No, not here, much further away from where we sleep.'

Beth took great deep breaths and, reassured by Alex's promise, began to calm down.

Caroline sent Alex down to make tea for the four of them. 'We'll all go sit in our bedroom, Beth, and have a cup of tea, right? Now you're feeling better.'

Peter disappeared to pull the little table out in their bedroom ready for the tray of tea. Caroline persuaded Beth to put dry jimjams on and then they slowly made their way across the landing. Every now and again she gave great gulps as though endeavouring to still her fast-beating heart.

There was nothing to say. Peter knew, Alex knew and obviously Beth knew, but Caroline didn't, because she'd never been told what had happened in Africa to so seriously traumatise Beth. But for some reason the event, whatever it was, had reared its ugly head again. What on earth had triggered it? Bury him, bury who? And heavens above, how had the two of them finished up with a dead body to dispose of in the first place?

Caroline poured the tea out with hands that shook with distress. She knew it was six years that the three of them had kept this secret because Beth and Alex were thirteen just before they left for Africa. Some secret.

Very softly Caroline said, 'Don't you think it's time I knew?'

'Not right now, Caroline, please.'

'Not right now, Peter? When then?'

Peter shook his head. 'Just not right now.'

Alex handed Beth the biscuit tin. 'Nothing like a biscuit with a cup of tea. Take one, go on.'

But Beth refused.

'Mum?'

'No, thanks, Alex. I'm asking questions here and I haven't heard anyone answer me yet.'

Peter said, 'In the circumstances there is no answer for you at the moment. Later?'

Caroline shrugged and turned her mind to

practicalities. 'Finished your tea, Beth? I'm going to change the sheets on your bed — they're so damp. Would you like Dad to sleep in your bed, and you sleep with me? Just for tonight.'

Beth nodded. She didn't say anything because she couldn't rely on speaking in case she began screaming again. Really she wished her mum knew. Out of deep concern for her mother they'd all kept it a secret for far too long. But would it make Mum not love Alex for what he'd had to do to save her?

The cool dry jimjams and Mum's lovely sweet-smelling bed linen combined with the security of her mother holding her hand, calmed Beth. She was ready to talk now and without Caroline asking she began to reveal the whole story. 'You see, Mum, while the preacher who'd given us a lift home from school that weekend was being dragged from the car and well . . . you know . . . was being killed, Alex and I slipped out of the back seat and straight into the trees at the side of the road. We ran and ran away as far as we could; it was dense jungle, kind of, but we knew they'd be after us if we didn't hide.

'Sometimes we heard the terrorists — well, either them or the government forces looking for them going by, but we kept so quiet they never found us. Then one man came off the road and found us. I gave him my watch, thinking he'd go away, but he didn't. He didn't speak English so we couldn't communicate. That's when he wanted me to take my dress off. Then I knew. Mum!'

Caroline hugged her tight, but it didn't stop the tears coming, nor ease the great effort Beth

240

had to make to stop herself screaming again. The memories of that dreadful day were so clear, it might have happened yesterday.

'Don't tell me any more. You hold my hand and try to sleep; remember you're absolutely safe now. You've got both Alex and Dad here, and me. You're such a brave girl, such a very brave girl. Hush! Hush! Gently now. Gently.' Slowly, slowly, Beth fell asleep, the rapid breathing ceased, the grip of her hands on her mother relaxed and when Caroline was certain Beth was sleeping deeply, she extricated her hand from Beth's and quietly crept out to confront Peter and Alex, whom she found in the attic bedroom. Obviously they must have been discussing things.

Alex was sitting up in bed and Peter was perched on the end of it, which left the desk chair for Caroline.

'Well, now,' she said. 'Are you going to tell me?' She looked at the two of them, waiting for their reply.

'I will, Mum, because I was there and it was me who did it.' So the whole story came out into the light in that attic bedroom that belonged to the brother who, in defence of his twin sister, had killed the terrorist hell bent on raping her.

'This was when you were hiding, waiting for help?'

Alex nodded. 'We'd tried walking down the road to get back home but it was dangerous; if it wasn't the terrorists it was the soldiers using it, and I don't know which were more dangerous, to be honest. He had the rifle and some ammunition; he wasn't interested in me. It was Beth he was after. We'd had to be quiet all the time because in daylight the terrorists passed close by in small groups every little while. But he spotted us and he told Beth to take her dress off. He laid the gun down while he . . . you know . . . and I grabbed it. And that was that. I swung the butt against his head really hard . . . ' He patted the back of his head as though remembering only too vividly. 'He never managed to touch her; I made sure of that. I hit him twice, really hard to be certain.' Alex rubbed his face with both hands as though trying to erase the memory from his brain.

Caroline sprang from the chair and embraced Alex. 'Oh! My God! What a brave boy. My darling, darling boy!'

Peter was compelled to speak up. 'That's the secret, Caroline. You know now why they didn't want to tell you. It was all my fault for wanting to go to Africa in the first place. I've told them the guilt is mine, wholly mine.'

Caroline turned to Alex to ask, 'But then what happened?'

'We had to get rid of the body and Beth helped me. We dragged him through the undergrowth, did the best we could. We buried the gun too.'

'You've carried the burden of this secret six whole years! I can't believe it, and I never guessed.' She slumped down on the chair again, hardly daring to listen to the answer to her next question. 'Have you told anyone else besides your dad?'

'Absolutely not.'

'Well, don't. Ever. As long as you live. Dad

and I, but no one else. What you had to do was dreadful, appalling and not what Dad and I would contemplate you having to do, not in a million years, but you knew what had to be done and you did it.' Caroline hugged him, hard. 'You meant to stop him, not to kill him, so your intentions were the best. I'm so sorry it happened, but as Dad told you when he came home, you mustn't carry guilt for it the rest of your life. It wasn't your fault; you did what any man would do in defence of a little girl. Goodnight, Alex, sleep tight. Sleep safe. At least I might be able to help Beth, now I know.'

He'd been too grown up for a long while to welcome his mum giving him a kiss and a hug but Caroline did just that right there and then. 'Thank you for what you did, Alex. Your dad and I and Beth are eternally grateful. Believe me. Goodnight. I'll get back to Beth.'

# 20

In the days leading up to Christmas everyone in the village was busy and happy, except for Craddock and Kate Fitch. The big new advertising initiative had been launched and though a few millionaires asked to have a look round Turnham House and liked it, none of them showed signs of real interest. He had only one offer, which was derisory, and that was it.

Craddock took to going on long walks around his estate alone; he bought a puppy from the Jack Russell Rescue and though it entertained him Kate sensed his heart wasn't captivated by it and after a few weeks he allowed the puppy to go out on its own, just like Sykes had always done, and he changed its name from Benny to Sykes and only very occasionally made the effort to escort it out of doors.

Johnny went twice to see about buying the house from him and both times he refused. The second time he told Johnny never to come again. 'You're wasting my time and yours. Just stay away.'

'Right. I'll forget it.' There was a finality in his voice which upset Kate. He sounded so positive, she was certain Johnny had finally given up on buying the house.

'I shan't come again. Like you said, I'm wasting my time. Hope you find a buyer soon; obviously it won't be me.' He reached out to shake Craddock's hand, but he refused. Kate offered to shake hands and Johnny, clasping her hand in both of his, did so, saying how sorry he was for her sake that his offer was unsuccessful. He strode out of the house and never looked back. From upstairs in the flat she watched him leaving and could tell even from his back view that he'd given up. She felt so sorry for him. Even sorrier for Craddock. Very gently she said, 'There are times, Craddock, when you are your own worst enemy. You have the house he wants, you want rid of it asap and still you won't sell. His is the only genuine offer you've had. He's not even using Ralph's money.'

'The housing market will be picking up soon, you wait and see.'

'If you go on like this, I doubt you'll live long enough to see it.'

'Me! I'll live for years yet. I will not let that blasted creep set foot in this house as its owner while I have breath in my body.'

'So be it, then.' Kate shook her head in despair and slowly made for the door, turning back to say, 'Not having a Christmas party for everyone has certainly cut down on the work, so I suppose I should be grateful, but I'm not. And the thought of moving into that appalling Glebe House that has the stamp of Neville Neal in every inch of it is making my skin crawl; there's never been a truer word than that saying, 'beggars can't be choosers'.'

Beggars: that word stung him. How could a man like him, with his astute business brain, finish up in such a mess? Extravagance?

245

Overindulgence? Not keeping a careful eye on his cash flow? Allowing staff too much leeway? None of those. No, it was a culmination of several things all coming at once. Should he really sell to Johnny Templeton? How much did it matter that he was related to Ralph? His Kate a beggar? That did hurt, for he loved her deeply.

Young Sykes came rushing in; he never did anything slowly, always at full tilt. Craddock bent down to stroke him. He picked him up and the two of them sat together in an easy chair where the heat of the open fire reached them both. Young Sykes felt cold to the touch, having just come in from his morning tramp round the estate, so he settled down willingly and the two of them stared into the living flames, enjoying their warmth and the sound of the wood crackling as it burned.

Craddock felt young Sykes relax and he smiled. Dogs could be great companions. He really ought to spend more time with this dog. Or was he growing senile, reaching that stage when he was looking back and there was very little looking ahead in his tired brain?

Maybe he should sell it to Johnny; maybe he was being a foolish old man being so stubborn. But memories of humiliation at Ralph Templeton's hands and in front of the whole village came into his mind. That time when he'd given the planning officer on the council a brown envelope full of fifty-pound notes to ignore the pulling down of that ancient hedgerow so he could build a housing estate in the field behind the Rectory. The diggers were in place when Sir

Ralph and the council members turned up and put paid to the whole project. Humiliation, total humiliation that had been. The incident of the cricket pavilion he'd built for the village, when the whole lot of them wanted Ralph's name on it, not his, or the time when he found that wonderful church silver that had been hidden in the house at the beginning of the Second World War in that secret room for fear of the Germans invading, and the villagers had stopped him selling it and keeping the money. He'd bought the house, hadn't he? The leaking roof and the woodworm were his, so why not the silver? That had been his reasoning . . .

A log fell noisily from the fire grate and young Sykes, startled, leapt off his knee in fright. Craddock hastily got to his feet and, with the antique tongs in both hands, heaved the log back into the grate.

This old man musing would have to stop. One more attempt at selling and then he might, *might* consider selling it to him. But only *might* because it would crucify him to do so.

★   ★   ★

Johnny went home defeated. He'd tried, how he'd tried, to get Craddock Fitch's agreement, but it simply hadn't worked. His feelings must run deep to refuse his offer — not just an offer but the full asking price, he reminded himself. To be so strapped for cash and still refuse the full price made Johnny know at last that the house, certainly at the moment, would not be his in

247

time for his son being born. What he really wanted to do was take his son, now only two weeks away from being born, from the hospital straight to the big house, so that he would have lived in his inheritance almost from his very first day.

However, Alice would be pleased. Now that was something he couldn't understand: how could she not want to live there? It was so beautiful and so important to him. If she loved him why didn't she want to do as he asked? But that was immaterial now.

He turned into the village store for a few things they needed and his spirits lifted immediately. It was that special indefinable something about the store that made you want to buy, buy, buy. He loved the displays, the lighting, the coffee machine. Johnny made himself a coffee and sat down to enjoy it. Jimbo appeared like a rabbit out of a hat.

'You startled me.'

Jimbo sat down beside him. 'Just the man I want to see. It's about money.'

Laughing, Johnny asked, 'Needing a loan?'

Jimbo denied he needed a loan. 'No, it's about the Old Barn. It's a real money spinner for me, but . . . ' He took off his hat to straighten the ribbon, then smoothed his hands over his bald head while he wondered how to phrase what he had to say. 'There's old Fitch up there sweating about selling the estate and there's you with money; why don't you buy what so obviously should be yours? Suit you with a son to inherit.'

Johnny shook his head. 'No go. I'm afraid he

won't sell to me. I've tried, several times.'

'Damn it. I'd hoped to sort my problem with the Old Barn. I'm taking bookings which I shall have to cancel and that's not a very good idea — bad for trade as they say, having to cancel.'

'I can see your point, but he definitely won't sell to me.' Johnny got to his feet. 'Sorry. Can I pay for these?' He held out the shiny red apples he'd chosen. 'Alice loves these apples at the moment; nothing else will do.' He smiled indulgently at the fruit. Jimbo stood up, downhearted by yet another idea for saving his bacon having gone down the drain. Stubborn old Fitch.

Johnny went home to Alice frustrated with Craddock Fitch and wishing, wishing his dream could become reality. It was just as he put his right foot on the doorstep to Alice's cottage that inspiration struck Johnny and he all but lit up from head to foot. Hesitating while the first flush of inspiration calmed a little, he ambled into the cottage sober faced. 'Hello! Anyone home?'

'I am! I'm trying to be calm and composed but I'm putting my wash bag in my holdall because I think today is baby day. Just in time for Christmas!'

This was Alice as he always thought of her: in charge, calm, organised.

'I'll get the car out then.'

'Not just yet; the contractions are coming every ten minutes so there's time.'

'Every ten minutes! Let's ring the hospital and tell them to expect you.'

'I have already. They said wait till they're five

249

minutes and then come.'

'Isn't that cutting it a bit fine?'

'No. It's what they want. We'll have lunch and then — ' Johnny was horrified at the prospect of lunch. Sit down and quietly eat lunch? This was taking calm and composed to whole new heights. He tried to keep his horror to himself but he didn't. 'Have lunch? Surely not.'

'Johnny. Keep calm.' She was standing at the top of the stairs, bag in hand.

'Wait there. I'll carry your bag down.' He charged upstairs two steps at a time and snatched it from her. 'Now I'll go down backwards and you hang on to me; I don't want you falling down.'

But she had a contraction and paused for a moment while it passed. Alice kissed him as he reached the bottom of the stairs. She was two steps above him and she stopped to cup his chin in her hand and say, 'Darling Johnny, this is going to be the happiest day of my life. Meeting you was the first happiest day, and giving birth to your baby is my second happiest day. I love you so deeply I can't find the words to explain it. But believe me happiness is at the top of my agenda today and for ever.'

Johnny swallowed hard. 'Thank you, my darling, thank you. It's my happiest day too. But come on, if we're having lunch we're having lunch pronto, then we're clear to go when . . . ' he was going to say 'when I say so' but he realised that today was Alice's day and he was merely a bit player, so he changed that to 'when you give the word.'

They finally left at half past three with Johnny

trying hard to drive sensibly when all he wanted to do was fly there before anything serious began.

He sat with her the rest of the afternoon, holding her hand, giving her drinks, talking about South America, which he rarely did nowadays because he'd become so involved in his life in the village. Alice exhibited absolute control over her labour and by half past six she was saying she felt she wanted to push. It was Johnny's turn to sweat and need a drink and want comfort, but taking his cue from Alice he remained helpful and cooperative. The nurses were full of praise for Alice and when his son slid into the world screaming vigorously, looking perfect with ten toes and ten fingers, two legs and two arms, a chubby bottom and sturdy shoulders and a face that mirrored his, Johnny wept for joy. He didn't see the midwife cut the cord — she'd offered him the scissors to cut it with but he couldn't see for tears and shook his head.

She wiped his baby's face and head, wrapped him in a sheet and handed him to Alice. 'My word, Alice,' said the midwife, 'you can have a few more of these if you like; you were a model patient. He's beautiful — a big strong laddie. We'll weigh him when you've had a cuddle. Have ye chosen a name?'

Alice said, 'Not really, but Ralph will be one of them, I think, maybe.' She smiled at Johnny and said, 'Aren't we clever? He's so beautiful. Some newborns are ugly and crinkly and need a few days for their skin to get used to the world, but

251

he's so beautiful right now.'

Master Templeton sneezed and frightened himself but Alice laughed and comforted him. 'Fancy being so young that a sneeze gives you a fright. He has so much to learn, hasn't he? He's so like you there's no doubt who his daddy is. Even his nose is right.' She'd had this ridiculous thought all the time she was carrying him that her punishment for being unfaithful to Marcus would be that he looked a little like Marcus and that it would haunt her all her life, yet it was impossible and she knew that and he wasn't and for that she was so grateful. In fact she almost wished she hadn't been so stubborn about the big house and Johnny had been able to buy it for him to inherit. But he couldn't anyway, so she'd no need to beat herself up about it. But was that how new mothers behaved? Wanting the very best for their children the minute they were born?

The midwife took him from her to weigh him and bathe him and Alice's arms already yearned to have James back where he belonged, snuggled against her bare skin. James! She'd called him James. 'Johnny, can we call him James?'

'That sounds wonderful. Yes, James it will be. He's wonderful, isn't he?'

'Are you all right? You're very quiet.'

He grinned. 'I think it's shock. I'm someone called Daddy now, when I wasn't before. You seem a natural.'

'It's what I've always wanted.' The sweating and the pain and the need for tremendous will power already fading, Alice dozed for a while.

And so did Johnny, and he dreamed about his son inheriting Turnham House Estate and woke with a smile of deep satisfaction on his face to find Alice starting James breast feeding and the sound of his son sucking hard and Alice laughing with delight at her success. Could there be a more satisfying sound than that in all the world?

Johnny went home about nine o'clock because Alice needed to sleep and there was nothing more he could do. It was deflating driving home on his own to an empty house. Should he sleep in Alice's house or in his own? He needed someone to talk to.

Johnny checked his watch and decided to ring the doorbell at the Rectory.

Caroline answered and when she saw who it was she raised her eyebrows, asking without words.

'A boy and he's beautiful! I've got some pictures. Would you . . . ?'

'Of course, come in. Is Alice OK?'

'She's fine. You'd never believe he is her first baby; she got it right all the way through.'

Caroline took him into the kitchen. 'Sit down. Tell me all.'

And he did, leaving nothing out and full of praise for Alice. 'So this is him. We're calling him James.'

Caroline studied the photos intensely, then said, 'Congratulations, Johnny. That's wonderful and I'm so pleased for you, so very pleased. He is so like you! It's amazing, there's no doubting who his father is. Oh! I beg your pardon — I didn't mean to be indiscreet, but he is the spitting image. Alice has longed for a baby and

253

now you've given her one. Peter will be delighted. He's . . . sick visiting otherwise he'd be here wetting the baby's head.'

'Sick visiting at this time of night?'

'Well, it's not so much sick visiting . . . anyway now's not the time.'

'Oh! Right.'

'So the two of us will wet his head.' She looked at the photos again and said, 'He's so like you. Ralph would have been delighted.'

'Ralph?'

'Yes, your great-uncle, or is it great-great? The thought of an heir being born. It was one of his great regrets that he didn't have a son and heir. Very important to someone titled. Wonderful man, you would have liked him. Very proud, very honest, very principled and I sense that's you, isn't it? I haven't got champagne so — '

'I have, in the fridge already waiting. Shall I go get it?'

'It seems scandalous just for the two of us.'

'Peter will be coming back soon. I'll go get it. Just wait there.'

Johnny left before Caroline could protest again. Inspired, she rang the Charter-Placketts and invited Grandmama if she wasn't already in bed, Gilbert and Louise, Tom and Evie and Zack and Marie, and Dicky and Georgie to the Rectory to make something like a party for Johnny. Secretly she wished Ralph and Muriel would be there but . . . where was Johnny? How long did it take to snatch a bottle from the fridge?

Eventually he arrived after the others, who had

already scurried across and established themselves in the Rectory sitting room.

Johnny was astounded when he walked in and found them all there. Jimbo had brought a bottle of champagne too and was glad he had because it was definitely needed.

But Johnny also had two cakes and paper napkins too. So they had a real celebration all together, raising their glasses to the future Sir James Ralph Templeton. There was a lot of laughter and then a demand for a speech from the new father.

Johnny, never at a loss for words, said, 'Our son weighs in at eight pounds fifteen ounces, he has blond hair, and he can sneeze! According to the midwife the birth was easy, though it didn't seem like that to me.'

'The contractions were bad for you were they, Johnny?' This from Jimbo, who laughed his head off at his own joke.

'You know what I mean! It's not funny being a dad for the first time, and you ought to know! I thought I was going home to celebrate all by myself, but I ought to have known better. Thank you so much all of you for coming; Alice will be delighted to hear about all this. We are so proud to be parents and look forward to bringing him up and any brothers and sisters he might have, in the midst of all of our friends.'

A huge burst of laughter greeted this casual remark, accompanied by questions like, 'Does Alice know about this?' and 'A bit early to be saying that!'

'All right, all right! But it is true we do want

255

more than one. No doubt you will have lots of advice to give us in the coming months and no doubt we shall be in need of it. To Alice and to our beautiful son, James Ralph Templeton. To James!!'

The party broke up at midnight and Johnny went home to sleep, feeling very lonely. To give himself some comfort he went to bed hugging a nightgown of Alice's and a blanket they'd bought for James. Tomorrow they'd be home! Johnny couldn't wait. If only Craddock Fitch had given in and let him buy Turnham House James could have been going home to his inheritance, but as Johnny thought that he was glad there was no one there to see him smiling, as though he hugged a secret.

# 21

Peter and Caroline went straight to bed when the others had left, doing nothing more than clearing up the sitting room and the kitchen enough to make life easy the following morning.

'So what happened, then, at Turnham House?'

Peter, just back from the bathroom, climbed into bed, and said, 'He's very low, very very low. I've never seen him so depressed; that's why Kate asked me to go see him.'

'It's all of his own making, Peter; let's be honest here. If he sells to Johnny, who is eager to buy, the whole matter will be resolved, won't it?'

'It's not as clear cut as that, darling.'

'I never realised just how deeply he hated Ralph. It hardly showed at all, did it?'

'In some ways it's not just Ralph stopping him; he remembers the times when the whole village stood against him. Remember when he wanted to build the houses in Rectory Meadow? And Muriel lay down in front of the diggers? To him Muriel's motive was ridiculous, saying she'd met a little wren sitting on a nest in the hedgerow and she didn't want its nest destroyed. He's motivated by making money and she prevented him. What made it worse was the village supporting her.'

'Did you get him to see sense?'

Peter turned towards her and smiled into her eyes. 'I may be good at persuading people to let their better side come to the surface but this time I was unsuccessful. It's also partly to do with Ralph's ability to persuade people to behave well with no brown envelopes being passed round. Apparently Craddock's paid out thousands that way.'

'Craddock gave the church a lot of money too, don't forget.'

'He did and I always thought it was because he lived where he lived and it was all part of being Lord of the Manor, but tonight I began to wonder if it was something to do with keeping the door of heaven ajar for when he arrived there . . . or conscience money.'

Caroline sat up abruptly. 'Conscience money? What do you think he's done then? Did he say?'

Peter pulled her back down again, saying, 'You've lived in this village far too long. You're a gossip.'

'I am not, I'm just taking an interest in your work.' Caroline grinned at him. 'Well?'

'He may be depressed but not so depressed he let out any secrets. My guess is during the course of his meteoric rise to riches he has done a few sleight of hands which are not strictly on the right side of the law.'

'Peter! Don't you think it would be lovely to have a real Lord of the Manor in situ in Turnham House? All sort of medieval and paternal. Johnny would be excellent at that, especially when he's so rich.' She sighed with longing at her flight of fancy.

'I'm right, you've been too long in this village. We don't really need some kind of father figure in the big house, Craddock Fitch is much more interesting! Even when he's not well, poor chap.'

'I bet if you asked, every single villager would prefer Johnny to Craddock Fitch.'

'Well, it isn't going to be. Believe me, he'd burn it down before let him have it. He's said so.'

'Bad as that?'

'Yes. Goodnight, darling.'

'Goodnight, Peter. See you in the morning.'

Had they known what was happening at the big house at that precise moment they would not have said 'Goodnight' so cheerfully.

★　★　★

After Peter had left, Craddock supposedly went to bed. Kate, exhausted by the terrible day she'd had, vowed to stay awake until she was sure Craddock had finally gone to sleep. But her weariness overcame her and within ten minutes she was deeply asleep.

Craddock glanced at his clock and decided to wait five more minutes and then get up to say 'Goodbye' to his house. His beloved house. He hadn't wanted to sell it but he had to, thought he'd got a buyer — a disagreeable one but nevertheless a buyer — but after weeks of new advertising campaigns, fresh strategies, new initiatives he was exactly where he was when he first wanted to sell. So now his latest idea was about to come into being.

He slid carefully out of bed, slotted his feet into his slippers, put on his dressing gown because it was damned cold when the heating went off for the night, and quietly left the bedroom. He'd come back for her when everything was in place. As he walked down the beautiful Tudor staircase which was the joy of his heart he tenderly smoothed his hand along the banister, and thought how could he possibly allow his wonderful home to be owned by that crass idiot, Johnny Templeton. It wasn't just the Templeton blood that flowed in Johnny's veins, it was the whole upper crust business in which his country was still embroiled, despite the attempts over the last fifty years to rid the whole country of such claptrap. He smiled to himself and wondered for a moment: if he'd been born into the upper crust would he have wanted rid of the whole shebang?

He smiled. No, he wouldn't. He'd have gloried in it, gloried in the privileges, the prestige, the power, the old school tie. He gazed round the huge kitchen that Jimbo had installed as part of his contract to cook the meals for the Fitch Construction students. How to do it? Chip pan left on? No, because the kitchen hadn't been used for several weeks now. Electric ring left on and a tea towel left hanging had slipped off on to it? Same good reason for it not to work. What the blazes could he do?

Log fire. He remembered about poor young Sykes jumping off his knee in panic when the burning log slipped off the sitting room grate. That was it: that was the simplest thing to do.

He went back upstairs into the sitting room in their flat, closed the door, switched on the light and stood contemplating it. Kate had put the guard round the fire as she always did before she went to bed. He moved the guard away. There was a meagre glow coming from the ashes, not enough to start a fire and no logs big enough to roll down onto the rug and really start a blaze.

Craddock knelt on the rug and dragged the log basket towards him. He couldn't believe it. There were exactly two logs left, hardly enough to set fire to a dog kennel, never mind a house. Where the blazes was the log store? Such trivial housekeeping matters he left entirely to Kate. They simply appeared as though from nowhere, replenished every day. He'd go ask her. Ah! No, he couldn't, mustn't, give her the details of the fire because he wanted her to remain innocent. He had to safeguard her; he would be able to tolerate prison but she wouldn't be able to cope. Would he? He'd have to.

The thought of how low he'd sunk crushed his determination. He went to sit in his favourite well-upholstered armchair. He'd sit and have a think. Somehow he'd come up with the right answer before long. Just as he lowered himself into the chair young Sykes leapt up from it and jumped to the floor. Only just in time, for Craddock was about to drop the last ten inches rather heavily. Young Sykes yelped loudly and landed clumsily on the rug, shaking himself awake. He hastily wagged his tail, as sitting in armchairs was forbidden and he knew it all too well.

Craddock picked him up and tucked young Sykes onto his knee. Gave him a talking to and asked his advice about setting fire to the house.

261

But young Sykes had no solutions for him; he simply looked his favourite human being straight in the eye and wagged his tail, asking to be forgiven for trespassing where he shouldn't.

The sitting room door was thrust open and there stood Kate, at once frightened yet relieved to have found him. 'Darling! The lights are on downstairs. Are you all right? Can I get you anything?'

In a voice thick with emotion Craddock asked her to come and sit by the fire with him. 'We need to talk.'

Kate suggested she should stir the fire up and put a log on. 'It's too cold to sit here. Were you about to do that?'

Craddock nodded. 'Yes.' Now he'd been reduced to a liar to his own wife, something they'd always eschewed — absolute honesty they'd always said.

'Talk to me then, Craddock, really talk.'

But he didn't. So she did. 'All this anguish could be sorted inside ten minutes tomorrow when the world has woken up. It's making you physically ill and you know it. Crouched over the fire, your shoulder blades are beginning to stick out. It's not right what you are doing to yourself, darling. I'm not ready to be a widow yet.'

Craddock, startled by her forthright remark, straightened his back. 'And I'm not ready to die yet, either. And I won't. But I am beginning to hate this place. There, I've said it. Something I never ever thought I would say in the whole of my life about this house. Kate, my dear, what on earth am I going to do?'

'Sell it to Johnny. He has the money, he has the will, it is fitting for it to be his. In your saner moments you know I'm right. Then we'll have a holiday; we'll rent a cottage by the sea somewhere in England to avoid the pressure of delayed planes and crowded airports and take young Sykes for walks. He'll love it and so will you.'

'But it's winter. We can't go in winter.' He grabbed at another valid excuse. 'In any case you've got school; you can't just take time off in the middle of term, so that's that.'

He sat back, relieved at finding a cast iron reason for not going on holiday.

'Can't I just. I have someone who would be glad to take over while I'm away and — '

'I don't believe you.'

'It's true. I shall take unpaid leave and she'll take over.'

'Who's she?'

'Zoe Phillips. I was at college with her. She's been widowed and desperately wants to get back into teaching; she stood in when Hetty had that operation in the summer. Remember?'

Craddock nodded, thinking, damn the woman.

'So, sell to Johnny and let's have no more of this anguish, please.'

Kate waited patiently for his reply. He blew his nose, stroked young Sykes's head, stared at the fire, made himself more comfortable by resting his head on the back of his chair and then said, 'I'll have one more go at advertising and then . . . I might, might sell to him if I don't get a buyer. But only might.'

'You will. You've promised just now, and

263

there's no going back on it. Come to bed. This minute. Sykes, come on, in your bed. Now!'

Young Sykes obeyed her, trotting obediently into the flat kitchen without protest and curling up in his basket, but Craddock delayed, thinking only Kate could have trapped him like this. He couldn't even remember saying he would sell to Johnny. What were the words he used to make her think that? He hadn't said it, but . . . this could be his escape route if he did change his mind. My wife insists I sell to a Templeton. What had he come to? Hiding behind a woman's skirts?

He heaved himself out of the chair, put his arm around Kate's shoulders, gave them a squeeze, placed a kiss on her cheek and humbly made his way to their bedroom. In his head he knew that the idea of the burning log falling on the rug was still the best route to take. In the cold light of morning Craddock realised that one fire in the flat would not suffice to spread to the whole house and destroy it beyond all hope. It was too big, too lofty, so he decided to wait until after Christmas, hoping a better idea might present itself or a buyer might miraculously appear on the horizon.

★ ★ ★

Everyone else, blithely unaware of his torment, put their minds to enjoying Christmas. It was always a happy time in Turnham Malpas, for not only were there beautiful and inspiring church services to attend, for Peter had not lost his

264

magic touch, but endless parties. The one at the Rectory was top of the list for most people. Caroline had given a Christmas party each and every year once the twins were any size at all and it was much coveted. It was on the basis that whoever was free on the night was most welcome to turn up, but some people got invitations and that meant they could arrive by eight o'clock. At ten o'clock it was a free-for-all.

This particular Christmas Beth had her own guests, namely Jake and his father, and this made her more than interested in the food being provided. About half of it was bought from the village store and the rest Caroline organised. When ten o'clock struck she replenished the food on the buffet table, laid out fresh glasses and drinks, paper napkins and cutlery and waited for the invasion. She needn't have worried that perhaps this might be a year when those expected simply wouldn't turn up. They came in droves and the food and the drinks rapidly dwindled. By midnight, when the church bells began to ring to welcome the birth of Jesus, an annual tradition not to be missed, Jake and Beth were sitting in his dad's car outside the Rectory talking.

In the peace that followed the final peal Jake said, 'You know, don't you, that you're very special to me. I'm very sorry if I ever gave you cause to be distressed by anything I did. You know what I mean . . . with Janey. At the time I didn't see anything wrong in having two girls in tow, except you were special even if I never said so to you. I can't believe how cheaply I treated

Janey. I'm ashamed about the whole episode.'

'She's in a scruffy flat in Culworth; I saw her a few weeks ago. She seems happy enough. With a scruffy boyfriend who's out of work, so she's the wage earner.'

'Beth! No! Where's she working?'

'She's a skivvy in the kitchen at that pub at the bottom of Micklegate. Working very long hours.'

'That makes me feel guilty.'

Beth turned to face him. 'Did you send her there? She's a free agent, free to do whatever she likes. Just like you. And me.'

'I know she is, but I still feel guilty. Have you thought any more about . . . ?'

'I know what you're going to ask and I have thought about it and I am going back next October. I've decided I must. For my own sake and no one else's.'

'Not because I said you should?'

Beth smiled into the dark night. 'Absolutely not! It's my decision.'

Jake kissed her. 'I'm glad; I know it's right for you.' They both heard the front door open. Disappointed their time together was being cut short, Jake muttered, 'There's Dad wanting to be off. I'll go in and say my thanks. Have a wonderful Christmas Day, Beth.'

To her embarrassment he kissed her with his dad waiting outside, right by the driver's window. Beth got out and said, 'Happy Christmas, Mr Harding.' His dad shook her hand saying, 'Thank you, Beth. We've had a lovely Christmas Eve, Jake and I. It's been perfectly splendid. Tomorrow is

Christmas Day with Granny, like it's been since Jake was born. Thank you again.' He leaned forward and kissed her forehead, whispering, 'Keep that boy of mine in check. He does like his own way far too much.' They both laughed.

Beth went to bed happier now that her mother knew the truth about Africa. It somehow had brought them even closer, but her puzzlement about her feelings for Jake still lingered.

★ ★ ★

While listening to the church bells, Johnny was walking up and down, up and down with his son propped against his shoulder, trying to get him to sleep. He didn't mind because he loved the feel of this new life laid so helplessly against him. They'd had him home, entirely reliant upon them, for exactly twenty-four hours and he already felt a powerful attachment to him. Charles Ralph Templeton they'd finally decided upon. It had been James, then out of the blue Alice changed her mind and asked him if he liked Charles better. 'We could call him Charlie for everyday and Charles when he's been naughty, or Charles all the time. Charles Templeton. It sounds rather grand, doesn't it?'

At the time Johnny would have said yes to any name, he loved her so much, and as for their baby son . . . he couldn't find the words to describe his joy at his arrival. The sooner they had another one the better, or Charles would be spoiled to death. He felt Charles's soft breath on his bare shoulder and thought there was no feeling anywhere in the world as beautiful as that: nor the sweet smell of him, nor his tiny hands softly clenched, nor his weeny toes resting on his chest. Was this paradise? Very gently he laid him in his cradle, pulled his blankets up round his shoulders and tucked him in. Johnny climbed into bed, into the waiting arms of his soon-to-be-wife and felt the happiest he had ever been in the whole of his life.

There was one more thing to achieve and then his life would be complete, and Johnny fell asleep with a vision of him swimming in the lake, with Alice standing beside it holding on tightly to the handle of Charles's pram. He couldn't wait for that day.

★   ★   ★

Finally at half past one the last light in the houses around the green was switched off and the whole village slept. The geese round the pond were silent and still; the only discernible movement was a small swirl of smoke curling upwards in the chill night air from the Charter-Placketts' chimney. They'd been the very last to go to bed because Grandmama was spending the night with them and she'd kept them up when they got back from the Rectory party telling them tales of Jimbo's father in his salad days. Her grandchildren loved the stories she told about him, but at the same time couldn't forgive his treatment of her and their dad. How could he have what amounted to two wives and two families and keep his integrity? So they loved the stories but thoroughly disliked the man. Yet Grandmama spoke of him with humour and contentment; only very occasionally did the bitterness show through.

# 22

The post held up over Christmas came early on the first day back at work and Craddock Fitch was in his office as though everything was fine and dandy when he knew full well it wasn't. He hadn't set fire to the house as he'd promised himself, because he knew his chances of getting away with it scot free were very slight.

The first letter he chose to open had a thick, expensive envelope and the letter was written on thick, expensive paper too. It was an enquiry about his newest advertisement from a company that owned . . . well, let's be honest, thought Craddock: homes for elderly people. Except these elderly people must be well-heeled, for it mentioned two in the south-east they already ran, and Craddock knew from the addresses they were stately homes that had been sold because the owners could no longer sustain them. And if anyone knew what that meant it was him. He assumed they were hoping he would be ready to end his days in one of their properties. The insolence! He wasn't ready to give up like that! No, sir, he was not!

Then he sprang to his feet faster than he'd done for weeks. My God! They wanted to come to see Turnham House with a view to buying it? Within the week! Why hadn't he thought of it? But he hadn't, but they had. His mind raced through the facilities available and he realised that what had once been for students and promising employees would easily convert to a home for the elderly. Well, the rich elderly. The brochure wasn't for him personally, but enclosed so he could gauge for himself what was on offer.

They concentrated on improving the general health and well-being of their residents, expecting them to swim and walk and in limited ways do pilates and aerobics, they organised a bridge club and once a month had guest speakers, and outings were organised too so they all got out and about and weren't sitting round the room in upholstered armchairs gawping at TV all day. They provided regular theatre trips, welcomed family guests to stay (at extra cost). Of course, thought Craddock, it would be at extra cost. By the time he'd read the literature he quite fancied staying in one of their homes himself. That was until he pulled himself together and dug out his diary to make sure when best to make an appointment.

Since Anne had at last got another job — he'd been rather flattered by the fact that she wanted to stay with him, but he'd finally persuaded her to go — the diary was now his affair. He impatiently waited until the very end of the day before he rang, not wanting to appear too eager. He pretended he would be going abroad on business shortly, so it was either this week or not for another three weeks. Fingers crossed while he waited for the reply. Day after tomorrow! Brilliant!

'That's great. You have the address for your sat nav from the advertisement so I won't bother

271

you with instructions on how to find us. Very much looking forward to seeing you. You won't be disappointed. May I ask who will be coming?'

He wrote down their names, put down the receiver and, clenching his fist, punched the air.

'I'll show that so and so Templeton where to get off. This could be it if I play my cards right! My God! At last!' Mimicking an American accent he said, 'Sorry! Johnny Templeton! No can do!' He could even face the prospect of Glebe House and that terrible décor knowing he wasn't lording it over everyone.

When she got back from school Kate found him drinking whisky from his secret supply in his office.

'What's this?' She sensed his excitement. 'Good news?'

He flung the brochure onto the desk for her to read. For one dreadful, shattering moment she thought he was thinking of moving into it. 'You're not . . . ?'

'They're coming on Friday to see about buying this place for another home for the elderly. That's what they do. Homes for the rich elderly! Can you believe it?'

Kate dropped into a chair and began to read while she recovered from the surprise of it all. It was supremely better than that Freedom Blade. Lovely elderly people with money. Good for the church. Good for the village. Good for the village store. Ideal in every way. A whole new start for the village, for everyone.

'Oh! My word. If it comes off!'

Craddock said grimly, 'It will. I'll see to that. I

knew we'd do it eventually.'

'Darling! Don't count your chickens before they're hatched, please. We won't tell anyone, just in case.'

'Oh! Ye of little faith! I'll go to the store to tell Jimbo; he's the soul of discretion. He won't let on, but I must tell someone. Is there anything we need?'

'A litre of milk. But not a word. Promise.'

'What's a litre in English money?'

'Two pints, roughly. Promise me, please, not to say a word or it will be round the village before we go to bed and they haven't even seen it yet.'

Craddock laughed at her. 'All right then. Must go.'

He straightened his face and solemnly went into the store just as Jimbo was tidying the shelves ready for the assistant who looked after things for the last couple of hours in the day, enabling Tom and Jimbo to finish at five, and Tom had gone in the back to count the day's takings.

'Just in time. I only want a litre of milk. Semi-skimmed, please. If it's not too much trouble.'

If he thought Jimbo wouldn't notice the change in him, that he looked ten years younger, had a spring in his step and a smile on his face, he was mistaken. 'You look surprisingly perky. Got some good news?'

The appearance of Craddock Fitch in the store was surprising to say the least, but to the one customer still loitering by the tinned

273

soup shelves trying to decide which of Jimbo's offers suited her best, it was a heaven-sent opportunity to eavesdrop.

'Good news? As a matter of fact yes, I've got a very promising buyer coming on Friday. A company looking to buy a property suitable for a residential home for rich elderly people; not a word to anyone, right? No one else knows but Kate. So please, mum's the word.'

'Oh! Absolutely. Much better option than Freedom Blade, believe me. I'm very glad for you. I'll keep my fingers crossed. Here's your milk. Hope you're successful this time. Sounds very suitable that: rich elderly, yes very suitable.'

The lone customer didn't make herself visible until well after Craddock Fitch had left the store and when she did go to the till she paid, said thank you and melted away into the dark, bubbling over with this latest snippet of news, leaving Jimbo rubbing his hands with glee while he contemplated what kind of stock he would need to get in for rich elderly people. More malt whisky? Gin for the ladies? Vodka? Everything of the very best? Double his order for *Country Life?* The future looked bright.

★ ★ ★

By eight o'clock that night, seated at the old table with the oak settle down one side was Maggie Dobbs, eagerly checking her watch every five minutes waiting for her usual clique of friends to turn up. They were later than usual and she was bursting with her news.

Who would have thought it? There'd be jobs there for people and not half! Bit of a blow for Jimbo, but he'd had it his own way for years so perhaps it was someone else's turn now. She took another sip of her white wine, the latest in her long line of favourite drinks. What was it last time? Oh! Yes, lager. Then she'd gone off that, tried various other drinks and finally settled on white wine. Ah! Here they were!

Willie, Sylvia, Vera, Barry and Pat simultaneously piled in through the door. Maggie waited until they'd got settled with their drinks and then told her news. 'Have you heard the latest?'

'If it's about the big house and who's buying it we're all ears,' said Willie.

'*Well*, there's to be another supermarket out on the bypass.'

'Another supermarket? Whatever for? One's enough.'

'Apparently we need another, and the council intend giving permission. More competition will bring down the prices, they say.'

Barry asked whereabouts. 'Which end?'

'Our end, apparently.'

'Who did you hear this from?'

'You know our Kev? Used to be in the planning department? The one Mr Fitch had in his pocket? Got caught taking bribes and not just from Mr Fitch? Well, I met his mother yesterday at the car boot — she hasn't half put weight on by the way — I hardly recognised her. Anyway, he's working for this chain of supermarkets now, searching out land suitable for future expansion and the farmer who owns the field where the car

275

boot always is has sold out to this supermarket company, so now it's one of their future projects. It'll be half as big again as the one we've already got. They say the farmer will never need to work again; he's got a fortune for it.'

Barry finally said, 'It could be years before it happens. They do this, apparently: all the supermarkets have land they've bought up with the intention, when the time is ripe, of building another branch.'

Maggie loudly declared whose side she was on. 'I feel sorry for Jimbo. He's lost the students up at the big house, and now this. What a blow for him.'

Willie declared that 'Jimbo's had it all his own way for years now. Maybe some more competition will bring his prices down. I tell Sylvia, don't I? She shouldn't shop there. Culworth market's the best.'

'Oh yes! And who is it you expect to heave all the shopping home now I'm not driving any more? Mmm? Me! Because you hate all the hustle and bustle of the market. My back! My legs! Isn't that enough? How much more? Bleating every single minute, you are, if you come with me. Which you hardly ever do.'

Maggie and Pat sympathised with Sylvia so Willie took no further part in the conversation because he knew she was right: he did complain, all the time, about every blessed thing.

To their delight Greta and Vince Jones came in. They were rare visitors to the Royal Oak and headed straight for faces that they knew. Two more chairs were pulled up, Barry offered to get

276

his mother and dad a drink as well as anyone else in need and went to the bar to sort them all out.

'Don't often see you in here, Greta, nor you, Vince.'

Vince agreed. 'Well, you know, we get comfy in the warm in the winter and the thought of climbing the hill into the village is more than we can face. And then in the summer it's the only time we have to keep the garden and my allotment up to scratch. Time flies when you're both working.'

'Had a good Christmas?' asked Sylvia.

'We did. Thanks. And you?'

'We went to my sister Jean's.'

'Good time then?'

'Excellent, always good for a laugh is our Jean. Oh! Thanks, Barry.' They sorted out the drinks, wished each other 'A Happy New Year!' and then Greta, unable to wait another second to impart her news, said, 'Have you heard the latest?'

'About another supermarket, you mean?' said Maggie, delighted her news was going to get another airing.

'No. About the big house.'

'What about it? Don't tell me he's sold it,' Pat said, astonished her Barry hadn't been the first with this bit of news.

'I was in the store looking for a soup that Vince loves — and they hadn't got any; isn't it amazing you go in for — '

Thoroughly deflated by the surprise being tinned soup that Jimbo hadn't even got, Barry interrupted Greta. 'Mum! Is it about tinned soup? Is that all?'

'No. I was searching in the tinned soup shelves

when in came old Fitch. I guessed it could be something special, he so rarely goes shopping, so I hung about kind of and he said . . . '

'Yes-s-s?' they chorused.

'That he has a man coming to go over the big house with a view to buying it for a residential home for rich elderly people.'

'No-o-o!'

'Rich elderly people? I like the sound of rich elderly people,' said Vera, thinking there might be some part-time work cleaning and such, which would supplement her pension a treat.

'Now that does sound promising, very promising. In fact it could be the best news in months. More bottoms on seats in church.' This idea from Sylvia.

'More high-class business for Jimbo,' said Greta.

'More people for the Saturday coffee mornings,' said Vera.

'More helpers for everything, even flower arranging. Sheila Bissett will be delighted.'

'Will she though?' said Sylvia. 'She loves being in charge and rich elderly ladies might think she's not quite good enough.'

'Surely to goodness she can't carry on much longer in charge; she's well past her sell-by date.'

Barry raised his glass. 'Let's drink a toast to the big house. If it comes off I'll be pleased. Might mean my job's secure; they'll be sure to need a maintenance man. It's been a while since old Fitch spent money on it.'

Dottie joined them and had to be brought up to date with the news about the big house. 'I wonder if they will want Jimbo to carry on with the weddings and events in the Old Barn. I shall miss earning that extra money if not.'

'Still, they haven't bought it yet. It might not suit. We'll have to wait and see.' Barry added, 'But some rich elderly people coming to the village sounds to me like a good idea. More compatible than that Freedom Blade bloke.'

Sylvia piped up with a remark about a piece in her morning paper. 'He's being charged with all sorts, it says in the paper, some of which I don't even understand.'

Barry patted Sylvia's knee. 'Best not. If you did I'd not like you as much as I do now.'

They smiled at each other, and the conversation picked up again, and they all went home convinced that the rich elderly people would transform the village and best of all bring a whole fresh stream of interest and gossip.

★   ★   ★

The day for the visit dawned. Kate had put huge pots of plants from the greenhouses about the house, and large flower arrangements dotted here and there, which was difficult, with it being the depth of winter. She whisked about the rooms, polishing furniture to bring a freshness that had been lacking since the house had been empty and the cleaners departed.

Twelve noon they'd said, so Jimbo had been asked to organise a buffet lunch in the dining room. They'd been told to expect three members of the board along with a couple of finance people, and Jimbo had excelled himself. Craddock was mightily impressed when he put his head round the dining room door and saw the beautiful spread, and the linen napkins and the impressive lace cloth. For the first time in the long weeks the house had been up for sale he felt his spirits rising. He settled himself at his desk and made to look busy. He'd looked up the company on the internet and he was very impressed with what he read. Sound, solid company, he thought, not likely to crumble just as they were about to sign. He read the names of the directors, none of whom he knew, but that didn't matter so long as they had money and drive.

They were a bright and breezy lot, typical London businessmen, charming but ruthless, well-mannered but curt, but what thrilled Craddock was their obvious delight in the house.

'May we take photographs? Just a few of the impressive parts?'

Craddock nodded his agreement. What the hell, he thought. They can take as many as they like. Anything to push the business on.

They complimented him on this and that. Admired the staircase, loved Jimbo's kitchen, realising that that was one big expense they'd be spared, obviously thrilled by the swimming pool and the gym. 'Just exactly what we want. We encourage our guests to keep active, you see. Our report back to the board will be full of praise. Can we look round the grounds? Just a little way; not quite the sort of day for us to amble right the way over every inch.'

Craddock Fitch suggested they walk towards

the lake. As they set off one of the finance directors with a lean face and a thin moustache, who reminded Craddock of a rat he met once when he was having a cigar outside one hot summer evening, asked what about that Old Barn halfway up the drive? With all the worry he'd had Craddock hadn't actually decided about the Old Barn. In a flash of inspiration he said, 'That would be an extra to the advertised price. It's currently very successfully run by a talented neighbour in the village and provides a very substantial rental income, with no disturbance to anyone living in the house itself. It's licensed for weddings and people book it for parties and business meetings. All very high-class and expensive. You might be glad of the rent . . . that is if you go ahead with your plans.'

None of them either approved or disapproved, and they trailed along behind Craddock to go view the lake. They were very impressed, taking in the beauty of it and thinking up the possibility of rowing boats for their guests to use.

'They could row to the other side and picnic; it's just far enough, not too far, ideal. Few rustic tables and chairs scattered about.'

'With sun umbrellas,' someone added, warming to the idea.

The one who appeared to be in charge said carefully, keeping any hint of serious enthusiasm out of his voice, 'This place is excellent. Everything about it is just what we want.'

Craddock heard the enthusiasm which the chap tried to keep under wraps but didn't succeed.

By the time they left Craddock's spirits were the highest they'd been in months. He was convinced that this time he'd got a buyer. After a friendly lunch they departed with promises of being in touch as soon as. 'The time for a new venture is now, and if we get the approval of the rest of the board we shall move on it immediately. Subject of course to the local council approving of our plans. And believe me, we shall give them a very convincing report.' There were nods of agreement from everyone. 'I can't shake hands on it, I'm afraid, until we have their approval. Thank you for lunch; thank you for showing us round.' It was friendly hand-shakes all round and Craddock stood out on the terrace to wave them off. Their two massive Bentleys purred their way down the drive and as they disappeared from sight Craddock raised his fist and shouted to the heavens, 'Yes!'

Kate rang him at a quarter to three from the school office and asked how things had gone.

'Kate! I do believe we've got a buyer. Everything about the house was just right for them. The bedrooms being en suite, the sitting rooms, the kitchen, the pool. Just what they want. They've even taken photographs. Believe me, darling, I'm pretty sure we shall be in Glebe House before long.'

'I'm delighted. What a relief. But we shan't celebrate till they've signed on the dotted line, though.'

'Of course not. I've been long enough in business to know that, but it looks very promising. Bye! Thanks for ringing.'

Kate pressed the off button on her phone and took a moment to stare out of the window. That dreadful Glebe House. Just imagine! Living with all that marble! She felt depressed and wished for one mad moment that these residential home people, rich or not, would decide not to buy it. She'd been so happy living in that magnificent house, so comfortable, so secure.

The school suddenly came to life again as the children came back in from their afternoon play. Which meant it was story time now. She went with a heavy heart, even though she knew to sell was the only solution to their financial problems. If only it had been Johnny Templeton buying it. She caught sight of herself in the wall mirror in her office and saw she was smiling ruefully. The result would have been the same though, her and Craddock living in Glebe House. Maybe in a while they could sell up and move somewhere more compatible. Leave Turnham Malpas? Perhaps not.

Craddock waited ten impatient days before he heard. During which every day without any contact felt like a year, every post without a nice thick envelope from London a wasted one, then finally it came. His hands shook as he struggled to open it, and then he read the fateful words. An offer! The asking price! Three million!

# 23

Being totally absorbed by the baby and Johnny's joy at being a father, Alice was unaware of the village happenings. When she did surface, momentarily, she came to the conclusion that where once music had filled her life, now it was baby Charles who filled it, with Johnny running a very close second. She felt motherhood was the most brilliant occupation and wondered how on earth she would be able to pick up her career again, or even find time for it. Best of all, it was the first time in her adult life she didn't need to worry about money. With Marcus it had been a daily anxiety; now Johnny had solved all that and she was at liberty to indulge herself.

He spent long hours on the phone talking to his brothers about the hotel business; they appeared to pick up every opportunity to expand, to acquire, to come up with new ideas for making even more money. She'd never met them but they were coming over at the end of the month so she would be able to show them what really mattered in life: a settled home, a family, love.

And she had all three, whereas Johnny's brothers had nothing else to think about but making money and then more money. Johnny appeared to have dropped the whole idea of buying the big house and making it the Templeton family home and she was glad, though every now and again it did occur to her that maybe she'd been too decisive about that. The romantic side of her rather fancied the idea of the Templetons being back where they belonged, but maybe having Johnny endlessly on the phone about acquisitions abroad was a better option. She tried to imagine what it would be like to live there and the day that Craddock Fitch heard about the offer from the residential home people she decided to take Charles round the lake at the big house for his daily quota of fresh air and see how she really felt about it. Alice knew, before she set off, that she wouldn't like it, but for Johnny's sake she went.

It was a crisp January day. The sun shone but gave no heat and she was glad she'd put on her wool hat and thickest gloves. Charles was asleep even before she'd set foot on the long drive that led up to the house.

The trees didn't hide the house like they did in the summer, and here and there they still bore the hoar frost from the bitter cold of the night and reminded her of fairytale trees. The intense cold wind made it difficult to breathe and she had to turn her back for a moment to ease the constriction in her chest. It was much colder than she'd realised and the thought of Charles getting too cold worried her, but with the hood up and his blankets tucked in right up to his chin he appeared perfectly happy. With her back to the house Alice saw the long vista of the approach and was surprised when her heart stirred. No! She wouldn't allow it; it wasn't going to happen. She was not coming to live in this house. He'd find a buyer, would Mr Fitch.

He wouldn't be beaten by anyone, being the man he was. She set off again and came across Barry Jones having a quiet smoke, hidden from prying eyes, leaning against the trunk of one of the beech trees that lined each side of the drive.

'Caught yer! Who are you hiding from, Barry?'

'Alice! You made me jump!'

'Sorry!'

Barry straightened up so he wasn't leaning against the tree trunk. 'Just been told,' he nodded his head in the direction of the house, 'by old Fitch that I've more than likely lost my job. All the gardeners have been told the same. That means we lose the Gardener's House; it's the end of life as we know it.' Barry looked away from her as though he couldn't face her seeing his distress.

'Oh! Barry, I'm so sorry. Has he got a buyer then?'

Barry nodded. 'He has.'

'But surely the gardens will need looking after, the house will still need repairs, and painting and such. He can't mean it.'

'He does. It's the residential home people — they've offered the full price. Says they have their own team of handymen and such and they won't need us. He's beside himself with delight. Not very delightful for us though. Unemployment in the village is serious. Everyone suffers.'

'But — '

'No buts; there's no work round here other than Jimbo and Mr Fitch employing people. The cleaners and the kitchen hands all went weeks ago when the students left and now it's us with skills and that.'

Alice felt all chewed up inside. She'd been so absorbed by the baby — she leaned over the pram to check his cheeks felt warm — she'd never really thought about how everyone would be affected by all the changes. If Johnny had bought it he'd have employed them all over again. Well, not the kitchen staff, but maintenance and the gardeners. You couldn't have a house this size with its flowerbeds, its huge lawns and the extensive glasshouses without experienced workers, otherwise the whole garden area would be overrun inside two years. The thought horrified her. Still, at least there'd be someone looking after it all, with these new people owning it.

'I hope things turn out better than you think, Barry. Must press on.'

'Baby doing all right?' He leaned forward to peer under the pram hood. 'My, but he's the spitting image of Johnny; no doubt about who his dad is. See yer around.'

'Of course. Bye, Barry.'

'Bye!'

Alice managed one trip round the lake and then hurried home to the warmth and comfort of her cottage. Although invigorated by her walk, she was depressed by the situation Barry and the others found themselves in.

As usual Johnny was on the telephone; she dreaded the quarterly bill coming, but then she remembered money was no longer a problem and the relief was enormous.

Johnny finished the conversation very quickly and emerged from the sitting room beaming with pleasure. 'Darling, you've been ages. I was

287

just about to come to find you. Where did you go?'

'Up to the big house and round the lake. It's definite — he's sold it to that residential home for rich people. The confirmation arrived today. I don't expect they'll want all the village wandering through the woods and the parkland like we've all of us always done. Pity that. It is truly beautiful up there. I met Barry Jones.'

'Nice chap is Barry.'

'He's very upset. Mr Fitch has more or less told him he'll be sacked and all the garden staff too. Mr Fitch is one of the big employers round here, and there's not much employment apart from the big house, except Jimbo, and he's insignificant by comparison. Oh!' Alice's eyes filled with tears.

Johnny put an arm round her shoulders. 'Don't upset yourself. There's always work to be found for skilled people and he might be good at skiving but he's skilled and he'll easily find other work.'

'Yes, but they'll lose the head gardener's house too; that's the worry. Old Grandad, Pat's dad, still supervises the gardening staff and a modern up-to-date company won't make room for an old man with serious arthritis, despite his experience. There's nothing paternalistic about modern business, is there? If Ralph had been there he'd keep him on, tradition and all that stuff.'

'You approve of tradition then?'

Alice laughed at herself. 'Since I had Charles my brain has gone mushy and sentimental, and yes, I do believe in tradition. We just have to be thankful we haven't got Freedom Blade coming. It's the end of an era, even so. I can't see a residential home, even if it is for the rich elderly, giving money to the church like Mr Fitch always did. It could mean the church having to close, though Peter has made a tremendous improvement to the attendance. The cost of everything, like heating the church, has rocketed. It's really quite depressing.'

'Don't let it worry you. It'll get sorted all in good time.'

'Do you know you've never mentioned us moving to your house for ages. Have you changed your mind, and we're going to keep on living in this one?'

'I thought it best to stay put until you felt more in charge of things.'

'OK! I do feel more in charge of things now. So, I've been thinking, now the big house is no longer on the agenda, we could move into yours, lock stock and barrel, because this one is too small for a family, especially as you want more children. Not just one.'

Johnny agreed he wanted a family. 'I do want a family, four children at least.'

'Four! Really?'

'Is that too many?'

'No,' Alice replied cautiously. 'No, it's a nice round number.'

'But we're all right where we are for now, Alice. Let's leave things as they are.'

Alice looked curiously at him, thinking he'd always wanted to move on with an idea immediately, but she said nothing more. Maybe having the baby had made him more settled and moving right now would be murder, with Charles's feed-on-demand routine anyway, so perhaps . . . as she thought this Charles began wailing for a feed. There was an urgency about his crying when he needed feeding, that always made Johnny laugh. But this time he made no comment, only, 'I'll make lunch for us.' And he disappeared into the kitchen.

★   ★   ★

Jimbo, having been told by Alice when she was shopping that the precious letter making an offer for the estate had arrived and the solicitors had got the go ahead, presented himself at the big house as soon as he could. He needed his position with the Old Barn clarified; would he be able to pay rent as before and keep taking bookings? Would he be thrown out or would his rent go up to some astronomical height which would make it invalid as an ongoing business?

He rang the huge old bell at the front door and waited. Anne had already left, so he wasn't quite sure who would answer. To his amusement it was Craddock Fitch who heaved the door open. 'Come in, come in, Jimbo. I was just about to ring you. You've arrived most opportunely.'

Jimbo followed him into his office and was ushered to one of the easy chairs by the big log fire. This was a change of habit; he'd never seen Craddock sitting anywhere other than behind his impressive desk.

'What can I do for you?' Craddock leaned

back in his chair and waited.

'I've come because I've heard a rumour that you've got a buyer, this residential home company, whatever it's called. Is it true or just another figment of the village imagination?'

Craddock Fitch nodded. 'It's true. So you want to know your position?'

Jimbo nodded. 'Of course.'

'You have almost a year to go until the agreement we had is concluded; after that you will need to negotiate with the new owners. They want to find out just how disruptive the events are to their guests, but as we've never had a problem I suspect they won't either and they'll agree. Come to think of it though, that rugby do was a disturbance in more ways than one. Must have cost you, employing that company to clear up the grounds, to say nothing of the damage inside.'

'Believe me, they won't be coming again. I understand they've been banned from almost every venue for ten miles around and no wonder.'

'Quite right too; they were hooligans. Your rent will be welcome, I'm sure. No doubt it will go up just like everything has gone up these last few years, but I'm sure it will be a fair increase.'

'Phew! That's excellent news. Thank you for arranging that. That's brilliant and puts my mind at rest. I shall need something in writing from them to assure me. They seem reasonable chaps, do they?'

'Hard as nails, tough negotiators, but I've got what they want and they're willing to pay for it. Full asking price. It's like a miracle.'

'You certainly look better than you did.'

'I feel better, believe me. The worst part about it all is losing my business. I felt so secure, everything turning out well and then . . . but I've had a good time all these years. I can't complain. Just lots of factors over which I had no control all came together at the same moment and bang! The whole lot went up in smoke, so to say.'

'You'll feel even better when the money appears in your bank account.'

Craddock nodded his agreement. 'Have a celebratory drink with me? Bit early for whisky but who cares?'

Craddock, who had never served whisky to himself in office hours before, always having some skivvy to do it for him, leapt up and did the business. The finest whisky money could buy served in antique glasses from a silver tray: what more could a man ask? They sat comfortably together, each grateful for the way in which disaster had miraculously turned into victory. Jimbo was relieved, Craddock unashamedly triumphant.

'Do you know this company that's bought the estate?'

'Not personally, but they already have two other stately homes doing well in the London area. I looked them up on the internet.'

'Stroke of luck them seeing your advertisement, eh?'

Craddock shrugged. 'Who cares? When the money's handed over they can go to kingdom come as far as I'm concerned. You'd be the same, in the circumstances.'

Jimbo laughed. 'I suspect I would, but my

daughter Fran is taking over the business, she says. She can't wait to get her hands on it.' The change in Craddock Fitch's face surprised Jimbo and he wished he'd never mentioned about Flick's intentions.

'Sorry, Jimbo, must press on. Things to do . . . do you mind?'

Jimbo swallowed the last drop of his whisky and got to his feet, puzzled by his abrupt dismissal. They shook hands, Jimbo thanked him again for sorting out his problem with the Old Barn, but Craddock appeared to have no time to listen and Jimbo left hurriedly, wondering what on earth he'd said to upset him so.

When he got home, Harriet put him straight on that score. 'Don't you remember when he first came here he mentioned his sons, two I think, but they've never appeared, have they? What you said must have reminded him about them. They'll be adults now of course. Obviously. Poor chap. First time I have ever felt sorry for him.'

'At least we know we're OK, thank goodness. I don't think I could have borne losing providing food for the students and the Old Barn, that would have been a tremendous blow. I love the events we do. When I decide to hand over to Fran the Old Barn, not the store, will be what I miss the most. It's so damned interesting.'

Harriet, clattering about in the kitchen preparing dinner, laughed to herself, remembering the glee with which he loved to relate the latest gossip going the rounds in the store to her. He would miss that.

★ ★ ★

Six weeks later Craddock Pitch was thrilled to find the agreement for the sale of the big house amongst his morning post. He caressed the envelope, thick and expensive as usual, dug his letter opener out from the top drawer of his desk, unused for weeks, and slit the envelope open. He drew the sheets of paper out and began to read. The letter on the top said all the usual claptrap, which normally he would have ignored. But he solemnly read every word of the sale contract minutely, and wallowed in the signatures at the end. One was an illegible dash of a signature done by an executive who obviously signed his name so often that his signature had grown into nothing more than a vast scribble taking up a lot of space. He sighed with satisfaction as he returned it all to its envelope, took it out again and examined his own signature in small neat and tidy handwriting, and legible. This then was the end of living like a lord. Back to normality and thank God for that; no more pretending. Glebe House here we come!

Craddock read the letter again and saw that a week to the day the company would be taking possession of the house. A lot to do. Thank goodness it was Easter and Kate would be off from school. What a splendid organiser she was. Boxes of belongings were already packed and waiting for the move. He wrote in his diary in capitals, *MOVING DAY*. The money was already in his solicitor's bank account and soon would be transferred to his. Three million

294

pounds. Who's the beggar now? Certainly not Craddock Fitch. When he started his company with a stolen wheelbarrow and a shovel, he never imagined for one moment that he could possibly be worth that. Well, not quite — there were a lot of bills awaiting payment — but with sensible investments they would be able to live quite comfortably.

He rang his bell for his secretary and too late remembered no one would answer. Well, damn it, he could make his own coffee; he was perfectly capable of doing so. It took a while and the first lot was too strong so he poured it down the sink and made the second batch much more palatable. He sat in front of his big log fire, now unlit and uninviting and drank two cups while he wondered what he could do to fill his day. Young Sykes came up with the idea of going for a walk with him. He stood looking invitingly up at him — he'd even brought his leash to make sure Craddock knew what he intended. He'd dropped it at his feet and stood waiting.

'Not right now, Sykes; it's lunchtime and Kate will be here shortly if those blessed children will give her time. We'll go after lunch. OK?'

The doorbell rang and as there was no one in the house except himself Craddock went to see who was there.

'You! What do you want? Mmm? If it's about the house you're far too late.'

Johnny Templeton stood his ground. 'It is about the house.'

'Then you can — ' Craddock was about to use a very crude word, but just in time stopped

295

himself, 'buzz off back to South America where you belong. I've sold it, got the paperwork this morning and the money in a day or two. So — '

'I know.'

'You can't know. No one knows except me and Kate and my solicitors.'

'I've arranged it all. Full asking price. Like I said I would.'

Craddock Fitch shook with anger. 'Is this some kind of joke? I've sold it to Heights Homes, not you.'

'I know it appeared so. But they acted on my behalf. Business acquaintances. It was the only way. I told you I wanted it, told you I'd pay the asking price and still you wouldn't sell it to me, so . . . '

Craddock went red-faced with rage. He turned from the door and headed straight for his office, followed by an amused Johnny.

Craddock snatched up the big expensive envelope from his desk and dragged the sales contract out, shuffling through the pages till he came to the penultimate page where the signatures were. 'My God! My God! You devil, you! This . . . fl . . . flamboyant signature is yours.'

Johnny moved towards him, looked at the signatures and nodded gravely. 'See the name printed in very small letters beneath: J. R. Templeton. That's me.'

Craddock Fitch dropped heavily into his chair, picked up the magnifying glass he'd begun using for reading small print and saw he was right. J.R. Templeton.

Johnny waited while Craddock absorbed the

devilish trick that had been played on him. 'Do you own the company, this Heights Homes?'

'No. The ones who came here are company executives from Heights Homes; they played out their roles rather well, didn't they? Taking photos, liking the lake, admiring the furniture, appreciating the suitability of the house.'

'It's not going to be a residential home then?'

Johnny laughed. 'No, it's going to be my home and my children's home for generations. Just like I wanted it to be. Templetons living in Turnham House, as it should be. I had to be devious in order to buy it. There was no other way to get it. I've wanted it since the first time I clapped eyes on it over a year ago. I was determined.' He beamed like a small boy who'd just received the biggest and best Christmas present of his whole life. 'Couldn't help it. That was how it felt. The Templetons coming home to their birthright after all these years. The satisfaction of pulling it off was mind-blowing.'

Craddock Fitch flung the contract onto his desk, looked up at this young man who'd tricked him beyond anything he himself had ever done in his own business life. But he recognised the triumph and more so the passion in his face and saw a man he liked. Nothing would stop Johnny Templeton succeeding and he admired that.

Johnny spoke up on behalf of himself. 'Believe me, I shall care for this house with great love. You'll be free to keep an eye on me, because I know you love it like I do, with an abiding passion.'

'Your uncle Ralph wouldn't approve of what

you've done, not at all. The way you've pulled a fast one on me wasn't the action of a gentleman and he was always a gentleman. In fact there was nothing honourable about your methods at all. Nothing! You crafty beggar. Ruthless! You're ruthless! Absolutely ruthless. That's what you are, and if Ralph had been alive he would not have allowed it. Still . . . so long as the money's good!'

Then Henry Craddock Fitch convulsed with laughter. He hadn't laughed so loudly, so joyously in years and he couldn't stop; he almost felt the triumph was his because for once Sir Ralph's principles had been disregarded and it had been a Templeton who'd done it. When he finally stopped laughing, he said, 'You're a man after my own heart. What a coup! Your uncle Ralph must be spinning in his grave.'

★   ★   ★

The evening before Johnny and Alice moved into Turnham House Johnny walked slowly up the drive, relishing every step of the way. The sun was about to set and the sky was dramatic, vast streaks of scarlet, pink and turquoise colouring the roof, the walls, the windows, the trees, the grass. His heart almost burst with pride. This was his at last. He wished he could embrace it, cradle it in his arms, hold it to him, cherish it.

For a split second he didn't know who he loved the most: Alice and Charles, or the house. Well, obviously Alice and his son, but the house came a very, very close second.

298

Johnny could almost feel generations of his ancestors approving what he'd done. He'd spent hours researching his family tree, seeking out tombs in the church, looking for graves in the churchyard with names familiar to him now: Ralph, Tristan, Muriel. He hardly dared to hope that perhaps in the attics he might find boxes of letters or trivia that had never been discovered by Craddock Fitch's workmen, and he could indulge himself in his family history to an even greater depth.

Craddock Fitch. He'd taken it so well when he found out a Templeton had bought the house from him. How he'd laughed! How he'd delighted at the idea of a Templeton with a devilish streak in him, prepared to be dishonourable, which his uncle Ralph would never have been. They were friends now, he and Craddock Fitch, a somewhat tentative friendship, but friends nevertheless.

Johnny stood with his back to the front door, looking out over the lawns towards Home Farm. A farm. He'd never had anything to do with animals, because he'd been brought up in a smart high-rise flat in the middle of Rio, where even a tank of tropical fish would have been inappropriate. He'd a lot to learn about animals, but in his mind's eye he saw himself lifting Charles on to a pony, and walking with him round the lake.

Even more to learn about being Lord of the Manor. His brothers had teased him endlessly when they came to visit that time, but he didn't care: this was where he belonged and he intended making a good job of being Lord of the

299

Manor. He'd re-establish the annual things like the bonfire night party, the village show and the stocks day celebration, which had all been allowed to lapse in the last eighteen months. The older ones in the pub who sat at that table with the old oak settle down one side of it, they'd help him restart village traditions. In fact they'd be the very ones at the forefront reminding him. He heard a footstep close by, felt a warm, comforting hand in his. 'Alice!'

'I couldn't let you come alone on such an auspicious day, so we've both come to be with you. Happy?' Alice asked.

He put an arm around her shoulders. 'Couldn't be happier. And you?'

'The same. It's the right decision. I don't know how I shall manage to change from a humble music teacher to Lady of the Manor but I'll give it my best shot.'

'Of course you will. We'll both learn together. Not so much of the humble. You're the best of the best.'

'Thank you.' She pressed his hand to her cheek in gratitude. 'It's getting too cold for Charles. Let's get home; tomorrow is our new beginning.'

Full of pride, Johnny turned to look back at the house. 'I wonder if Uncle Ralph knows we've bought his house back for him?'

'I think maybe he does,' Alice replied with a smile.